The Shocking Experiments of
MISS MARY BENNET

✳ ✳ ✳

The Shocking Experiments of
MISS MARY BENNET

✳ ✳ ✳

a novel

MELINDA TAUB

GRAND CENTRAL

New York Boston

This book is a work of fiction. Names, characters, places, and incidents are the product of the author's imagination or are used fictitiously. Any resemblance to actual events, locales, or persons, living or dead, is coincidental.

Copyright © 2025 by East Pole, Inc.

Jacket design and illustration by Caitlin Sacks.
Jacket copyright © 2025 by Hachette Book Group, Inc.

Hachette Book Group supports the right to free expression and the value of copyright. The purpose of copyright is to encourage writers and artists to produce the creative works that enrich our culture.

The scanning, uploading, and distribution of this book without permission is a theft of the author's intellectual property. If you would like permission to use material from the book (other than for review purposes), please contact permissions@hbgusa.com. Thank you for your support of the author's rights.

Grand Central Publishing
Hachette Book Group
1290 Avenue of the Americas, New York, NY 10104
grandcentralpublishing.com
@grandcentralpub

First Edition: September 2025

Grand Central Publishing is a division of Hachette Book Group, Inc. The Grand Central Publishing name and logo is a registered trademark of Hachette Book Group, Inc.

The publisher is not responsible for websites (or their content) that are not owned by the publisher.

Grand Central Publishing books may be purchased in bulk for business, educational, or promotional use. For information, please contact your local bookseller or the Hachette Book Group Special Markets Department at special.markets@hbgusa.com.

Print book interior design by Jeff Stiefel

Library of Congress Cataloging-in-Publication Data

Names: Taub, Melinda, author.
Title: The shocking experiments of Miss Mary Bennet : a novel / Melinda Taub.
Description: First edition. | New York : Grand Central Publishing, 2025.
Identifiers: LCCN 2025016340 | ISBN 9781538768297 (hardcover) | ISBN 9781538768310 (ebook)
Subjects: LCGFT: Paranormal fiction. | Novels.
Classification: LCC PS3620.A8944 S56 2025 | DDC 813/.6—dc23/eng/20250414
LC record available at https://lccn.loc.gov/2025016340

ISBNs: 9781538768297 (hardcover), 9781538768310 (ebook)

Printed in the United States of America

LSC-C

Printing 1, 2025

To Stella

PART I
✶ ✶ ✶

Chapter 1

A Request for Assistance

It does not matter at all that my mother never loved me. I have always known it; it has never signified. *Reverend Quindley's Admonishments for Godly Young Ladies* says, "You are commanded to honor your father and mother, but there is no reciprocal demand placed upon them. Therefore love humbly, obediently, and without expectation." Why should it distress me? I have never found much to interest me when it comes to her conversation, either. When one thinks about it from a purely logical perspective—which as you know, Herr Holzmann, I strive always to do—it is absurd that mothers and daughters are expected to be so firmly attached to one another solely because of the connection of blood. My mother did her duty by me; she fed me and clothed me and brought me up (nearly) to respectability. Certain species of newt, you know, eat their young, especially if there is a danger of overpopulation. My mother, herself cursed with far too many offspring and all of us daughters, is comparatively merciful.

I lead with this, Holzmann, well aware that it will confuse you, for I have something very shocking to tell you, and I do not wish for you to draw the wrong conclusions. No doubt you are now quite bewildered: Why should your friend and colleague Sir Gregory suddenly write as though he were a young lady with difficult parents?

(Do I sound pompous? I am told I often sound pompous. You have never said so, though. It tends to happen when I am nervous.)

Here is the truth, my friend: The country squire Sir Gregory G——, with whom you have corresponded for many months on subjects ranging from mathematics to chemistry to the movement of celestial bodies, is actually a gentleman's daughter of nineteen years. That is—me. My name is Miss Mary Bennet, third of five daughters of Mr. Bennet of Longbourn, Hertfordshire.

There. I have told you at last.

Dear Holzmann, do not be angry. If you have not already thrown this letter in the fire in disgust, I shall explain.

I did not mean to deceive you, my friend—at least, not for long. After I read your enchanting little partial proof of Goldbach in the —— *Journal*, I was so taken with the neatness and creativity of it that I felt I simply must write you. However, I had by then learned not to expose my true identity when writing to men of letters. I will not bore you with the details, but had I not written under my true name, the isolation of rhodium would properly be attributed to me, not to Mr. Wollaston. I singed my eyebrows off for nothing.

I meant only for "Sir Gregory" to pay you his compliments and then disappear again. I meant it as a favor to you as well—I did not intend to bring scandal upon you for corresponding with an unmarried female, for I did not know your domestic situation (and indeed still do not).

I thought, truly, that that initial letter would be the beginning and end of Sir Gregory. But you wrote back, Holzmann. You not only wrote back, but you had the most gratifying things to say about the points I had raised in my letter, and—best of all—questions of your own.

Is there anything better than a question you do not yet know the answer to? I could not help but let "Sir Gregory" take up the pen once more.

The Shocking Experiments of MISS MARY BENNET

It grieved me to deceive you, for I soon found in you such a friend as I have never known in all my life, even if we never wrote of anything personal. I do not know if you are twenty-five or sixty, married or single, rich or poor—only that you are a Swiss gentleman of letters. And yet I know you draw your integrals with little curls at the end to distinguish them from your S's. I know that you prefer Leibniz to Newton, and that you look with as much scorn as I do upon the theory of phlogiston. In short, my friend, I know you better than I have ever known anyone, and you know me better than anyone has ever cared to.

(I included the bit about my mother because I believe that cases of wayward young ladies such as I are often blamed on the mother. I assure you that no mother in the world could have prevented my being like this.)

I tell you the truth now because I am in great danger. You will have noticed that this letter is burnt in places and smells more strongly of chemicals than usual. I must beg you to come here without delay, for matters are moving beyond my control. I believe you will, my friend, for even if you despise my deception, you will be unable to resist the knowledge I have to offer.

If that does not draw you, I do not know you at all. Pray come quick, for if you do not, you may come not to aid me but to avenge my memory. Even now—

But no, the sun is almost up, and I must post this without delay. I will tell you the rest when I see you.

Yours sincerely,
MISS MARY BENNET

I expected you by now, Holzmann.

It is now nearly three weeks since my last letter. Not only have you not appeared in Meryton, but you have not even responded. I must own, sir, I am rather disappointed in you. I thought a man of such intellect would be better able to see past the prison of my sex in the name of the meeting of the minds that we have hitherto shared. In that, it seems, I am mistaken.

I am *not* being pompous. When a friend has made it clear he no longer desires any intimacy, a withdrawal into frosty formality is, I believe, indicated.

I suppose, Holzmann, I owe you a debt of gratitude. You have not, at least, written to my parents. Nor have I heard word of any of the theories or discoveries I shared with you as Sir Gregory making their way to the public under your name.

Goodbye, Holzmann. I wish you all the best in your future endeavors. At least I wish I wished you the best. At the moment I own that my fondest wish is that you will forget all your Latin and discover a fossil that has been discovered a dozen times before. And then fall down a well.

(Later)

Before I could post this letter, matters changed. I intended to let you go; I am afraid that will not now be possible. The situation has progressed; perhaps even where you make your home (London? As I always write to you care of the ——— *Journal*, I've no idea where you live) you have heard of some of the strange events that have transpired around Meryton. The peculiar affair of the Netherfield piano, I believe, made the papers.

Holzmann, you *must* come. It is your own work as much as mine that went into the creation of my—no, our—project. Indeed, were it not for your enthusiasm when I first proposed the idea of personal elementation, I am not sure I should have pursued the matter at all. Your warm support for the idea that human personalities, like matter, could be broken down into essential building blocks was, on the more frustrating days, what spurred me forward. That, and the wonderful book. I know, I know—I never told you in so many words that I planned to put our theories into practice.

Well, I did, and I have, and now he has escaped and I do not know what I shall do.

I remain,

Your respectful colleague,

MARY BENNET.

P.S. Do, do, do come. If we can bring matters under control, I daresay our names will be inscribed in the annals of science alongside Newton and Cavendish and Copernicus. Yours will, at any rate.

P.P.S. If it is the female issue that worries you, I assure you it needn't. I have neither beauty nor charm. You will not, I promise, fall in love with me.

P.P.P.S. Nor I with you.

P.P.P.P.S. As you know I have never included a postscript before; now I have included four. From this you may deduce how my usually (I flatter myself) organized mind is in the greatest disorder. *Please*, Holzmann. I need you.

Chapter 2

The Early Life of Mary Bennet

Well. So this is how it is to be.

Holzmann, I suppose you did me a favor by never responding to my pleas for help. Your complete silence has taught me a lesson that I ought to have learned long ago: There is no one in the world one can rely on but oneself.

(Does that sound bitter? I do not mean to be bitter.)

The situation is under control for the moment, you will be interested—or not—to know. It took considerable effort, and I daresay the neighbors will never look at me the same again, but it is done.

Whether he will remain docile, or whether our problems are just beginning, I cannot say. However, I have decided to continue updating you. Perhaps you really do wish to reply to my letters but cannot for some reason—a long illness, maybe, or you performed that experiment with pure sodium that I advised against and blew your hands off. And if matters do worsen again, perhaps at the expense of my own life, I believe someone ought to know how this mess came about, even if that someone is handless.

Holzmann, you have been my constant correspondent for many

months; when it comes to the technicalities of my process, you already possess most of the particulars. However, since your own experiments have henceforth been unsuccessful, I suppose I should give you an explanation of how I came to study this subject. Perhaps a fuller account of the origin of my theories and my development as a woman of science will allow you to reproduce my work at last—or, as seems more likely to be necessary, to destroy my work.

I learned to read before I could talk. I was unusually late to speak, nearly four years old; in our large family no one seems to have been much concerned about this. I imagine it was considered a blessing in our noisy house.

I was approaching my fourth birthday, and unease was at last growing that something might be truly wrong with my head, when a fateful spanking changed matters considerably.

I had read all the books I could find, from my elder sisters' primers to Mamma's novels from the circulating library to even the housekeeper's book of accounts—anything I could get my small hands on. No one believed I was really reading, of course, since I had never uttered a word, but they let me amuse myself by "pretending" to read.

The trouble came when I ran out of books. I remember reading the last page of Mrs. Burney's *Evelina* and starting to cry—not because I was moved by that ridiculous tale, but because I had read it four times already and sucked all the savor out of it. I felt that if I could not get some new ones my life would not be worth living. Unfortunately, the remaining unconsumed books were in my father's study.

My father's study was my Shangri-La, my Camelot. It was the one place I was strictly forbidden to go. I was not a disobedient child, but I was also quite convinced in my baby mind that if I did not get something new to read I would die, so I felt I had no choice.

At first I was discreet. I would slip in when no one was looking, grab a volume at random, and secret myself under the credenza. There I would read a few pages, just enough to take the edge off my thirst, then I would put it back in its place and slip out with no one the wiser. I even carefully maintained my father's faults of alphabetization, though they drove me mad.

As time went on and I was not caught, I grew bolder. I read more and more, longer and longer, until one day I became so absorbed in my volume of Dalton that I failed to hear my father come in, and he found me cross-legged on the floor with a volume nearly as large as myself open on my lap.

I can remember the way my heart thumped in terror when I looked up and saw his astonished face, which quickly changed to fury. He grabbed the book, snapping it shut so fast that it pinched my fingers. When he found his voice, he roared, "Mrs. Bennet!"

My mother came fluttering in, still holding the shirt she was sewing. "My dear, what is it—oh! Mary, you naughty girl, what are you doing with that?"

"Mrs. Bennet," he said, very sarcastically, "it matters little if your idiot daughter plays with your Gothic romances, but these are real books. She must not be allowed to damage them." And he turned me over his knee and rapidly spanked me thrice.

"I do not care if you s-spank me," I sobbed as my mother wrenched me free. "O-only let me r-r-read the rest of the p-page. I want to know what Dalton said about the relative weights of carbon and phosphorus."

At this, both my parents stared at me, dumbfounded. My father let the book of Dalton's fall from his hands in astonishment; I caught it with a look of reproof.

"Mary," said my mother, "you can talk?"

"It appears so," I said. "I never tried before."

"Good God," said my father. "Did the child really read all that?"

"Of course I did," I said, wiping my nose.

"And why not?" my mother demanded, replacing my sleeve with a clean handkerchief. "She is *your* child, Mr. Bennet. If *you* are clever enough to read such things, why should not she be? Good heavens, Mary, stop sniffling in that disgusting fashion."

"Yes," said my father faintly. "Why not."

You may imagine that all this created a bond between my father and me, but it did not fall out that way. Oh, for a time he enjoyed showing me off to his friends; I was even allowed in his library on occasion. But I soon ran through all the volumes he had, and when I tried to discuss them with him, it became clear that, at least when it came to volumes of natural philosophy, I understood them a great deal better than he did. Papa fancies himself a gentleman of letters, but really, his library, while broad, is shallow. His Latin and German are poor, and—pardon the unfilial sentiment—his mathematics execrable.

My father was not jealous that I understood more than he did. He simply did not believe it. When I began to beg, with increasing urgency, for more books to continue my studies of the natural sciences, he simply decided that I did not understand them, that I had been putting on airs, and that that was quite enough of that.

What is a young natural philosopher to do? Well, I could only make the best of things. Mamma, having discovered that shoving an unread book into my hands would keep me quiet for hours at a stretch, borrowed as many as she could from the neighbors. Few of them had libraries even as fine as Papa's, though, and I had soon read every book within ten miles that was deemed suitable for a young lady's eyes (and quite a few that were not).

But the one true ally I had in my quest for more advanced knowledge: my father's cousin, Rev. Henry Bennet—known in our household as Harry. He was rector to our small parish, and his passion for learning made him a staunch friend to both myself and my father. He even persuaded my father to take me along to an electrical salon.

I can still remember how my heart pounded with excitement as the carriage lurched along toward Harry's friend's house. I was bursting with questions about electrical fire, but as my father, who hated leaving home, grew more sarcastic with every bump in the road, I held my tongue.

"Still don't see why we must bring the child all this way," my father grumbled. "This sort of exhibition was old in my father's day."

Harry winked at me. He was shy and stammering with most adults, but grew steadier when speaking to me or Papa. "Mary was not here in your father's day," he pointed out. "Besides, electrical fire still contains many mysteries. Perhaps one of us shall be the next Franklin or Galvani."

"Hmph," said Papa, but he looked pleased, and I stopped worrying he would turn the carriage around.

There were perhaps a dozen of us crowded into a small salon. The electrician, a tired-looking man in a stained cravat, seemed as bored by his own demonstrations as Papa claimed to be, but I was in heaven. His apparatus consisted mainly of a great glass globe held by a metal frame and attached to a crank, and it required all Mamma's lessons in etiquette to keep me from rushing forward to get my hands on it. From the moment he had the servants draw the curtains, leaving us in darkness, I felt a thrill go through me. There was a soft *whirr* as he turned his glass globe against the cloth, then we all went *ooh* (even Papa) as he waved his metal wand, lighting up this artificial night with a shower of sparks.

He showed us all the old standbys—the artificial aurora, arcing blue-green between two poles; using electrical power to turn a book's pages without touching it. It was all new to me, and I felt I was nothing but eyes and ears and tongue, existing only to see the sparks, hear the sizzle, taste the strange tang in the air.

He concluded by having us all hold hands in a line. I took hold of my father on one side. On the other, a small and rather sweaty hand slipped into mine, and I realized in surprise that there was another young girl in attendance. I had been so busy staring at the electrician's equipment that I had scarcely noted the other guests. We exchanged shy smiles, and then the electrician closed the hand of the man at the end of the line around a jar wrapped in some kind of metal foil. He himself took the hand of the lady at the end, and dipped a metal rod into the jar.

Zzzzap!

A tingle raced through me. A flutter, like nervousness, or excitement, flooded my body starting from the stranger's hand. There was minor pain, too, shooting through my chest like longing. Her fingers twitched against mine and she gave a soft *oh*.

The adults were not so poised. "I say!" said Papa, and several ladies screamed and one swooned. The electrician immediately set about apologizing—it seemed the shock had been rather stronger than he intended. I turned away, wondering if I could get him to do it again. It had hurt, but only a little, and what was that next to the thrill of touching the mysteries of creation?

I looked at the girl. The perfect ringlets that had hung around her face were now in some disarray. Short hairs stood out all around her face, like a sort of electrical halo. I reached out to touch it without thinking and we gasped as another shock went through us both. We had neglected to let go of each other's hands.

Holzmann, I cannot tell you what this first taste of electrical fire did to me. Mind and body, I felt consumed by it. I felt as if I *had* a body for the first time, as if the spark had created me instead of merely passing through me. The sensations I felt—I am a young lady, so I shall mention only my fingertips, a warmth in my cheeks, and a tingle in the tip of my nose, but please believe that every part of me felt—well, it *felt*. On the carriage ride home it still shivered over and through me. My fingers clenched around the remembered sensation of that shock passing from the stranger's hand into mine, up my arm, and thrilling through my chest until my father carried it away again.

"Admit it, cousin," Harry teased Papa. "You enjoyed yourself."

"Yes, well, it's always a very gaudy display. That young showman, though, what a charlatan. Did you hear him spinning tales to that young lady? Telling her electrical fire could be used to transform one metal to another, or even create living insects from nothing! Preposterous."

"Yes," Harry admitted. "Most of it."

"Most?"

"I know this talk of spontaneous generation is nonsense, but when he called it 'the spark of life,' well, we do not really know what electrical fire is, do we?"

"Nonsense."

"Biblical scholars talk of the 'spark of the divine.'"

"Oh, don't go all churchy on me."

Harry just laughed. "What do you think, cousin Mary?" he asked.

"I should like one of those great glass globes," I said.

Papa laughed as though I'd made a joke. I leaned back against the seat, ignoring the jouncing. *The spark of the divine. The stuff of life itself.*

Harry was a good friend to me all that year, most kind. No, not kind—*kindness* implies doing something one would rather not, and Harry, I think, genuinely enjoyed my company. He often solicited my opinion on scientific matters, first with the mock gravity of one humoring a child, and then with real interest. He was like me in many ways: shy, odd, clever, passionate about answering the questions the world posed. Sadly he caught consumption and we lost him. His death, in the very room where I now reside, was for me a harrowing ▮▮▮

Apologies, Holzmann, I let my pen run away with me. It is my research you care about, not my juvenile melancholy. I have scratched out the extraneous details. I mention Harry only because he influenced the path of my experiments in several ways:

The Shocking Experiments of MISS MARY BENNET

I. As previously mentioned, he introduced me to electrical fire.
   A. His subsequent passing associated it forever in my mind with life and death. The phrase *the spark has gone out* echoed in my mind for months after.
   B. It seemed as though that strange awakening the shock brought about never entirely went away. Whenever I see a girl or lady who reminds me of my electrical companion, I feel a phantom shock pass through me. Electricity is never far from my mind, for it seems to have imprinted permanently upon my physiology. I soon began to wonder what else it could do.
II. My father, who was also very fond of Harry, had tolerated my interest in the sciences whilst he lived. However, he never truly believed I understood as much as Harry claimed. Afterward, without our mutual friend to tie us together, I was exiled from his library for good.
III. In his will, Harry left each of us Bennet girls a legacy. The others got a few pounds each. I alone got something special. Harry left me a book. *Reverend Quindley's Admonishments for Godly Young Ladies.* It has been my constant companion ever since.

CHAPTER 3

Sanctum Sanctorum

Harry was not the only relation who took an interest in us Bennet girls. My uncle Gardiner, Mamma's brother, was a wealthy manufacturer in town. He and my aunt were great favorites with us. When my elder sisters Jane and Lizzy each turned twelve, the Gardiners began to take special interest in them. Each was invited to visit the Gardiners in town shortly after her twelfth birthday, and continued to visit frequently after that. Naturally, when they came to visit shortly after my twelfth birthday, I assumed my turn had come. They were sophisticated London people; surely, in them, I would find like-minded friends at last.

I had never been to London, and longed to see it, but I think the principal reason for my excitement was simply the prospect of being distinguished for special attention. Since Harry died, I had never had any to speak of. At best, I was one of an undifferentiated mass of Bennet sisters. At worst, my attempts at society provoked blank stares, awkward silences, and even titters behind gloved hands. There is a trick to being easy in company, and I have never been able to learn it.

I believe that when the Gardiners arrived, they did have the intention I imagined. They had never spent much time with me, and from the first day of my visit, they did much to distinguish and encourage me: bringing me on carriage rides, asking me to play for them, and doing their best to draw me into conversation. They even talked to me about science. My uncle's factories were concerned with the dying of cloth, and as such he was fairly well versed in chemical processes and could converse sensibly about the latest advances. He seemed impressed by my understanding of them.

His wife, in particular, fascinated me. She was a little younger than he was, and still very beautiful—so beautiful, I felt at the time, that it hurt to look at her. At twelve, I had a fascination with female elegance. I often found my gaze lingering on their faces and forms, which I realized must be because of a sort of collegial curiosity. I was the only one of my sisters who was not pretty, but I had not yet given up hope that I might achieve it. With study and effort I had left my sisters in the dust at embroidery, music, and mathematics—why should beauty be any different? So everything my aunt did, I studied, from her laugh to the way she absently brushed back the charming little curl that kept springing forth from her coiffure. To be singled out by someone so elegant—what lady of twelve can ask for more?

I fear the effect of all this unaccustomed attention upon me was rather overwhelming. My excitement at spending time with these clever, cosmopolitan people thrilled me like a drop of water in the desert; if no one in Meryton liked me, I decided, it was simply because they were sleepy and stupid, not because I myself was inadequate. Here at last were people who understood. I had visions of them adopting me, asking me to stay with them forever. I longed to hear them say I was their favorite niece.

Unfortunately, my excitement undammed the considerable force of my personality. It is so hard, don't you find, not to be too much? Or perhaps that is a problem only young ladies face. In any case, I was excessive in every way a twelve-year-old can be. I followed them about, talking to them of calculus, and demanding that they listen to more and more music. I studied hard to make my conversation sophisticated and pleasing, using my aunt's genteel manners as my guide. I believed I had succeeded until one day I overheard them talking.

"We are agreed then?" my uncle was saying. "We won't ask little Mary back to town with us?"

My aunt sighed. "Indeed not. It is too bad, for she badly needs the polish, but I declare I cannot spend one more day in her company. Such a profoundly irritating, bragging manner she has! Always putting herself forward! It is most unseemly."

"Too true," said my uncle. "And that strange, affected way she talks—my dear, I believe she is imitating you!"

"Good heavens," she said. "No, I cannot face it. I should like to do something for her, for plain as she is she will need all our help, poor thing. But one has one's limits. Let us ask Elizabeth again instead." (The next day they did.)

As I listened to their conversation, my face grew hot and prickled with mortification. I fled to my room, closed the door softly, flung myself on the bed, and cried.

Do not feel sorry for me. My aunt's careless words were the best thing that could have happened to me. As I cried, you see, I began to worry that someone would walk in and see my tears. Perhaps Mamma would even deduce what had happened, and prevail upon them to invite me after all; if that happened I would die of shame. No one must know.

Smothering my sobs, I burrowed to the back of my closet, intending to cry myself out where no one could see.

There I sat, for minutes or hours, my tears cresting and ebbing and returning again. No one indulges in self-pity like the twelve-year-old female. At last I had cried myself out and lay there in a weak and exhausted daze, feeling a thousand years older than I had that morning. Gradually, my fingers began worrying at a crack on the back wall.

Tracing it, I found it was too regular to be a mere flaw. There was no latch or knob, but there was a section about three inches long where the groove ran a little broader and deeper, just the right width for slim little fingers to dig in.

My heart was by now pounding with excitement. What had I found? I told myself sternly that it was nothing, that I had simply found the scars of long-ago renovations, but my sorely bruised heart would not believe it. I needed something, *something* to be for me.

And He must have heard a miserable child's prayer, because the next moment, there was a shriek of protest from the wall and the section bounded by the crack swung outward an inch. A breath of musty, ancient air puffed forth. It was a door.

It was by now evening and the sun was down. (Tea must have come and gone without anyone thinking to look for me.) I returned to my room for a moment to take up a candle—how lucky I was that none of my sisters shared my chamber!—and then I pried the door the rest of the way open.

It is a good thing I have no fear of spiders or mice, for quite a few of both made their home in that forgotten chamber. I could not avoid their webs, which brushed my face and clothing as I fumbled forward. Raising the candle, I found I was at the foot of a spiral stair, so narrow and steep that it was more like a sort of ladder. At the top I found another door, stuck as tight as the first, but this one had a knob at least. After managing to pry it open, I took up the candle again and stepped beyond the threshold.

It was a small chamber, but high-ceilinged. A small skylight displayed a few stars, and a pair of grimy windows looked out onto the roof of the kitchen. The room held a sturdy wooden table and a few chairs, and there was another door at the back, but this one was stuck tight.

I do not know what that secret room was for. Perhaps some ancestor of mine had used it to hide priests in, or as a smuggler's bolt-hole. It was cramped, and musty, and bare. I did not care. I had wanted something that was mine; well, here it was.

Luckily, I do not need as much sleep as most do. Each night, after the household went to bed, I would steal up to my sanctuary. Gradually, I cleared the dust and grime of decades, and made the place my own. (The maids could not understand how my nightclothes got so dirty. I let them believe I had been sleepwalking.) By spiriting away some old glass jars, and the remains of some chemicals and equipment that my father had ordered and then lost interest in, I soon had the beginnings of a makeshift laboratory.

I was in heaven. My aunt and uncle's rejection was all but forgotten. Why had I been trying so hard? My aunt was right; it was intolerable. I did not like other people any more than they liked me. I saw that I ought to stop trying to force myself into the mold of a pretty young lady they would approve of, and instead simply abjure company altogether. My lack of beauty would distress no one if there was no one to see it. If I did not press my presence upon them, they would be relieved and I would be free.

The shaking in my hand is growing worse. I am getting one of my sick headaches. For some reason they often seem to appear when the subject of my looks arises. I had better lay down my pen for now. I shall take up the tale tomorrow.

CHAPTER 4

Enter Septimus Pike

At first my little laboratory was not fit for much. I had scant supplies. I reproduced the simple experiments I found in my reading, but I soon satisfied myself that the candle under the bell jar would, indeed, snuff itself, that the period of the pendulum remained the same even as its length decreased, and that the juice of a red cabbage would change color based on whether a solution was acid or alkaline.

I wanted more. I needed more.

Do you have any idea, Holzmann, how much a glass phial costs? I hope not. I hope you are a gentleman of independent means, and that the cost is nothing to you. Or perhaps you are affiliated with some university and need not fear the cost of breakage because they will replace it for you. Heavens, what a luxury that must be! Alas, I have little money. My allowance is not designed to stretch to more than shoe roses and the occasional bun. It was enough for a few phials and a gas lamp, no more.

I quickly sold such possessions as I had, which amounted to some hair ornaments I never wore and a few pieces of ugly jewelry. In my desperation, I even turned to alchemy. This, too, failed me, though not for the reason you might expect—I actually found it quite easy to turn lead into gold, but have you seen the price of lead these days? Highway robbery. I would almost do better to turn gold into lead. It is all those lead musket balls, I suppose, that have to be forged to blow Napoleon's head off.

It did not help that the equipment I longed for the most was delicate and must be ordered specially from America. Yes, more than anything, I craved a proper electrical apparatus. Where most young girls dream of handsome swains, I lusted after a great glass globe, a copper rod, and Leyden jars. Such things cost a great deal more than a pair of shoe roses.

It took a great deal of thought, but I did come up with a solution—one that, if not exactly socially sanctioned, was at least socially invisible.

It unfortunately involved becoming more closely acquainted with a certain Mr. Septimus Pike.

Mr. Pike was one of the clerks of a Meryton lawyer called Phillips, who was married to my mother's sister. Poor Pike! Even when alive, he was never terribly appealing. Not to me, at least. I believe he was generally considered handsome enough, but I could never see it. I disliked the way he smelled. I dislike the way most people smell, especially men—a sensitive nose is a boon in a laboratory but a curse in daily life. Pike smelled of the tools of his trade—ink, paste, and old ledgers not dusted recently enough. I did, however, find him interesting. He was tall, with the slightly pinched tallness of a young man who had grown beyond what his master was willing to feed him, and his wrists stuck out of his sleeves an inch or more. I had often found myself going in to dinner on his arm, after the more eligible young men had maneuvered to escort my prettier sisters. A young man in his position—"Hanging on to a place in society by his fingernails," my aunt once sniffed—might have tried too hard to please, but he rarely smiled and never flattered. His gaze was clever and appraising, more the young squire than the penniless apprentice.

Of course, I was appraising him right back.

I chose Mr. Pike as my accomplice of all the people in Meryton for several reasons.

I. I could see he would welcome a bit of extra income. I'd often seen him glaring sullenly at the young gentlemen of the village strutting about in boots polished to a high shine and blinding white cravats. Mr. Pike dressed neatly but shabbily. Anyone with eyes could see how he hated it.
II. No one paid much attention to him. He was not common enough to associate with servants and tradesmen, nor fine enough to move in genteel circles. He was, to a large extent, invisible. This suited my purpose admirably.
III. I could easily speak to him privately. It was the simplest thing in the world to claim I had a message or a parcel for my uncle and slip into his office; everyone knew that he spent most of his afternoons dozing in his parlor. If I went on the third Thursday of the month, the senior clerk's day off, I would usually find it empty except for Pike.

The first time I slipped in to see him, he was surprised. "Your uncle's inside," he said.

"Yes, I know. I came to see you."

His eyebrows shot up. He carefully put his pen back in the inkwell and leaned back from the ledger he was copying. "Me? I am flattered. What can I do for you, Miss Mary?"

"You can sell this for me." I put a sack about the size of my fist on his desk.

Pike chuckled. "What is it? Hair ribbons? Some fine embroidery, perhaps?"

"It's gunpowder."

Pike froze. After a moment, he opened the sack and sniffed it, then took a few granules between his fingers. Carefully he closed it and looked back at me.

"Where did you get this?" he asked.

I considered lying. However, most of the essays and sermons I read caution against deceit, especially in females. Since I am often obliged to lie anyway, I do try to be honest when I can. Hopefully the scales will still balance. I have a great abundance of some other virtues, such as chastity.

"I made it," I said. "It is easy enough if you know how, if rather messy." It's true, by the by. The process involves charcoal, a tract of land where rotting flesh has been buried, and—well—the contents of chamber pots. All of those are, of course, easily found on a farm. Anyone with patience and a strong nose could do it. Let me know if you would like the recipe, Holzmann.

Pike gave a snort of incredulous laughter. "Cooked it up in the kitchen, I suppose, alongside the day's soup."

"Certainly not. My mother would never allow me to make soup."

"But gunpowder is permitted?"

"Ah. Well." This was the delicate bit. "She doesn't know, actually. As a matter of fact, Mr. Pike, I would prefer that you not mention this to—well, anyone."

"And you wish me to sell it?"

"Well—yes." I shifted from foot to foot. "It will sell, won't it? There are all those soldiers about, and it's almost hunting season…" I felt a twinge of uncertainty. I had never considered that my months of disgusting labor might be for nothing. I stretched out a hand to take the bag back.

He swiftly pulled it back toward him. "Oh, it'll sell all right, for a pretty penny, too, if it's the real stuff."

"It is."

"Come now, where did you really get it? Raided your father's hunting chest, I suppose."

"No! I told you. I made it."

He eyed me. "You're a strange one, Miss Mary."

"So I have many times been told."

It was a strange conversation we were having, too. There are certain proprieties when a young man speaks to a single young lady. We were observing none of them.

"It's very fine gunpowder," I said. "I tried it out in the woods, using one of my father's rifles. It fires very smoothly. I shot two pheasants."

He said nothing. He was still staring into the bag.

"Well," I said, "good day to you," and I retrieved the bag and turned to go. A hand shot out and grabbed my wrist.

I jumped. Turning, I snatched my hand back. "Sir?"

"No deal until we test the merchandise, miss," he said, and, before I could cry out, he grabbed the bag and threw a pinch of my gunpowder into the fire.

Gunpowder on its own is not terribly explosive. It requires compression by a bullet or bomb before it can tear flesh. But of course it will put on a show. There was a sharp *bangbangBANG* and a series of rapid flashes of white light that made me throw an arm across my face.

"Well," he said calmly. "That seems to be in order."

"Mr. Pike! Why would you do that?"

For the first time since I'd known him, he smiled. "It is an improvement over copying out contracts in triplicate."

"Ah." I pressed a hand to my racing heart.

"Very well," he said. "I'll sell it for you. I daresay Sir William's steward will buy it. The Lucases are always inviting too many guests to hunt."

"Thank you, sir," I said. "You may keep half of my profits, as a token of my gratitude."

He looked amused again. "How gracious. Now get out of here; the noise may draw Poll from the kitchen."

I left, but the bright spots danced in front of my vision for some time. Later I found that the cinders had burnt holes in my petticoat. Mamma scolded me for my carelessness.

A week later I slipped into Uncle's office again. Pike had four shillings, which we split as promised. We soon had a regular arrangement. I would bring him gunpowder or other creations, and he would sell them. With my portion of the funds I sent away for glassware and a proper burner and everything else I needed for my laboratory.

For a time, there was between me and Pike a comradeship of sorts. I found that, though he had been forced to terminate his education early, he had a quick understanding. I lent him my journals, and soon he was not only sourcing supplies for me but suggesting alternatives. He seemed to enjoy having a secret with me, and I admit I did, too. Sometimes when my family dined at my uncle's, he would catch my eye and say something smooth and respectful that nevertheless guided my uncle to greater heights of pontification. Then he would catch my eye and I would be forced to smother a laugh in a napkin.

But I was growing older. I came out very young, as all my sisters did, for my mother could not abide the thought of missing the chance to snare a husband. Soon hair curlers and dancing lessons were most seriously impinging on my research time. I found I loathed dancing at balls. I hated getting a step wrong, hated the stilted conversation with some partner or other who had only asked me in order to ingratiate himself with one of my sisters, and most of all, I hated the moment when the dance ended, and I sat down and overheard those about me praising the grace and charm and beauty of every Miss Bennet but I.

If there was one guest enjoying Meryton balls as little as I, it was Pike. Few mammas would allow their daughters to waste their time with a lowly clerk. Of course they could not refuse a request to dance unless they wished to sit down the rest of the evening, so I often watched them flee before he could greet them.

And so, at many a ball, Pike and I had no one to speak with but each other.

"It is not your fault, you know," I assured him on one occasion.

He fidgeted with his cuffs, tucking away a loose thread. "It's only their presumption that irritates me. They flee to avoid a request I had no intention of making."

"You do not dance?"

"Not with these—" He bit back the end of the thought. "These ladies."

"Ah."

"I will dance with you, if you like," he said, glancing at me sideways.

I made a face. "Must I?"

"I suppose you, too, have been instructed not to waste your time with me."

"I may have been. Mamma talks so much that one loses track. But it's not you. I would much rather not dance at all. It is a torture for me, those who watch me, and the feet of the young man who partners me."

He laughed at that. "It is true. You are quite the worst dancer in the county."

I found his honesty rather a relief.

"So why did you speak to me?"

"I wanted to ask if you could get me some more sheep's blood. You see—oh, drat, here comes Mamma. And she's got Tim Lucas in tow. Pretend you have just offered to turn for me at the piano after supper."

"Why pretend?" he asked, and took my arm and led me over to the piano, where we perused sheet music and discussed the price of sheep's blood.

Ball after ball passed this way. Months turned to years. My sisters acquired suitors; I did not. I could not regret any man in particular—they invariably failed to please my sensitive nose—but it was rather humiliating, to be left standing alone time and again. Nor did my dancing improve.

I very soon gave relief to all of Meryton society by deciding that I would dance no more. Pike and I used our meetings at balls to conduct business and ignored the way everyone else was ignoring us.

Abetted by the small but steady revenue of my business with Pike, I was able to modestly improve my little laboratory. A full sized electrical rig remained a distant dream, but I got hold of some makeshift Leyden jars and a bit of chemical equipment. I was attempting to discover what made up the living self—not the mere dead flesh, but the *spark of life*, as I'd heard all those year ago. The theory of bodily humors is, of course, considered hopelessly old-fashioned, but I believed it might have been discarded too quickly. You see, I was inspired by the great strides humanity was making in the study of chemistry. Every day, it seemed, new elemental chemicals were identified and isolated. If the physical world was made up of such building blocks, I reasoned, ought it not be possible to distill humanity down to its purest components as well? There must be reasons, after all, why we were the way we were. Suppose I could derive the source of Jane's sweetness, or Elizabeth's charm, or Papa's indolence, and bottle them up to study in their purest form? Imagine what a relief it would be if, before a ball, I could simply take a spoonful of medicine that would transform me into the sort of girl who liked balls!

It remained purely theoretical. However, I did find that by subjecting the blood of farm animals (procured for me by Pike) to a process I designed of dilution, basification, exposure to a mild charge, and induced precipitation, I obtained very different results based upon the species and, indeed, even the individual. Some had a meaty stink and were nearly as clear as water; others smelled sweet and were thick and dark; and everything in between. They had strange properties. One batch of serum remained an eerie blood-warm temperature no matter how long it remained in a phial. Another looked almost metallic and seemed to move in response to my voice.

My results were inconsistent, however, and nearly impossible to quantify. I was sure that I was on track to discovering what might be called the elements of life; but how to prove it? I could find no way to use these serums, interesting as they were, nor to demonstrate that they were the building blocks I believed—until a lucky bit of feline carnage. I refer to the bird Cariad.

Cariad was the first recipient of what I now call the Procedure. You see, I had been performing the usual electrical experiments—making the legs of a recently deceased frog twitch and jump, etc.—when one day I heard a thump overhead. I opened the skylight and in sauntered a great black tomcat from the barn with something struggling in his jaws. I got there just as the poor little bird, with a desperate flutter, expired under Jack's needle-sharp teeth. He then lost interest and, seeing me, laid the little corpse at my feet with a proud swish of his tail. It was a tiny finch—*Carduelis spinus*, if I am not mistaken—and its brilliant green-yellow feathers practically glowed against the dull floorboards. It would have made a pretty painting, were it not for the bloody hole in its chest.

I looked from the poor little finch to my electrical equipment. *The stuff of life.*

I laid its little body in a tub of salve I had recently synthesized from pig's blood, which seemed to have some interesting conductive qualities. I wrapped wires around its exposed heart. Then I turned the crank on my little electrostatic generator.

I expected no more than the kind of grisly twitch I got from the frog's legs. But after a moment, the creature fluttered its eyes open. Frantically it pecked at the wires trailing into its chest, which luckily were not attached very tightly or else it might have ripped its own heart out. I held it down and carefully freed it from the wires. It flew around the room in a frenzy, and then landed on a beam overhead. I held out a finger. Cautiously, it flew down and perched.

I examined it, holding as still as I could. It cocked its head, examining me with one bright little eye that had been dull moments before. I had initiated the Procedure at the instant of death—but it *had* been dead. Electricity and one of my serums had brought it back.

Subsequent attempts to replicate the bird's revival were unsuccessful. Either I had not isolated the role of the serum, or the animals were too far past the point of death, or—as I increasingly suspected—my current equipment was not powerful enough. My little bird colleague remained, though, reminding me that it was possible. It lived on seeds and nuts like a normal bird, and though it sometimes grew listless, I found that a few sips of the dark sweet serum soon had it chirping and alert. And yet, the gaping hole in its chest never healed. It never seemed to distress it, though I could see its little heart fluttering in the open air. I longed more than ever for a proper rig. With more power, who knew what I might do?

I know I ought not to have named it. It is a research subject, not a pet. But it happened by accident. Cariad sings so much, you see, and his whistles and chirps reminded me of one of the postboys who come through Meryton. He is Welsh and very musical—always singing or whistling is Owen. And when he helps change the tired horses, he talks to them. "There now, cariad," he croons. "You've done a good day's work. Time to rest now, cariad."

It means "beloved" in his tongue. Once it popped into my head, I could not seem to shake it off—the bird was Cariad, and that was final. He soon learned to perch on my shoulder, singing merrily, heedless of the hole in his chest.

So captivated was I by this development, and so bent upon repeating it, that I failed to notice that my business associate had begun to regard me in a new light.

As I had grown into a plain young woman, Pike had become rather a handsome young man. Several times he abandoned me for weeks on end in pursuit of some young lady or another. I did not mind; he had, I thought, excellent taste, and I liked watching their pretty faces laugh and blush and sigh. It seemed he could be quite charming when he chose. Still, those liaisons always ended the same way. Pike was too poor even to make a go of it as a fortune hunter. After a ball or two, the flirtation would be cut off, and Pike would end up back at my side.

And then he had to go and ruin it all by asking me to marry him.

It began—as practically everything does in this stultifying town—at a ball. During supper I played two most difficult concertos, as usual, and Mr. Pike turned for me, but when the musicians came back from their rest he abruptly held out his arm and said, "Miss Mary, will you do me the honor of dancing the next set?"

"What?" I said.

He looked faintly annoyed. "I asked you to dance."

"I know. I am not deaf. Why?"

Again, that flicker of irritation. But he smoothed it away. "Is it strange," he said, with a smooth little bow, "that I should wish to dance a reel with the loveliest and most amiable young lady in the room tonight?"

Ah. Now I believed I understood. He wished to practice his gallantry upon me. Perhaps there was some young lady in the crowd tonight to whom he wished to make his addresses, and he wanted to try them out on me.

Well. I supposed I owed him for all the page-turning, not to mention the sheep's blood. "Oh, all right," I said, "but only one set, mind," and I gave him my arm.

I tried not to look too bored as he led me through the dance. He was really not such a bad dancer, but I could not conceive of why he would waste our time this way.

"Your uncle has a fine house," he said.

"Hmm? Oh. I suppose." My uncle's house had no room suitable for a laboratory, and the lights of town would quite likely obscure any attempts at viewing the rings of Saturn.

"It would be an excellent home for a respectable gentleman's family. It is too bad that they never had any children of their own." He did not sound very sorry.

"Do you think so?" My aunt Phillips, at least, had always seemed perfectly content to borrow my younger sisters, Lydia and Kitty, and send them home when she tired of them. I wondered if any natural philosophers had ever examined the motherhood-by-proxy instincts of childless aunts. I was sure I had observed it in sheep as well as humans. Perhaps mother love was so strong that it must find an object, even an unnatural one, as with the ewe in our barn that I had observed insistently raising a chicken.

Whilst musing upon this I realized belatedly that my dancing partner had continued talking. "—not imagine a more charming helpmeet," he was saying.

"Hm? Oh. Certainly." The music had stopped. "Will you take me back to the piano, please?"

He bowed over my hand and—this was a novel affectation—kissed it. I took little note. My mind was on the ewe.

At the next few balls, however, his performance was repeated. After supper he would rise from the piano, bow, and ask me to dance. It grew quite tedious, listening to him talk of his future prospects instead of something sensible, like the price of fox blood, while doing my best not to turn the wrong way and slam into some Lucas's behind. I looked forward to the day he would talk sense again.

I began to notice, between counting steps and nodding to Pike, that we were attracting no little attention. When we danced I felt many pairs of eyes upon us. There were whispers, too.

"...throwing herself away..."

"...likely to be an old maid, otherwise."

"The cheek of him!"

"Best she can hope for."

I know, I know. I am not so unworldly that I cannot understand such talk. I simply never imagined they were talking of *me*. No one had ever speculated before that I was forming a romantic connection, suitable or not. Besides, I had hit upon a method of using stars of equivalent brightness to estimate the age of the earth. The calculations occupied my mind even on the dance floor.

It was at a public ball when the truth was thrust upon me. I was dancing with Pike—well, my feet were dancing; my head was concerned with the brightness of Polaris—when suddenly I became aware of what my partner was saying.

"Be sure to be at home tomorrow afternoon," he told me. "I mean to come and speak to your father."

"How nice," I said, then, "What? What can you have to speak to my father about?"

He smiled tightly. The dance pulled us apart, and when we were back together he tugged me a little closer. "To ask for your hand, of course," he said. "Come, do not be coy."

"Coy?" I hissed. "My *hand*? Do not be absurd."

"I beg your pardon?" His hand, hot and sweaty, gripped mine too tight. "You have done nothing but encourage my advances."

"Stuff." I tried to pull away, but he held me too tight. He made a visible effort to master himself.

"You have sat with me for hours."

"*You* sat with *me*."

"You dance only with me."

"Yes, because I hate dancing. I was being *nice*."

His jaw clenched. "I am entirely beneath your notice, is that it?"

"No, I just—"

"It is an excellent alliance for you. I flatter myself that you will not find a better," he said. "Pray think on it. I am probably your only chance at matrimony. You are too plain and too poor to expect another."

With that I wrenched my hand from his and stopped moving. Maria Lucas bumped into me from behind with an *oof*. I was disrupting the dance, but I did not care. "I would not marry you if you were the richest, handsomest man in England!" I hissed in a whisper, and although the dance was only half done, I stalked away without waiting for an escort.

CHAPTER 5

Mr. Pike's Attentions

After our little display I thought Pike was done with me. I could not have been more wrong. He was determined to have me.

From then on, whenever we were in the same room, his eyes were always on me. His attentions, while never quite rising to the level of open courtship, were unmistakable and unavoidable.

Perhaps I should have been flattered. At seventeen, I had never attracted so much as the whisper of a suitor. Instead, I felt rather insulted. I missed our old companionship. We had never exactly been affectionate friends, but I could talk to him without getting a headache. Now he seemed determined that I should leave any encounter with a blinding one.

Why *didn't* I want to marry Mr. Pike, you may wonder? So, too, have I. It was hardly a brilliant match, but as he said, I was unlikely to attract a better, and we did have a rapport of sorts. And yet—there was that smell of paste and ink that clung to him. There was the way he'd tossed the gunpowder into the fire without heed for singeing my petticoat. When we danced, sometimes he held my hand so hard it hurt, as though he feared I'd run away.

And there was my research, my answers fluttering just out of reach as

Cariad fluttered above me. If I married him, or anyone, I'd no doubt be obliged to stop. Of course I would marry someday—but surely it needn't be so soon.

Pike, however, had other ideas. The young man who liked to throw gunpowder in the fire had a similar approach to flirtation.

Every time he bowed to me in the street, looking up at me through his lashes; every time he greeted my family with "Miss Bennet, Miss Elizabeth…Miss Mary," seeming to put a special emphasis on my name; every time he arranged matters so that he could walk me in to supper at Uncle's—oh, I hated it. Whenever he tucked my hand against his arm I envisioned kicking him in the shins. Yet I felt guilty, too. I could tell many people thought I ought to be grateful for his attentions.

That, I realized eventually, was why I hated it so much. *He* thought I ought to be grateful, too.

"Why are you doing this?" I asked him once while we were walking. The Lucases had arranged a walk through the hills, and of course Mr. Pike had managed to fall in next to me.

"I ask for very little in this life," he answered. "I know my place. But what I do ask for, I deserve."

For a time it greatly disconcerted me. However, I did my best to disregard it. Perhaps if I ignored it, it would cease, and Pike could go back to being simply my business partner and page turner. No need to borrow trouble. But a young lady of modest means cannot so easily banish the question of marriage. It was Elizabeth who made me see my situation clearly.

How to describe my older sister Elizabeth? There was a time, when we were younger, when we spent quite a bit of time together. She is the only one of my sisters who likes to read half as much as I do. We marveled over Mary Wollstonecraft together, and tore through John Bigland's *System of Geography and History*. She is really quite clever—not terribly interested in the sciences, but capable of an intelligent conversation.

But she grew up and became beautiful. I grew up and did not. What was more, she was my father's favorite. When I was banished from his library, she was suffered to remain. Soon we had very little to say to one another. She was busy going on visits to my uncle Gardiner's in town and to her other friends'. I was retreating whenever I could to my laboratory. If you plant two identical pea seeds and leave one full in the sun and the other in a murky corner, they will grow up anything but identical.

So I was quite surprised when, one night, she knocked on my bedroom door.

She was already in her nightclothes, her hair plaited down her back. I had not yet let mine down.

"Sit down," she said. "I'll do it for you."

I did. I was too surprised to do otherwise. It was rare that anyone from my family came up to my cramped little chamber. Lizzy took me by the shoulders and turned me a little away from her. Her long fingers deftly picked the pins from my hair.

"Mary," she said, "do you want to marry Septimus Pike?"

I jumped in surprise. "What?"

"I overheard Uncle and Aunt Phillips talking," she said. "They seemed to regard it as almost a settled thing."

"It isn't!"

"So I thought. Aunt Phillips said you would come around, though, when you realized there would be no other offers."

"Were our parents there?"

"Papa was."

"What did he say?"

"He said you were far too young, but that..." She hesitated. "He said he would talk to Mamma."

The room seemed to be growing smaller around me. Somehow what I felt most was embarrassment. That my sister, considered one of the local beauties, should know that this shameful thing was happening to me! I thought longingly of the secret door in my closet. Oh, to be in my laboratory, observing and unobserved.

"So," she said. The brush caught on a tangle that made my eyes smart; Lizzy held up the offending lock and brushed it in one hand so it could not hurt me. "Do you want to marry him?"

"You don't know if he even intends to offer."

"But if he does."

Of course the answer was no, but I found myself asking, "Do you think I ought to?"

"He has certain qualities that are amiable," she said neutrally.

"But what do you think?"

"It doesn't matter what I think. The choice is yours, Mary."

"We are commanded to be fruitful and multiply," I pointed out.

"That's so."

"However, the bard wrote, 'To thine own self be true.'"

She sighed. "Please, Mary, no more quotations."

If this poor fellow with his meager charms had approached Lizzy, she would have refused him immediately, and everyone would have backed her. But because it was me, it seemed they would consider it.

And what if I did refuse him? What would become of me? You must understand, Holzmann, what it is to be a fortuneless female. The thought of being a full-time poor relation made me shudder. And what if none of my sisters married well enough even for that? Could I support myself as a governess? Certainly I was learned enough, but I do not have a way with children. They seem always to be sticky. It disconcerted me even when I was a child myself.

And in either case, if I did not have a home of my own, how was I to continue my research?

Being a young lady is a bit like playing vingt-un. You start with certain cards, and then you try your best to improve your hand with what comes your way. But if you are too reckless or too arrogant—or too unsatisfied with a perfectly good lot—you may end up with nothing at all.

I hate cards.

"My God," I said. "I may really have to marry him."

She gave a sigh of relief. "So you don't want to."

"Of course I don't!"

"Well, I didn't know. You are friendlier with him than with any other young man."

"That is hardly saying much! I am extremely unfriendly!"

"All right then. I can tell Papa to refuse him, if he offers for you."

Of course. Lizzy, Papa's favorite, would intercede to save me. My laugh sounded bitter.

"How kind of you. He will probably point out that I won't get another offer to take me off his hands."

"Nonsense! Of course you will," Lizzy said, too heartily.

I grabbed the brush so hard the bristles stung my palm and turned to look at her. "Do you really believe I'll get a better offer? Tell me what you *think*."

She hesitated. "I don't know," she said quietly.

That was the first time I remember being properly, properly scared.

I suppose Lizzy could see it, for she hurried on: "It will be all right, though. Probably Jane will marry some terribly rich fellow and keep us all in her mansion."

"Poor Jane."

"I suppose. *I* am a delightful houseguest."

She was trying to cheer me up. I hate being cheered up. But it was kind, I supposed. I mustered a smile. "You can go downstairs. I'll finish my hair."

"All right." She stood and went to the door. "Good night, Mary."

"Good night." I hesitated. "Elizabeth?"

"Yes?"

"What if it's you?"

"What if it's me what?"

"What if it's you who marries a rich man?" I asked. "If I never marry—would you be pleased to have me live with you?"

There was just a flash of hesitation on her face before she smiled and said, "Perfectly pleased. We both know it will be Jane, though, don't we? Good night, Mary." And she went out and closed the door.

I am not proud to say it, Holzmann, but I threw my brush at the door so hard that the handle cracked in two.

CHAPTER 6

An Offer to Pike

After my talk with Elizabeth, I began to consider my future more seriously. When I felt myself succumbing to self-pity, I thought about the fate of the great scientists of the past. My lot was really not so bad compared to Galileo, who was imprisoned in his house for a decade, or poor Bruno who was burnt at the stake for the sin of correctly inferring that the earth orbits the sun. And let us not forget Newton, who went mad, though that was perhaps his own fault for drinking too much mercury.

Compared to the trials of these great men, being a young lady was nothing. Yes, as a man I could have gone to university and learned at the feet of the great thinkers of our age. And, of course, if I were a young man, I would not have to look around for a husband to save me when my father died and we lost the house. Longbourn would simply be mine.

Still, I decided I must remember poor Bruno, be grateful that there was no burning pyre in my future, and discover a solution.

The first question was what to do about Pike. My initial instinct was to run him off, once and for all. He had no idea how unpleasant a companion I could be when I chose (and sometimes when I did not).

However, I soon thought better of it. The thought of marrying him still made me shudder—but, I realized, the thought of marrying any man was nearly as bad. Even if I found a more amiable suitor than Pike, he was unlikely to be richer or better-smelling. I would spend my life cooking his dinners and having his progeny. My research career would end, and no matter how violently in love I managed to fall with this imagined spouse, I could not reconcile myself to that. Anyway, my preference was to keep Pike as a business partner, which he would hardly do if I made him loathe me. If not him, then who? And if I did not marry, how was I to live? As a poor relation? If I had to watch Lizzy bite her tongue in irritation with me all my life I was quite sure I would end by burning her house to the ground, which would be most wicked.

Think, Mary, I told myself day and night. *You are supposed to be clever. There must be another way out.*

And then, one day, I found one.

My aunt and uncle Phillips were dining with us at Longbourn. My uncle was always rather loud and braggish when they came to us. Maybe it was the superiority of Papa's cellar, which led him to drink deep, or maybe the grandeur of Papa's gentlemanly status that made him feel inferior. Whatever it was, he was even more overbearing than usual.

"It's been a very good year for the practice," he said. "A very good year. Lots of young men need their wills made, coming back from war with their pockets full of prizes, and I've been made solicitor to Lord Henry Charing." He paused to see if any of us would express admiration for this. No one did, so he continued, "A very good year indeed. But of course now I've the duty to sort out what to do with the excess! Ah, well, a prosperous man's work is never done." He laughed as though he'd told a great joke.

"Excellent pudding tonight," my father said.

"I've done not a little research," Uncle Gardiner said. "Of course I've thought of buying an estate of me own. How would that be, Bennet, eh? Two gentlemen in the family then, eh?"

"Mmm," said Papa. "That would be a welcome change."

"However, upon consideration, I felt that a life of idleness would not suit me. No, I must *invest*." He dropped his voice, as though there might be spies lurking beneath the table. "You mustn't tell anyone about this—but I've got word of a tremendous new factory enterprise up north. I've got it on excellent authority that if I commit my funds I am guaranteed to see returns of 13 percent."

"That would indeed be extraordinary," said Papa.

I was only half attending to this—my uncle lost his life savings every few years, but luckily my aunt never let him gamble more than they could afford to lose—when he said something that grabbed my attention.

"Think I'll send young Pike up north," he said. "He can keep an eye on my investment for a year or so."

"Did you say you are sending Septimus Pike up north?" I said.

My uncle gave me a disgustingly knowing smile. "The prospect disturbs you, eh, Miss Mary? You are not the only young person who does not want to be parted! Septimus himself refuses to go. Foolish boy doesn't see what a fine opportunity it is. I believe he is afraid I will forget about him." His smile was now so knowing it was almost a leer. "And perhaps he has other reasons as well."

I ignored my uncle's innuendoes. My mind was in a whirl. I knew how to rid myself of Septimus Pike once and for all—perhaps of any need for a husband.

The next afternoon, I walked into Meryton. When I stepped into my uncle's office, he was there and working, but he was very quick to tell Pike to take a break and take a turn about the town square with me.

Pike looked at me with a slight frown. "I'm in the middle of the letter to Captain Berwyck's executor," he said.

"Never mind that. Go, lad, go."

So Pike gave me his arm, and we went.

"Not the town square," I said. "Let us climb the hill." He looked at me with surprise but said, "Very well," and we left Meryton behind us.

When we reached the top, I sat on the puddingstone for a rest. Meryton's rooftops lay below us. No one was now close enough to hear.

"Why do you wish to marry me, Pike?" I asked.

He shrugged. "Why not? We have always got on. We suit."

"You do not seem to like me very much."

"Like? Oh, I don't know. But I mean to have you all the same." He had taken up a stick and was whacking the heads off dandelions.

"You won't give up, will you."

He turned to me with a sudden, wolfish grin. "Actually, I was on the fence about asking for your hand at all, until you left me on the dance floor. Since then it's all I can think of."

That startled a laugh out of me. At least he was honest. I could almost like him.

"It wouldn't be so bad," he said. "We've managed a very successful partnership as gunpowder traders. Why not expand it?"

This was my opening, and I seized it. "Actually," I said, "that is just what I'd like to do."

"Marry me?"

"No. Expand our partnership."

You will recall, Holzmann, my experiments with galvanization of blood. I had, unfortunately, hit a wall with my current research. My results had plateaued; I could make no accurate conclusions about what, actually, made up the thing called life, at least not without better equipment. The little jar in which I saved my coins for an electrical rig was, despite years of savings, only three-quarters full.

However, one of my attempts had produced a bright, tart green dye, the color of new spring leaves. I now brought out a handkerchief dyed with the stuff and showed it to Pike. I thought I might have to explain it to him, but to Pike's credit, he wasn't stupid. His eyes narrowed, and he turned the scrap over in his hands. "Mercy," he said softly. "That's ten times as green as any green cloth I've ever seen." He lifted his eyes to me. "You did this?"

I nodded.

"And it's fast?"

"I've washed and dried that scrap a dozen times. It's hardly faded."

"Expensive to make?"

"Not really."

He nodded. "What do you want for it?"

I drew a deep breath. "Don't marry me. Go up to Manchester, as Uncle asked you. There are dozens of cloth factories there. I am sure you could sell this stuff, don't you agree?"

"It's possible there'd be a market," he said cautiously.

"Good. Then the same arrangement as before." I nodded. "We split the profits down the middle. People are always making huge fortunes up north."

"I hardly think one little dye will net us a fortune. Do people really like green that much?"

"Yes," I said. I had no idea. "Anyhow, I don't need a fortune. Just enough to live comfortably. I imagine five thousand pounds or so ought to be enough."

"Oh, is that all." He drew the cloth between his fingers. "How will you account for your sudden windfall?"

"We can pretend some distant, eccentric relative left it to me. You can mock up a realistic enough will, can't you? My father pays little attention to his relations, except as it pertains to the entail. I do not think it is impossible."

"Wouldn't it be easier to just marry me? We could skip the fraud."

"Wouldn't you rather have five thousand pounds to your own name? You'd have many pretty prospects then."

He looked skeptical. "Forgive me if I lack your optimism."

I drew a deep breath. "All right," I said. "If...if the dye does not make us enough to live on...I...I'll marry you."

He rubbed a hand and regarded me with narrowed eyes, like I was a particularly complicated codicil in a will. That honest grin broke out again. "We have a bargain."

The next week, Pike went north. In his trunk, well-padded and carefully hidden, were six phials of my greenest dye.

CHAPTER 7

Mamma; Reviving Papa

My spirits were lifted immeasurably by Pike's departure. Not only had I rid myself of a troublesome suitor, but I might soon be possessed of an independence.

But a year passed, and Pike did not return. My uncle's investment paid out for once, though not to the tune of 13 percent; still, Pike did not return. When I ventured to ask my uncle about it, he harrumphed about the unreliability of today's young men. He soon hired another clerk.

It was extremely frustrating. I had no way of knowing exactly what had happened, but I assumed he had gone bust, as so many people do up there, and was either ashamed to show his face here or simply unable to afford the journey. It made me quite vexed—I was sure the dye would sell! If only I could have gone up there myself, I knew I could have made every factory owner from Manchester to Liverpool bid for it. Ladies, of course, do not go peddling dyes, though. My hopes of a fortune evaporated.

I soldiered on, though, as best I could. I was able to sustain a semblance of my gunpowder business through Miss Figg, the apothecary's sister—all the county knew about Mamma's myriad imaginary illnesses, so I never lacked an excuse to visit the apothecary's shop. That and my laboratory sustained me, and I began to think I might find my way without Pike's help. I even saved up enough to order proper electrostatic equipment at last. But then came the night of the accident.

It was at one of the dreary balls at the home of our neighbors the Lucases. Everyone hereabout complains about them—too hot, too little food, too many guests of dubious gentility—but everybody goes. I did not mind. I had been going about for weeks in a haze of happy anticipation. Soon my electrical rig would arrive. Oh, what might I do then! What would I soon discover! At last, at last, my life would begin.

Then, when we were leaving, Lady Lucas spoke to Mamma.

"How wonderful to have you all," she said. "Where is Mr. Bennet? Not indisposed, I hope?"

"No, no," said Mamma. "You know how he is. It can be fearfully difficult to rouse the dear man from his library. Such a clever scholar he is! He is in there day and night."

A clever scholar! Ha. It was true that Papa spent most of his time in his library, but much of it passed in front of the fire with his feet up on a stool, snoring.

"I think," Mamma went on, "that you are almost sure to see him at the next assembly, however. He had a particular reason to stay at home tonight." She dropped her voice importantly. "You see, he has been sent an *electrical*."

I stopped dead. I felt as though a bucket of ice water had been poured down my spine.

The electrostatical machine. It was here at last.

After long years of scrimping and saving and mucking about with quicklime, I had at last saved enough. As Pike was gone, I ordered it myself. I knew I was taking a risk, but since I was the one who walked out to meet the mail coach each day, I thought it was safe enough. I planned to store it in the garden shed, and then spirit it up to the laboratory when everyone else was asleep.

Only the afternoon mail had been late today. I thought I'd simply missed it, but evidently it found its way to Papa while I was submitting to having my hair styled.

I tugged on Mamma's arm. "Come, Mamma. Depriving oneself of sleep is not salutary. My reading on healthful habits says—"

"Yes, yes." She turned back to Lady Lucas. "Come over tomorrow and we can talk over the whole evening. Come, girls, it's late."

In the carriage, my mother snored, and Jane dozed on Lizzy's shoulder. My younger sisters, whose prattle might have kept us awake, were spending the night at my aunt's. I was wide awake. My heart pounded. Sweat stood out across my nose. My electrical machine. *He had my machine.*

My father's light was still on when we got home. He pretends to scorn Mamma's tendency to gossip, but he was just as curious about our neighbors as she was. Luckily, he soon tired of her chatter about who had danced with whom. By the time I had put on my nightclothes and braided my hair, the light in the library, visible from my window, had gone out.

I lay awake for another half hour, just to be sure. Then I crept downstairs.

I had long since learned which boards groaned, and my descent was utterly silent. I slipped into Papa's library, now lit only by the flicker of my candlestick. Dim though it was, I knew it well enough that I instantly discerned the change. On his desk, by the window, there now stood a large box.

My heart was now beating so fast that it felt like a bird's wings fluttering inside my chest. I crept toward the box. It was around four feet long and three feet wide, and I could just make out the words PHILADELPHIA FINE GLASSWORKS on the lid.

The words shivered as the candle trembled in my hand. This was it.

Carefully, I removed the lid. Inside was a nest of wood shavings, and nestled within it—*oh*.

It was not the finest or the largest rig in the land. In fact, it was the cheapest one I could find. Still, it was the most beautiful thing I had ever seen. The wooden and bronze body shone in neat collapsible segments. I set them carefully aside—oh, the smooth, competent weight of them!—and began to dig through the shavings for the pieces of the stand.

I sat back when my fingers found it. I lifted it carefully. A glass globe, heavy and clear, larger than a man's head. At either end—*the poles*, I thought giddily—there was a hole for the insertion of a screw.

"Mmph—ahem—why, what the devil do you think you're doing?"

I whirled around, clutching the globe to my chest. There, snorting and blinking in his chair, was my father.

"What are you doing?" he repeated. "Put that down at once, Mary. Carefully, mind. That's my new electrical equipment."

I ought to have done it at once, I know. He was my father. I owed him my obedience. Not only was it right; it was prudent: The moments of freedom I was able to snatch in my laboratory depended upon my activities being kept a secret.

But I had waited years for this. Years. I am afraid I lost my mind.

"It isn't yours," I said, pushing a whisper through my tight throat. "It's mine."

"Yours?" He laughed. "Don't be ridiculous."

"It is," I said. "There, my name is on the box."

He glanced at it. It read TO M. BENNET, LONGBOURN, HERTFORDSHIRE. "Meant to be Mr.," he said. He tried to take it from me. I stepped back. "I suppose it is a gift from your uncle, or from my old master at Oxford. Really, now, Mary. It isn't a toy."

"And I am not a child."

"You're acting like one." He smiled at me kindly. "Come, girl. I know how you love to feel learned. I promise I will set it up one of these days so that you and your sisters may see some sparks. You'd like that, eh?"

The blood was rushing in my ears. "It's mine!" I said. "It's mine!" and I yanked it out of his grasp.

His face darkened. "That's enough. Give it here."

I couldn't. My arms refused to pry loose from their desperate embrace of the globe, even when Papa grasped it. There was a ringing in my ears. We were tugging it back and forth between us, my father continuing to scold me in a whisper, and me unable to do anything but repeat that *it was mine*.

It ended as it must. You know the story of King Solomon and the baby, I assume? My father had not spent years dreaming of this very globe. I had. When his grasp became too rough, I did the only thing I could. I let him have it.

He staggered back a step when I let go. "Good," he wheezed. My father led a fairly sedentary life. He was red in the face and sweating. "Good girl. I knew you would see reason."

"You do not know anything about me," I said. *"Anything."* I had never looked at my father this way. I thought, *I wish you were dead*.

He laughed. "Your exhaustion has made you overdramatic, Mary. Go to bed, and tomorrow I—*unh*."

My father clutched his chest and staggered forward. I had a split second to decide which of them to save from a hard landing. I am ashamed to say I chose the globe. My father fell to the floor and was still.

With one hand, I clutched the globe close to my bosom. The other I pressed over my mouth in horror. My father wasn't moving. Even after bending down to examine him, I found no whisper of breath.

Oh, God! What had I done? I'd killed him.

Mentally I cursed the Mary of fifteen seconds before as a fool. I had wished him dead—well, now he was. And now everything would be lost. Our home. My laboratory. My sisters' chances at a match. What would become of us? We would split up, I supposed, to stay with grudging distant relatives or become governesses. I'd doomed us all.

Panic imbued me with a sort of white-hot clarity. Before I knew what I was about, I had lifted the lid on the galvanic equipment. My hands, as cool and steady as my mind was scattered and erratic, lifted the bronze framework, one piece after another after another, fitting them together, hanging the globe, until the complete rig stood before me. Then I lifted my skirts and ran silently up to my laboratory. Once more, my hands seemed to know what they needed before my mind did. I watched as they darted out to pick up various items. Scraps of cloth. Copper wire. A certain salve.

Back downstairs, I laid my father flat beneath the rig. I ripped open his shirt and spread the galvanic salve on his chest and temples and tongue.

I did not think. I did not allow myself to. I simply went about it as though my father was an unusually large Cariad. I placed bronze weights on his chest and temples, and turned the globe until the cloth that rubbed against it crackled with electric charge. I saw a spark jump and fizzle out in his chest hair. He remained still.

Faster and faster I turned the crank. A spark large enough to revive a finch might not be enough to revive a man. Again and again, I shocked him. His body jerked, but otherwise was still. At last I stopped. The strength drained from my body as I faced the full horror of what I had done. *He was dead.* Past reviving.

Then he coughed.

I crashed to my knees beside him. "Papa?"

He blinked and coughed again. One shaky hand came up quizzically to tug at the pad on his chest. "Mary? Is that you? Where am I?"

"Your library, Papa." I took off the pads and closed his shirt.

"Library?" He blinked more. "Mary? Is that you?"

"Yes, Papa. Come, let's get off the ground."

He remained confused as I helped him to his feet, but at least he was no longer dead weight. I soon perceived that he retained no memory of our fight and only the haziest recollections of the previous day. I put him back into his chair. He stared up at me in the flickering light of the candlestick I'd left on the desk. His face looked pale and his eyes were two great black holes. For a moment, I had the queer idea that I'd failed, and that he was dead after all.

Then, however, he muttered, "Don't touch my books, Mrs. Bennet," leaned his head against the chair, and immediately began to snore. I watched him for several hours to make sure he would not collapse again. He slept on peacefully, his snores the welcomest sound I had ever heard.

It is strange, watching a parent sleep. Parents seem so important when one is younger—like giants, or gods. But they're just people, after all.

When I was satisfied that he was out of danger, I put the globe back in its box. It made me shudder now to look at it. I'd saved money for years to buy it, but the price had almost been much, much higher.

Still, I thought, better not to leave him the reminder. I hauled the crate up to my attic. Afterward, sore, sweaty, covered in sawdust and salve, I did my best to wash in my basin and then crawled into bed.

As soon as I closed my eyes, my father's blank, staring eyes appeared before me. I'd killed him.

I opened my eyes again. Luckily I'd not yet blown out my candle. On my bedside table lay *Reverend Quindley's Admonishments for Godly Young Ladies*. I had always kept Harry's gift near me, but rarely looked inside it. Now I opened it and began to read.

Chapter 8

Papa's Condition

I watched my father closely the next morning. A few cautious questions established that he had no memory of anything that had happened the night before. He was a little tired and cross, but that was not unusual, for he had waited up for us long past his preferred hour of retiring.

In the light of day, I began to think I had been a bit silly. Of course he hadn't died. He had merely fainted, and my machine had revived him. Galvanic shocks would wake anyone up. No doubt in the dark, in my panic, I had missed the signs of him clinging to life. Still, he likely would have died if I had not interfered. It was a strange sensation, watching my family go about their business, knowing that it all could have come to an end.

In the days that followed, I felt myself fill with renewed love for them. It was brave of us, in a way, how we lived as though this house was ours, instead of merely borrowed from a stranger on a lease of uncertain length. I felt a new affection for my mother, a butterfly of a woman, frantic and brainless and beautiful. For my father, I felt a great swell of gratitude each time I looked at him. His life was so precious to us all.

I loved them all, but it *hurt*. Every time I heard Lydia and Kitty's footsteps thumping up and down the stairs, or watched Elizabeth and Jane read under their favorite tree in the garden, I felt a stab of guilt so profound that I wondered if it might do physical damage to my heart. I almost hoped it would. Everything we had was so fragile, and I had been so careless.

I walked about in a storm of misery so intense I could hardly speak. I found solace only one place: within the pages of *Reverend Quindley's Admonishments for Godly Young Ladies*.

It was exactly what I needed. Harry must have known that I would. I suppose he saw flaws in my character that alarmed him even then. How foolish I was not to turn to it before! Here were answers for my questions, and corrections for my faults. Even running my fingers down its table of contents, with headings like "On Modesty" and "On the Home" and "On Prayer," could bring me solace.

I was not irredeemable. This book could repair me. I could be the daughter and sister my family deserved. I read it cover to cover, imagining Harry's comforting hand on my shoulder, then read it again. My sisters sighed and rolled their eyes as Quindley's words filled my speech, but I ignored them. They were simple women. They did not contain such depths of depravity as I did.

I had time for these new pursuits. The night after what happened with Papa, I went up to my laboratory, put everything away in crates, then came downstairs and pushed a chest in front of the secret door. My final act was the hardest, but I knew I must. I took Cariad from my apron pocket, put him on the sill, and shooed him out the open window. Then I closed it. I soon heard him tapping at the glass, but I put a pillow over my head and read *Quindley's* until the sound went away.

CHAPTER 9

In Which Two Gentlemen Refuse My Proposals of Marriage

Bear with me a bit, Holzmann. This chapter has little to do with science. However, it has everything to do with how I came to create the chromae, so I'd better tell you.

What do you think it means to be in love, Holzmann? For the well-organized mind, I mean. Is it when you look at someone and see how he fits perfectly into the life that you want? How if you can just have him, it will unlock everything you need to be happy? If so, I was in love with Mr. Collins.

When my Collins-related derangement took hold, it had been approximately a year since my father's accident. I had watched Papa closely since then but detected no ill effects, aside from perhaps a certain anxiety at the sight of lightning.

I had watched myself closely, too, and was less sanguine about my observations. *Quindley's* said, "A young lady's primary duty is to prepare for her life as a mother and wife. Until the happy day when a man makes her his own, she must strive to make her father's home a happier, godlier, more pleasant place and be a helpmeet to her mother and brothers and sisters."

I had no gift for making anyone happy, but I could play pleasant music and share godly extracts. All that year I played and copied until my fingers ached. I saw Cariad once more, but I did not let him approach me—my little half-dead experiment could not improve any man's home. He flew into our carriage, chirping desperately, while I was on my way to a morning visit with Mamma. She shrieked and shooed him away, and after a moment of shock so did I, with twice as much vigor. I believe he was trying to sit upon my shoulder. After he'd flown away my head began to ache so fiercely that I begged Mamma to take me home.

A girl who gives all she has to her family shall become tranquil of spirit. So Quindley proclaims. Yet I found tranquility elusive. Some days I missed my lab so much I felt ill with it. The harder I strove for womanly perfection, the more insufficient I felt. Quindley would not approve of my strange, restless dreams, full of shocks and the scents of lightning and sweat, of sparks shining against disordered curls, nor of the way I would lay awake after, longing for I knew not what.

A husband. I must be longing for a husband.

And then, in our very midst, appeared Mr. Collins on the hunt for a Miss Bennet for a bride. It was so ideal it felt divinely ordained.

Mr. Collins was a cousin of my father's who came to visit us about a year after Papa's little accident. Due to the unfortunate entail, he was also Papa's heir. It quickly became apparent that he had come to Longbourn to choose a bride, and I knew—I *knew*—he would choose me. How could he not? He was a learned fellow and a clergyman. I was the only one of us remotely interested in the things he liked to talk about.

True, when I discounted all the material advantages and thought only of the man himself, my ardor cooled noticeably. His hair was rather greasy, and so was his ingratiating style of speech. But if he had no gift for conversation, that only made us better matched. Anyway, does anyone really fall in love with *just* a person? If that were true, we would not all know one another's incomes so precisely.

And if he chose me, I could keep Longbourn. Dear, dear Longbourn, with my dear, dear laboratory at the top. True, I had sworn off it—but if Mr. Collins chose me, would that not be a sign that my penance was paid, that I could go back to it?

That thought banished all remaining doubts. I was in love with Mr. Collins. He would be mine. He had to be. It was divinely ordained.

Unfortunately, the divine Ordinator failed to inform my beloved, who looked right past me to my prettier sisters. When I did manage to wave down his attention he called me "Cousin Kitty—Lydia—er—Mary." No matter. I had barely begun.

My campaign was threefold.

I. Hymns. I played them as often as I could, and all his favorite composers. I wished him to know that as a clergyman's wife I would share his interest in God, and that I could save the church money by playing the organ for free.
II. Beauty. Usually I strove only for a neat appearance, but now I did my best to appear to advantage. I cannot pretend that it was an unqualified success.
   A. I tried pinching my cheeks for an elegant flush, as I had seen my sisters do, but I pinched too hard and broke out in spots.
   B. I experimented with curl papers, but instead of producing elegant ringlets to hang prettily round my ears, I ended up with a riot of curls that stood out all around my face, a bit like a lion's mane. Mamma made Hill take me back upstairs

and slick it all back down with pomade. Too bad. I thought the effect was rather interesting.

III. Conversation. This was the most important angle of attack, and, I thought, the easiest. Mr. Collins would soon find that I was far more ready and able to share his interests than my sisters. In fact, I found it difficult to hold his attention for more than a sentence or two. He would speak to me only when Jane and Elizabeth had left the room, and even then he did his best to accompany them, sometimes forcing them to say quite plainly that they were going to the bottom of the garden.

Despite these setbacks I persisted. After a day or two, I felt my efforts were beginning to pay off. I was standing by the window, dressed for a ball at nearby Netherfield, when Mr. Collins's voice said from behind me, "Fair cousin, you look enchanting. That color becomes you most elegantly. It reminds me of the hue of the chaise cushions at Rosings."

I turned around. It was happening! It was working! I had to work to keep my smile moderate and ladylike. "Thank you, Mr. Collins."

But when he saw my face, his turned to confusion. "I thought you were Miss Elizabeth," he mumbled. "Pardon me, cousin—er—cousin." He fled back to the guest room, not emerging until the others had come down.

I was not repressed. Very well, he thought I was Elizabeth. But if my backside was enough like hers to make him wax rhapsodic about Rosings, then I was getting closer, wasn't I?

I spent the first part of the evening drifting around the ballroom after him, hoping he would ask me to dance. And he did! True, it was only to ask about what sort of hymns Elizabeth liked best, but still, I did my best to use the time to my advantage.

"I hope you are enjoying your future home," I told him.

"Hmm? What?" He had been trying to bow to Elizabeth and dance with me at the same time, and as a consequence was several steps behind. "Oh, yes, quite lovely." He turned to look at me and started. "Are you quite well?"

I have a tendency to frown when trying to remember the steps to a dance, and hence was making a great effort to smile instead. The effect may have been disconcerting. "Yes, quite well." I turned and curtsied and cast about for something to say. "Longbourn was built in 1685."

"Very commendable," he said, "for a young lady to be so knowledgeable about her house. Why, on the subject of Rosings, Lady Catherine de Bourgh—"

"Oh, yes, I love Longbourn." We were going down the line of the dance now, perhaps the longest uninterrupted moment I would have with him. I seized it. "I hope I shall never have to leave."

He gave me an approving smile. "A pleasure to hear such retiring sentiments from a young lady. Too many young ladies these days are pert and forward."

"Yes!" I said. "So I have read! On the subject, Fordyce says—"

"You know Fordyce? He is a great favorite!"

"Very well indeed! He says that excess pertness in the female will drive young men into such a frenzy that they will riot in the streets. I strive never to be pert."

He beamed upon me and patted my hand. "Miss Mary, you are an upstanding young lady indeed. It is a delight to converse with one with such a well-developed mind. You will make some man an excellent wife someday."

The dance was drawing to a close. I could not risk losing this chance. I knew I ought to wait for him to speak, but I had tired of talking around the subject.

"Why not yours?" I blurted.

He whipped his head around to look at me. "What?"

"I'd be a fine wife to you," I said. "Really I would. Much better than Lizzy, I assure you."

"You…Wife…?" he said faintly.

"Forgive my bluntness, but someone has to tell you. I am really the only one that will suit you. Jane is in love, Kitty and Lydia are idiots, and Lizzy is pert enough to launch a thousand riots. Do marry me instead. You will find me quite modest and meek."

His mouth was open. With an apparent effort, he shut it again. "Miss Mary," he said, "you are charming in every respect. I hope one day as your brother to introduce you at Rosings." He patted my hand again. "As your *brother*."

He had walked me over to the punch bowl. Now he dropped my arm with all speed. The next thing I knew he was across the room. That was clear enough.

In my mind's eye I saw my laboratory retreating into the darkness. My heart throbbed sickly in my throat. I fought the urge to chase Collins across the room, to press my suit. Surely if I could just make him understand—but no. *Try harder*, that was always my solution, but in this I had already tried too hard.

I was just about to return to the refreshments table when I heard a voice say, "Why, it's Miss Mary Bennet."

I turned around. Septimus Pike was standing before me.

He had changed a great deal in the years we'd been apart. His face no longer bore the hungry, pinched look he'd had under my uncle's employ. His smile was easier, less sly. He looked older, too—more a man than a boy, now. His bow was smooth and assured, that of one who moved comfortably in society. He straightened up and I noted the biggest change: his clothes. They were not as fine as the rich gentlemen's suits, but his coat was well cut and nearly new, his gloves spotless, and his cravat a brilliant white. Not a rich man, but a prosperous one. All hints of his bygone shabbiness were banished.

In his pocket, he wore a square of silk of the deepest green.

"How wonderful to see you," he exclaimed. "You were always so kind to a poor clerk." His eyes twinkled. "I was quite grateful in those days to be distinguished by your attentions!"

"Mr. Pike!" I exclaimed. "Are you back? What are you—do you have—"

"Excuse me, Miss Mary." He cut me off. "I should be very pleased to reminisce with you about our childhood days, but I promised Miss Ella Long a dance. I must beg your pardon." He bowed again and moved away.

I wanted to follow him, but a lady does not follow a man she barely knows. He danced with Ella Long, then with Charlotte Lucas, then Margaret Cross; all the time, I had the feeling he was really watching me, to see how I would react. Perhaps, though, that was only because of how hard I was watching him. I could not help it. Surely he knew I must be dying to hear about our venture? From the looks of him it had gone well. His dancing was much improved, and he danced nearly every dance. I thought he might ask me—it would give us a chance to talk, after all—but he did not. If he meant to avoid me all evening, however, fortune did not favor him. We found ourselves seated tête-à-tête for dinner.

Luckily for me, it was as noisy and chaotic an affair as such things always are. Mamma was bellowing down at one end of the table about Jane's probable marriage to Bingley. At the other, my younger sisters were giggling with Aunt Phillips. In between, everyone else in Meryton was making merry with all the restraint that three glasses of wine usually bring. It was a perfect opportunity.

Dropping my voice and leaning in to be heard, I asked Pike, "Well?"

He gave me a kind smile. "Well what, Miss Mary?"

"You've obviously done well for yourself." He merely inclined his head microscopically. "So what's my share, Pike?"

His eyebrows lifted in surprise. "Your…share?" Then he gave an incredulous laugh. "Oh! You mean that little box of 'dye' you sent me north with?

Heavens, I'd forgotten that." He shook his head fondly. "Such fun we had together as children."

Fun? Children? My stomach sank. "It didn't sell?"

"Hmm…let's see…No, I rather think it did sell. The owner of a small factory very kindly took an interest. Rather an eccentric fellow. He's since gone bust. But you are absolutely right, I do owe you a fee." His smile widened. "Come by your uncle's office this week, and I shall pay it. It comes to about four pounds."

Four pounds!

I swallowed hard. "Surely… surely it was worth more than that."

He looked apologetic now. "I'm sorry, Miss Mary. Really. Things are much cheaper up there, you know. And the bottles were really very small."

"But…but it was so concentrated. It should have been enough for hundreds of yards…"

Again, that regretful shake of the head. "I'm afraid it did not go so far as you imagined." He patted my hand. "Do not be too upset. It was really very clever as far as it went." My eyes burned a hole in his green pocket square. His gaze followed mine; he stroked it. "Plain old vegetable dye, I'm afraid," he said. "The techniques for deepening its hues are improving all the time."

Strange, Holzmann. An hour earlier I would have said I had given up completely on the dream of the green dye, but now that Pike was here and quashing it definitively, I felt as crushed as though I had been waiting for him every day. And maybe, I realized, I had. Maybe some deep, secret part of me had never stopped hoping that Pike would return with the fortune that would save me.

That hope was gone now.

Pike was still speaking, making the usual genteel inquiries after the health of my family.

My answers were so slow and monosyllabic that he soon turned away to speak with his other neighbor. By the time I had regained my wits, supper was drawing to a close. Pike, rising from the table, was making his way toward young Miss Abigail Charing, who was smiling at him invitingly. Clearly he meant to dance the rest of the evening away. It appeared that I was entirely gone from his thoughts.

Well. We would see about that.

"Why, certainly," I said loudly. "I should be very glad to oblige the company, if you insist upon it."

I spoke to no one in particular, but vaguely in the direction of Sir William Lucas. Dear Sir William, red in the face with drink and enjoyment, looked confused, but he never missed a chance to be gallant. "Yes—er—yes!" he cried. "You must, I say you *must* play for us, Miss Mary. Everyone, you are lucky, for this little creature plays the most complicated bits of tune I have ever heard. Do, do play for us, and sing, too!"

Bingley's sisters looked as though they had stumbled across my saltpeter pit, but in the face of Sir William's hurricane of civility all they could do was join in his entreaties.

"If you insist," I said again, sweetly (well, as sweetly as I know how). "And thank you, dear Mr. Pike, for agreeing to turn for me."

Pike looked as though he'd swallowed a toad, but I'd left him little choice, and he was obliged to come forward. "Your pardon, madam," he murmured to me quietly, as we looked through the sheet music available. "I do not seem to remember making such a promise, though I am of course glad to oblige."

I had no time for such civilities. "I can make more dye," I said under my breath. Sorry, Quindley.

He froze for an instant. "I told you, it only sold for eight pounds and the client went bust. I'm sorry."

"But—"

"I'm *sorry*."

Behind us, Caroline Bingley cleared her throat impatiently. Pike grabbed blindly at the sheet music in my hand. "An excellent choice, Miss Mary," he said, and set it on the music stand.

Trapped, I sat down and played. It was some stupid Scotch air of the kind that are so popular now. I am an excellent sight reader, but I did not know the piece, and I soon realized that the vocals were not comfortably in my range, which is rather lower than is fashionable.

Miserably, I got through it as best I could.

Piano benches are small. If someone is turning for you, they are obliged to press against your side from knee to shoulder. Pike was rigid as a stone, trying to lean away from me despite the impossibility of it. Whenever he turned a page, buying him a little time, his gaze drifted over to Miss Abigail Charing.

The last time I'd seen this man, he'd been willing to do anything to drag me into marriage with him. Now he was acting as though I was beneath his notice. The money he'd earned up north was enough to banish me from his mind and heart.

One good thing about Scotch airs is that they leave most of one's mind unoccupied. Mine was racing as I played and sang. When I reached the end of the song, grimly grasping that final high C like a hound bites the throat of a badger, I was rewarded with ten seconds of tepid applause. I felt Pike's muscles tense, ready to leap up and away from me.

"Good heavens, how marvelous," exclaimed Bingley. "I am sure no one I know can play half so quick. I've half a mind to demand another, Miss Mary!"

Elizabeth managed to catch my eye. She shook her head slightly. Elsewhere in the crowd Miss Bingley, who had started to come toward the piano herself, shot me a look of venom. "Certainly," I said, "if Mr. Pike will continue to turn for me," and I turned to the stack of music once more. Next to me, Pike slumped infinitesimally.

"I suppose," I said under my breath, "that you intend to enforce the other part of our bargain then."

He kept his gaze on the stack of music, as though advising me. "The other part?"

"I am to marry you." The titles swam in front of my eyes. I selected a piece at random and opened it. Perhaps this was a sign. I had been right to close my laboratory. As Quindley told me, true female happiness rested in marriage and family. No man would ever understand me better than Pike.

His look turned to pity. "Oh. Oh, Miss Mary. I never dreamed—well, we were just children playing, really. Weren't we?"

I turned away and slammed my fingers onto the keys in order to avoid smacking him in the face.

I do not know what I had in mind, exactly. I had some mad notion of holding him hostage until he gave in, I suppose. Certainly Meryton little knew what they got just then. Instead of a Scotch air I'd selected an Italian aria, but I found myself straying from the delicate tune on the page. I embellished it with rolling, thunderous chords that seemed to mock the simple, high vocals that my voice could barely carry in the first place.

The keys had probably never been played this hard. They buzzed beneath my fingers. It was not as though I had wanted to marry Pike. But oh, that look of pity on his face.

I slammed out a series of minor chords an octave lower than the piece called for.

I was so tired of seeing that look on everyone's face any time I asked not to be ignored. "*Che faro, oh, che faro*," I sang, and for a moment the light melody sounded more like a scream.

Before I knew it I had reached the end. The last chords still rang in the air as the silence greeted me. There was no language in Meryton for what I'd just done.

After a moment the crowd remembered their manners and began

timidly to clap. The thunder was still rolling in my chest. Without thinking about it, I brought my fingers back to the keys. They had more to say.

Out of the corner of my eye, I saw Elizabeth dart a look of alarm at Papa. He stepped forward. "That will do extremely well, child. You have delighted us long enough. Let the other young ladies have time to exhibit."

I heard Miss Bingley suppress a snicker. I would not look up. I knew that look of pity would be on a dozen faces. Staring at the floor, I fled. As I hid myself in a shadowed corner between the curtains and an open french window, I listened as Miss Bingley began to play the same aria, properly. The applause when she finished was considerably more enthusiastic.

I caught Elizabeth looking at me several times that evening. She, at least, looked a little ashamed. I was unmoved. What had she expected our father to do, if not that?

When we were in the carriage going home, she tried to squeeze my hand. I wrenched it away.

The next day, Mr. Collins proposed to Lizzy. I barely remember it, if I am honest. After the previous night's barrage of humiliations, I was utterly spent. I had made three attempts the night before to secure my future, two matrimonial and one entrepreneurial. All had been firmly rejected. It was as though I was standing on a melting iceberg. Would I ever find solid ground?

I mention this, Holzmann, only to make you understand what a desperate state I was in when Pike came to call.

CHAPTER 10

Pike's Offer

Septimus Pike came to call on a blustery Thursday. His riding clothes were quite as fine as his attire at the ball had been. Mamma looked quite comically perplexed when he bowed and claimed an old acquaintance with the family. Clearly, she'd entirely forgotten him. On any other day, she'd have stayed and tried with clumsy subterfuge to ascertain his income, but she had bigger prey to think of; she left me, Lydia, and Kitty to entertain him and flew off in pursuit of a rumor regarding when Bingley would return from London.

"It is a beautiful day," he lied, "and I have missed the countryside hereabouts. Shall we go for a walk?"

As usual, Lydia and Kitty had secret business of their own; despite the cough Kitty was developing, the two of them quickly outpaced us. I tried to keep up, but Septimus Pike took my arm and held me back a little.

"Let them skip ahead," he said. "I would like a word, Miss Mary."

"Oh?" I said. The road wound up the hill, with a steep drop to one side. I had a sudden, delightful vision of shoving him over the embankment to his doom.

He patted my hand. "I am sorry for the other night. Truly. I was so excited to be home, and, well—I see now that I was abominably rude. Can you forgive me?"

He really did look sheepish. I did not want to forgive him—but of course, leaving town a penniless boy and returning as a man of means would make anyone lose his head. "I understand," I said.

"Good." He drew a deep breath. "I believe I can make it up to you. How would you like to sell more dye?"

"But you said—"

He held up a hand. "I know. But I owe you, Miss Mary." He gave me that charming smile again. "You may not be the most profitable partner I have had, but you were the first to trust me to be one. I can certainly see my way to a small side business."

"I see." I fell silent. I could feel his eyes upon me. So much for the dream of five thousand pounds.

After a moment he sighed. "You are a gentleman's daughter, Miss Mary," he explained gently. "Every third person you know has a fortune of five or ten or fifty thousand. I am afraid that making that kind of money is not as common as it may appear."

My face grew hot. It was true. When I seized on the number of five thousand pounds, I was trying to be modest about what had seemed, to my younger self, to be a guaranteed success. If someone like Mr. Bingley, who appeared to have dandelion fluff for brains, could amass a large fortune from manufacturing, how could I fail to attain a small one?

Stupid, stupid, stupid. Arrogant, too. I was lucky Pike offered anything at all.

There was no reason not to say yes. I had nothing to lose. No reason, except the strange desolation that had rolled in my chest the night of the Netherfield ball.

He took my hesitation for business concerns. He sighed. "It is true, our profit margins would be slim. But—as I have said, you deserve my help."

I had not cried since the day I'd discovered my lab, but my throat began to feel sore and gummy. "Do not help me out of pity," I ground out.

"No, no, of course not." He cleared his throat. "Actually, there is… another reason. I… wish to marry." I looked at him, and he added hastily, "To marry someone else."

Ah. Of course. "So you do remember our bargain."

He looked sheepish, and said nothing. I actually felt a little better. It wasn't just pity; he felt obliged to help me to make up for breaking his promise to marry me. I had no objection to a fair exchange. "How much would you need?"

He gave me a relieved smile. "Shall we say…five bottles per month? I can pay you up front, so you needn't worry if I've found a buyer. Half a pound per bottle."

Something about all this was bothering me, but I had learned to doubt my own intuition. I supposed it was just the lost dream of five thousand pounds. I would be a fool, though, to turn down two and a half pounds per month to spite my vanished fantasy. If, as appeared increasingly certain, I was to be a poor relation all my life, I may as well try to be a fractionally less poor one.

And—my lab. I could go back to it. I would have to. Already I could almost smell it. Sawdust and chemicals and centuries of isolation.

Just a few hours per week, of course. Just to make the dye. Plenty of time to be a model of Quindley's womanhood the rest of the time.

"Very well," I said.

Chapter 11

My Year As a Factory

I admit, Holzmann, I spent more than a few hours per week in my laboratory. Can you blame me?

I nearly cried when I first mounted those creaky stairs again and found my dear old laboratory just as I'd left it. Well, a little dustier perhaps, but that was soon remedied, and then I unpacked my equipment without delay. After some hesitation, I left the larger electrostatic rig in its box. I had no need of it to make my dyes, and I thought it best not to indulge my own selfish desires. I knew where that led.

I also opened the window, despite the chill, and scattered some seeds on the sill. I kept half an eye on it as I cleaned, but only a few wrens came to peck at the feast, and a great bully of a raven. That was all. I swallowed down my disappointment. If Cariad still lived, he had every right to hate me.

I set straight to work making more dye. Immediately there was a problem. I had promised Pike a regular supply of the green dye, but what I had sent him away with had in truth taken months to amass. I needed more supplies. A great many more.

You will recall, Holzmann, that I get my parcels in care of the apothecary's niece Miss Figg. With Pike gone, I relied upon her more and more. She was a strange, sour creature, and her prices could be exorbitant, but I had no choice but to trust her, and she had proven reliable. She managed to find all that I needed—glassware, copper, chemical salts, and, most importantly, blood. Pig's blood was an important ingredient in the green dye, and at first she got me a regular supply, bottled like beer and smuggled home at the bottom of my basket. However, I soon realized that it wasn't enough. In order to produce as much dye as I'd promised Pike, I'd need pig's blood by the barrel, not the pint.

"That's the last of it," Miss Figg announced one day, plumping a bottle upon the counter. "Everyone's done their slaughtering for the year."

I stared at the little bottle in dismay. "That's all? But I must have more."

She shrugged. "Can't get it. You want this or no?"

"It isn't even full."

Her laugh sounded like a raven's chatter. "Wants her money's worth, does Miss Mary. Well, have this then." And by God, Holzmann, before I could protest, she whipped out a little silver knife, opened a cut along her palm, and squeezed the blood into the bottle.

"What are you doing?"

She'd filled the bottle. She stoppered it with her good hand, squeezing the other one tight. "You want it or no? Full price for a full bottle."

"You've contaminated it."

That laugh again. "I! Contaminated a pig? You are a flatterer, Miss Mary. Blood's blood. One drop's as good as another."

"No, it isn't," I muttered, but I had little choice, so I paid her usual price.

And I was right. It wasn't the same. For that batch of blood produced the truest, deepest green dye I had ever made, and ten times as much of it.

After that I relied less and less upon pig's blood. A few drops of Miss Figg were all I needed.

The Shocking Experiments of MISS MARY BENNET

It was a strange time. Joyful and torturous all at once. I had to make the dye, but I strictly forbade myself from doing any other experimentation. Still, I felt consumed with guilt for how much I was enjoying myself. To make up for it I threw myself into my accomplishments the rest of the time. The time I now spent away from the piano must not cause my playing to suffer by one false note. I slept little, and worked much, and talked almost entirely in quotes from sermons. Surely if I studied my *Quindley's* hard enough I could offset the wickedness of sneaking off to my lab.

Of course I had another source of guilty joy. That was you, Holzmann.

I read a great many journals that year. It helped distract me from my longing to return to research of my own. Writing you was the impulse of a moment, and when you wrote back, I could not resist. I reasoned that talking about research was a sort of weakened version of the real thing that would sate me and help me avoid temptation. A bit like a smallpox inoculation. Miss Figg soon became my postwoman as well as my supplier. Waiting for your letters was a sweet torment. No one, not even Pike, had ever grasped what I was truly trying to do. You did, and I savored it. I have here one of your letters from that time, creased with much rereading.

"It makes abundant sense, dear Sir Gregory," you wrote, "if you will only think about it a moment, that pig's blood is inferior to that of a woman. You say that you are interested in the *essence of life*, but I submit that you are really in search of the *many essences of many lives*—the building blocks, as you say, which must differ in proportion. You are wasting your time with this dye nonsense, sir. Focus on your original questions. What are we made of? Can it be altered? Your answers to these queries will interest many, including myself."

Now you know why I could not do as you asked. And yet, I could not keep from dwelling on it. My dreams had only grown sharper with fear and unknown longing. The electrostatical rig, still packed in its crate, mocked me from the corner. Do you remember how you used to tease me about alchemy? You said that my serums reminded you of ancient ideas about bodily humors and you sent me a massive old tome of alchemical nonsense as a joke. I am dismayed to now admit that some of its ideas improved my process significantly.

Something else did, too.

"Haven't you got enough of my blood?" Miss Figg complained the next time I went in to her uncle's shop.

"I only need a few drops each time."

"Yes, and it stings each time. Come, I'll sell you someone else's, how about it? Lord Henry Charing's, perhaps? Noble blood, that is."

I blinked. "How would you get Lord Henry's blood?"

She shrugged. "He was poorly this week. Got plenty." And she pulled out a large glass jar. I stared into it. Its dozen or so occupants, plump and glistening, against the glass, gave no sign that they cared.

"Leeches."

She nodded and pointed to one. "See there at the top? That one breakfasted on Lord Henry Charing this morning."

I leaned in close, fascinated. "It's still got his blood in its belly?"

"Course. Why d'you think it's so fat?"

"I'll take it," I said. Miss Figg deftly extracted it, slit it open, and squeezed its bloody contents into a little phial for me.

Adding Sir Henry's blood to an existing decoction of Miss Figg's entirely ruined the batch. It came out a nasty greenish brown. I had to throw it all out. I almost did not repeat the experiment.

Then I thought of your words. *Not the essence of life, but the many essences of many lives.*

I asked Miss Figg for more of Sir Henry's blood. (Luckily his gout had been troubling him a great deal.) This time I made a batch from him alone. The usual process yielded not the brilliant sour-apple green of Miss Figg, but a rich brown.

I opened a cut on my own hand. This time the dye came out as scarlet as the blood that went in.

I sent samples of the new dyes to Pike. His response was brief: "Send more."

I no longer relied just on Miss Figg's blood. Now she and I began in earnest to trade in human blood. All of Meryton's. Whenever I could, I slipped off to their shop and bought whatever fattened leeches they had on hand, carefully noting the name of their most recent donor. Back in my laboratory, it was the simplest thing in the world to slit the creature open and disgorge its contents into a mixing bowl. From this I was able to obtain a wide range of colors and study a wide range of personalities. This arrangement continues to this day. Sometimes she even slips me the leeches at home, for she comes often to tend to Mamma.

I still had attacks of conscience. As time passed, my sisters attracted suitors, but none stuck. Our position grew ever more precarious. I considered that perhaps I ought to turn my full attention to helping my family. But what could I do? Indeed, I reasoned, if none of us secured a good enough match, we might have to live on my dye money, paltry though it was. I kept on.

I continued to leave crumbs out on the sill, though more out of habit than hope. One morning I mounted the stairs to hear a familiar song. There on the sill was Cariad, hopping about and chirping like a small feathered king of seeds. I rushed to the window and threw it open. Cariad fluttered in and alit on my shoulder. He rubbed his head under my jaw as though he had never left. I am not one to seek out signs and portents, but if I did, I would take this to mean that heaven blessed my endeavors.

However, I was soon to receive evidence otherwise.

CHAPTER 12

A Fornicator Inspires Me to Take Up My Research Once More

It was summer. Rather an empty, lazy summer, for my littlest sister Lydia had gone off to Brighton chasing some officer beaux, and Lizzy was traveling with our aunt and uncle Gardiner. Only my eldest sister Jane and my younger sister Kitty remained at home with me, and they were both out of spirits. It suited me well enough.

One August day I went to meet the mail coach and found a letter for Papa from Colonel Forster, Lydia's host in Brighton. He went white when he opened it, then called Mamma in to his library. Her shriek could be heard all the way up in my laboratory.

My sister Lydia—aged sixteen, by the way—had run off with a penniless officer.

So much for rescuing our family through good marriages. After this, I thought, we would be lucky to wed at all.

I was furious with Lydia. Such *selfishness*! And for what? Some man? He was counted handsome, but he looked much like all the others to me. In truth, I almost never understand why the other girls sigh over this man and spurn that one. Unlike women, with their greater variety of gowns, ornaments, and coiffures, men all look more or less the same. One can stare at a pretty girl for hours and never run out of things to study; a man will bore one immediately. And now, for the sake of one such nonentity, Lydia had ruined us. Marriageable men were, for us Bennets, life rafts; stupid little Lydia had instead taken hold of an anchor.

When Lizzy arrived home in the midst of this cataclysm, she looked white as a sheet beneath her summer tan. Perhaps, I thought, she shared my feelings. She had always been the most sensible of my sisters. I sat by her at dinner and drew my chair close. "This is a most unfortunate affair, and will probably be much talked of," I whispered to her. "But we must stem the tide of malice, and pour into the wounded bosoms of each other the balm of sisterly consolation."

Lizzy stared at me, round-eyed. She did not look consoled, but Quindley seemed to have taken over my tongue, and I found myself continuing. "Unhappy as the event must be for Lydia, we may draw from it this useful lesson: that loss of virtue in a female is irretrievable; that one false step involves her in endless ruin; that her reputation is no less brittle than it is beautiful; and that she cannot be too much guarded in her behavior towards the undeserving of the other sex."

Lizzy still said nothing, but she drew her chair a little away from mine and stared silently at me. I managed, at last, to dam the flow of *Quindley's* expelling itself from my tongue. *Oh do shut up, Mary,* she did not say aloud, but I heard it clearly anyway. I felt my face grow hot.

That night I lay awake, my words seemed to ring in my ears and I almost winced. *This useful lesson? The balm of sisterly consolation?* I had thought I was bettering myself all these months. Abstaining from dangerous research, working to improve myself.

Was I improved?

I pulled *Quindley's* from my bedside and opened it to a random page. In the starlight I could barely make out the words, but I had no need—I practically knew them by heart anyway.

A young lady must remember that her constitution, however healthy, is more delicate than a young man's. The most enticing flowers only bloom if treated delicately. Take the time to refresh yourself, and you will in turn refresh those around you. Excessive exertion is both dangerous and unattractive.

Quindley was right as usual. I had tried for months for excellence in all areas of womanhood, and had only succeeded in making myself into a sort of irritating parrot.

It was not Quindley's fault. He'd tried to tell me. He'd given me all the tools I thought I needed—but even he could not mold the perfect woman if the raw materials were not there.

But what if the raw materials were added?

I sat up. Sleep had vanished. I slipped out of bed, into the closet, and, using my feet to feel my way in the dark, crept up to the lab.

Cariad chirped a sleepy question when I emerged. "Shh," I whispered. "It's all right."

By morning, I had assembled my full electrostatic rig.

Chapter 13

Green

Over the next few months, my arrangement with Pike continued. Each month, his agent would send me my five pounds. Each month, I sent him more dye. Lydia's disgrace turned out not to be as apocalyptic as we'd feared; Jane and Elizabeth made such triumphant matches that the stories of their courtships are now recounted like fables. Kitty began to court with a young clergyman, despite the fact that he was, as far as I could see, mediocre in every possible respect.

And me? Outwardly, nothing changed.

I stayed at home. Read my books. Ignored the pitying looks thrown my way now that three of my sisters were married and the fourth was courting. Tried to appear impressed when my father set up his telescope in the garden and showed me the moon.

In reality, though, I was throwing myself into my research in earnest.

Miss Figg proved an excellent accomplice, though hardly a cheap one. Soon I knew what color might result from the blood of nearly everyone in Meryton. An attempt at distilling Jane's sweetness of nature gave me a lovely cyan hue. Papa's complacency gave me a warm burnt orange, Mamma's anxiety was an eye-smarting magenta, and Kitty was a surprisingly elegant blue-gray. Though similar personalities often produced very similar hues, everyone seemed to have a unique color. I called it chroma.

However, my dye profits barely improved. I did not have time to produce more than one small batch of each color each month, and because of increasing competition in the dye market, Pike was obliged to shave down my fee several times. He was very apologetic. I hardly cared. Colors filled my head. What did the different hues mean? Could I somehow reverse the chromatic decoction—instead of using different temperaments to extract chromae, could I use the individual chromae to alter someone's temperament?

I had not yet found a way, though not for lack of trying. I dosed myself with innumerable solutions of dye. Some produced a change of mood, but only very briefly, and I could not reliably reproduce the effect. The most common result of ingesting them was an upset stomach, as I learned when I snuck a little bit of tincture into the family's soup one night. I felt a bit bad about that particular incident. Still, just to dig my hands into the problem again made me wake with a smile on my face.

If anyone noticed that I spent less time at the piano and spoke in fewer quotations, they did not say so. Of course it was a busy time.

Elizabeth and Jane carried off their prizes in joint triumph. They were married together on a blustery morning in late October. This was preceded by several weeks of bustle of which the little village of Longbourn had never seen the like. My sisters would have preferred a quiet wedding, but our mother would not be restrained from trumpeting her double matrimonial triumphs with as large a celebration as possible. Every possible family member on our side was enjoined to come to town, and soon our little inn was filled to the brim with Bennets, Gardiners, Fitzwilliams, and Bingleys. The Darcys stayed away, whether because they were snubbing us or because the groom failed to trouble them with invitations to the gauche affair, I do not know, but in any case, the most important Darcy relation did put in an appearance. It was the arrival of this new family member that shook me out of my complacency and changed things for good.

I met Miss Darcy at a luncheon held at Pemberley. She was quite ordinary in appearance. But as she curtsied and her head bent, I caught sight of something in her hair—a ribbon. A remarkable one.

It was green. *My green.* Unlike her sash, the ribbon was the bright hue I had only seen from my own dyes.

Often, when experimenting with my galvanic apparatus, I have accidentally given myself a shock. The sensation is quite singular. A sort of shaking, tingling weakness fills the affected limb. Sometimes there is pain. Sometimes my hairs stand on end. Sometimes it is a sort of thrill that leaves me wanting more. Perhaps you know the feeling, Holzmann.

All this shot through me when I first saw Miss Georgiana Darcy.

After my gasp, I actually stumbled a step toward her, my hand outstretched. Her gaze, startled, flew to mine. Another jolt rippled through me. Her dark eyes were piercing and intelligent, and I found it hard to look away. Caroline Bingley's sharp eyes followed hers. She threaded her arm through Georgiana's. "Dear Georgiana," she drawled. "May I make you acquainted with one of your new sisters? This is—" Her elegant nose crinkled in amusement. "I *do* beg your pardon, but which one are you again? There are so many Bennet ladies, one loses track."

Forgotten as usual. "Miss Mary Bennet," I said.

"Ah, of course." She smiled so broadly I could see a dozen gleaming teeth. "The accomplished one." She squeezed her companion's arm. "Miss Darcy, Miss Mary Bennet."

"Delighted," Miss Darcy whispered, and bobbed another curtsy.

"Likewise," I said. "Your hair ornament—it's very bright."

Her eyes went wide and her hand flew to the ribbon. "Oh," she said, in that same soft voice. She was, I realized, extremely shy. "I knew it was too…" Here she trailed off, mumbling something too soft to hear.

"Nonsense," said Miss Bingley. The Bingley sisters are perhaps the only people I have ever met who can glare ferociously at one without for one moment reducing the acreage of their polite smile. "You look charming. I daresay the new fashions have not made their way to this place yet."

Swiftly, Miss Bingley drew her away, but for the rest of the afternoon, I knew exactly where that green bow was in the room. Echoes of the shock fluttered my heart whenever I saw it.

I had ample opportunity over the next few days to observe the ribbon. Miss Darcy wore it frequently. She favored a childish, half-down hairstyle, and the ribbon was apparently a favorite. I found myself drifting after her in fascination, trying to get closer to what must be my own wares. Except, I reasoned, they could not be. Pike would have told me if ours was on the market. But then why did it look so exactly like that piercing green of the handkerchief I'd shown him that day? The debate raged on in my head, practically drowning out the polite prattle around me. All of Meryton and the wedding guests seemed to fade to a dull obscurity while only the ribbon, and by extension the girl under it, stood out in sharp relief. I could not even escape by turning away. The scent of her expensive French soap seemed to reach my nose from anywhere in the room, announcing her location to my senses. I could not help knowing where she was, whether I screwed my eyes shut or stared openly. My excitement over my wares made her a source of fascination to me. Even now I am sure I could draw her features from memory.

Once I was so caught up in my curiosity that I drifted far too close, and when she turned about suddenly, I was only inches from her face. I had to swiftly babble out a lie about how much I admired it. She nodded, looking unsurprised, which was worse. Then, with what I suppose was an attempt at smoothing over my gaucherie, she stepped behind me and examined my hair ornament from a similar proximity. It was a single tiny silk flower. Gravely she pronounced it very cunning. I suppose a Darcy is used to hangers-on making up lies to get close to her. Later, I saw her glance at me with curiosity.

Curse the life of a country gentleman's daughter! My thoughts chased themselves in endless circles with no hope for relief. I wrote to Pike, of course, but it might be weeks before I heard anything. For days, while Jane and Elizabeth laughed and cried and packed and sewed, while they prepared to leave our house forever, I could think of little but *is it my green?*

The day of the wedding, Miss Darcy attended Lizzy to church, and my sister Kitty and I attended Jane. I could feel Miss Darcy staring at me throughout the ceremony. Wondering what was wrong with me, no doubt. Imagine making a fool of oneself in front of a Darcy! And now I had done it twice.

She departed that afternoon, a little after Darcy and Lizzy, who were to honeymoon in the Lake District. A little parcel arrived for me soon after. I opened it to find the green, green ribbon and a note.

As you were kind enough to say you admired this little ornament, she wrote, *I wish you to have it.*

The ribbon, in my hands at last. I turned it over until I found a little tag stamped on one end. *Pike's Green.* But I knew the color. This was no vegetable dye.

He was selling my dyes at last.

I tied the ribbon in my hair and ran outside. Red and yellow leaves swirled off the trees as I ran down the lane. *My green, my green, my green.* Pike was selling it. Perhaps selling a great deal. Perhaps enough to make me independent.

I did not know where I was going until I found myself at the top of a hill overlooking the king's road. Miss Darcy's carriage thundered by beneath me. I raised a hand in farewell. A slim hand emerged from the window and waved back.

It was as though that one green ribbon was the first drop in a flood. Suddenly the hue was everywhere. Green ribbons in girls' hair. Green trim on gowns. Green ties on stocking braces, green shoe roses, green stripes on bunting. I even saw one young dandy go strutting out with a green cravat, though his fellows quickly bundled him back inside and he reemerged with a proper white one.

It was a true craze. The brilliant shade was nothing like the pale hues we were used to in our dyes. It smote the eye.

At first I went about in such a frenzy of excitement that my mother asked if I felt feverish. My green, everywhere! Pike must be getting rich. Which meant I was getting rich.

I wrote to Pike with my next batch of dye, offering my warmest thanks and congratulations, and asking how much I could expect my share to increase.

He did not immediately respond, but I was too busy to notice. My sister Jane asked me to spend a few weeks with her at her new home of Netherfield Hall, and whilst there I made a most thrilling discovery.

It was Christmas, and we were all lounging about in front of the fire. Jane was sewing, I was reading, and Bingley was playing a card game against himself and somehow managing to lose. Bingley's sisters were whispering to one another, occasionally casting glances in my direction, and I had a feeling I was supposed to mind my exclusion from their confidence, but I was too warm and cozy to care. Suddenly there was a great commotion. Bingley's groom could be heard yelling outside in the hall. Then the door banged open and, with a great skittering of claws, several of Bingley's hounds came bounding in.

Bingley, of course, only laughed, and helped the man round up the overgrown pups. But one of them evaded capture and, with a great *wouff* of triumph, heaved itself into Jane's lap.

Jane is as sweet to animals as she is to people, but the truth is she is rather frightened of dogs. She cried out and knocked over her sewing basket. A skein of bright green thread bounced into the fire.

I knew that skein. It had been part of my Christmas present to Jane. Part of a brightly colored bundle, which I had dyed myself.

Instantly, a puff of smoke filled the room. It had a sharp, sour smell, a bit like green apples. Bingley flung open a window, and the air quickly cleared. Jane, who had taken the brunt of it, sat coughing, her eyes streaming. Bingley was at her side in an instant, his hands on her shoulders.

"All right there, darling?"

Instead of smiling and squeezing his hand as usual, Jane flung off his touch. "I would be," she snapped, scowling, "if you could keep those mongrels of yours under control. Honestly, Mr. Bingley, is it too much to ask to keep the house and the barnyard separate?"

The look on Bingley's face was so exactly like one of those hounds when it was scolded that it was almost comical. If he'd had a tail, it would have been between his legs. "Right. Of course. I'm dreadfully sorry, dear."

Then Jane, who had caught her breath, shook her head and smiled. "No, I'm sorry. I do not know what came over me."

Bingley grinned in relief at that, and all was as it had been. But I watched Jane with unease for the rest of the night.

Jane does not snap at people. Not *ever*.

Unless, apparently, she inhales the fumes of the green dye.

Luckily, I had given her an entire rainbow of bright thread, and Netherfield had a great many fireplaces. Over the next week, I allowed my "clumsiness" to lead to the immolation of several other skeins. The fumes of the crimson allowed Bingley to actually beat me at chess, when before I had not even been sure he knew the rules. The pale gray derived from old Miss Charing turned Bingley's sisters, normally very arch and verbose, into shy, tongue-tied creatures (rather a relief). And the magenta of my mother's derivation gave us all rather pleasant, empty-headed giggles, which faded to a sense of dread that was in no way worth it. Here, it seemed, was what I'd sought: a way to transplant the chroma of one individual to another, without the inconvenient emetic effect. I'd have done more, but Jane began locking her sewing box.

The effects were pronounced but highly variable. None lasted longer than a few minutes. By the end of that visit I was longing to get home and try more experiments. I went home in great excitement. The additional funds I expected from Pike would allow me to attack the matter with greater ambition.

However, when I stopped by Miss Figg's for my correspondence, there was no increase in my remuneration. Nor had Pike responded to my letter.

I wrote him again. And again. His factory up north, his man of business in London, everywhere. As you know, Holzmann, the royal mails are extremely reliable, but I made every allowance for my letters being lost. It was not just the green anymore, either. Every time I walked through the village, I saw more of my brilliant hues adorning hats and pockets.

After two weeks of this, I finally had news of him. It seemed he danced three nights running with Miss Abigail Charing in London, and twice drove her through the park. They were practically engaged. He had leisure enough to swan about with her, but not to respond to my urgent inquiries? I had had enough. Another shipment of dye was due to Pike. I enclosed one more note.

Sir, it read. *This will be my final shipment. As you have not had the leisure to respond to my inquiries, I think it is best we dissolve our arrangement. I shall take my dyes elsewhere. Sincerely, MB.*

Perhaps "Sir Gregory" could write and form an arrangement with another man of business in the north. One a touch more honest. I had to admit it was unlikely, but my spirits were not depressed. I was on the verge of something glorious.

CHAPTER 14

It Happens

For two weeks I wandered about in a reverie. I half expected a letter from Pike—scolding me, perhaps, for breaking our agreement, or pleading for its renewal, or perhaps offering some excuse that explained away his failure to pay me my share.

There was no letter. He had been cheating me, that was all. He knew that a gentlewoman in the Home Counties had no way to prove business fraud or even claim it. I had moments of bitterness, of course, but I cheered myself with the reflection that Pike had cheated himself as well. He had no idea how to make my dyes. If I managed to bring them to market with a new partner, he would certainly be sorry. Very foolish of him. People are strange. Give me a phial of prussic acid any day.

I awoke one night to a sound from my laboratory.

At first I thought I was mistaken. There was a storm outside. I lay for some minutes listening to the wind and rain outside. A clap of thunder nearly made me jump out of my skin— surely that was what had woken me?

No. From behind the hidden door in my closet, it came again—a muffled but distinct *thump*.

It's probably just a squirrel, I told myself as I threw on my wrapper and lit a candle. *Or maybe a family of wood pigeons taking shelter from the rain.*

My assurances did nothing to calm the sickly pounding of my heart in my throat.

Even under the tumult of the storm, the *creeeaaak* of the secret door seemed unnaturally loud to my ears. Quietly as I could, I started up the stairs.

Thump. There it was again. The flame trembled as my hand shook. I seized my wrist with my other hand, and kept climbing.

THUMP. No squirrel or pigeon ever made that sound.

Despite my attempts at steadiness, the candle trembled violently when I reached the top. It was all I could do to keep from dropping it, and the furniture in my little hideaway seemed to dance in the frenzied light it threw. My eyes flew from one corner to another. *Turn back*, a voice inside me cried. *Get Papa. What on earth can you do against an intruder, whether man or beast?*

I was sorely tempted to listen to it. But if I told Papa what I had here, it would be the electrical rig all over again. Only I could defend what was mine.

For an instant I thought I really had imagined it all. Then a deafening crash of thunder was followed almost immediately by a flash of lightning that lit the room as bright as day for a fraction of an instant.

Septimus Pike was standing over my table.

He was a mess, soaked through to the skin. His hair was plastered to the sides of his face in dark blades. In his hands he held a messy sheaf of papers. My papers. He was clutching all the formulae for my dyes.

"Pike?"

He jumped at the sound of my voice. He turned to me in the gloom. His hands gave a guilty twitch, as though he might hastily drop the formulae now that the game was up.

Instead, he began to laugh.

It wasn't the genteel, charming laugh of Pike the well-to-do merchant. It was a harsher, crueler sound. More like the old Pike.

"Well, Miss Mary Bennet," he said. "This is a surprise, but not an unwelcome one. I have long dreamed of telling you the truth of it all."

"The truth of what? Pike, what are you doing? How did you get in?"

He answered only the last question, gesturing toward the ceiling with his chin. Another flash of lightning showed me a ladder, protruding from the skylight down to the floor of my laboratory. "Quite simple really. You ought to tell your father to trim the oak next to the house, you know. Its branches make it quite easy for any intruder to gain admission over the roof." He was stuffing my formulae into his pockets. "Not that they would bother, I suppose. I'd warrant I am leaving tonight with the only thing of value in this whole dreary house."

"Pike's green," I said.

"Quite so," he said. "And Pike's scarlet, and Pike's blue, and Pike's gold."

"Everything you've done," I said. "These past few years—it's all my dyes. Isn't it?"

"Remarkable, really, that you are a clever enough woman to concoct them, but too stupid to see that I was robbing you blind the whole time. They're most ingenious. We're the toast of Manchester." He gave me a sort of mocking leer. "Well. I am, at any rate."

"I did realize it in the end."

"Yes," he said. "But even then you thought you were at liberty to destroy my business." He waved the sheaf of papers again. "I should have taken these years ago."

It was different from the night of Papa and the electrical rig. I had completely lost control then. Now I felt no urge to weep or scream. Inside there was only a dry, dead calm.

He was right. I should have seen it long ago.

"I'm going to make a fortune off you, Miss Mary Bennet," he was saying. "And when you are some pitiful poor old maid, pinched and starved and always too far from the hearth, I shall visit you with my nobly-bred wife and my elegant children, and I shall *laugh*."

His face was twisted in something halfway between a grin and a snarl.

"Why?" I asked. I found that I was not so much angry as genuinely curious. There was a sort of fluttering along my left side though. Perhaps something in me was angry, if not my brain. "I was already your partner. If I had known, I could have been making more dyes all this time. Why cheat me in this way?"

"Why? *Why?*" He took a step toward me. "As if you did not know. You *humiliated* me."

"I did? When?"

He laughed. "Don't pretend you have forgotten! Or maybe you have. So many females delight in cruelty. Perhaps I am not the only man you have left with his tattered heart in his hands in the middle of the dance."

My eyes widened. "You mean—you mean all this is because I didn't finish a dance with you?"

Again, that bitter laugh. "All? You know very well it was all anyone talked of for months. I was a laughingstock. Because of you. Rejected by *Mary Bennet*. The plainest girl in the parish. Surely you see what an insult that was."

"I never heard anyone talk of it. I do not think anyone much noticed."

He was pacing now and ignored me. Rain was blowing through the half-open skylight above, spattering the floor and table with long droplets. "That is why I courted you," he said. "I was going to make you fall in love with me, and then jilt you. Plain as you are, you'd be alone and pining for me for the rest of your days. But *this* is so much better. Your cold heart will never be capable of love, but *these*..." He waved the sheaf of papers. "You will never recover from the loss of these. Goodbye, Miss Mary Bennet." And he started up the ladder again.

I have a few half-done diagrams for a fire safety system for my laboratory. One idea I think has merit is a sort of flame-dampening blanket. I would construct a heavy blanket of some flame-retardant material, you see, and if an experiment grows too lively I can throw it over everything and smother the flames. I felt as though such a blanket had been thrown over my insides, as though what had been ignited in me was too strong even to be safely perceived.

But when I saw Septimus Pike start to climb the ladder with years of my work shoved in his pockets, the flames started to creep out from under the blanket.

"Wait! Give them back!" I grabbed at the back of his jacket and tried to haul him down. He shrugged me off, and when I tried again, he kicked me. It was not much of a kick, just a firm, contemptuous shove, but the shock of it sent me sprawling back. Quick as a flash, he was up the ladder. He cast one last gloating glance over his shoulder, then he was out.

When the ladder began to vanish up after him, it broke through my shock. I threw myself after it and yanked it back down. "I said *wait*!"

His face appeared above. He tried again to haul the ladder up after him, which I prevented by climbing onto the first rung. I bunched up my nightgown and shimmied up after him.

Strange to be on one's roof. It is right there above one, but one rarely, if ever, sees the house from that vantage. Icy water was pouring over the slick slate tiles. Pike had his back to me, already making his way toward the oak tree that bent toward the roof.

The rain made a sodden mess of my hair and clothes immediately. It was hard to gain purchase on the slick, slanted surface, but I bunched up my nightclothes in one hand and used the other to keep my balance. But young ladies, even peculiar ones like me, have little experience in that sort of physical endeavor. Before I had crossed half the roof, he had reached the tree. He grasped the branch that extended over the eaves, but before climbing down, he turned to me once more.

"Give them back!" I screamed. "They're mine! Or so help me—"

The villain laughed. "Goodbye, Miss Mary Bennet," he said. "Thank you for making my fortune. You will never see another penny from it."

"Pike!" I screamed. "Don't do this! I swear to heaven you'll be sorry! *Pike!*"

He only laughed again. Took one more look at me, sodden, distraught, pathetic, as though to fix the image in his mind. He grasped the bough with both hands.

Then it happened.

CRACK!

The loudest crash of thunder I had ever heard in my life was accompanied by a blinding flash. A jagged arrow of light tore the sky straight down to our oak tree.

There was a shower of sparks and a strange, chemical smell, mixed with the scent of burning wood. Pike flew backward from where he'd been grasping the branch. His body struck the tiles so hard I saw a dent. Then it slid down to the edge of the eaves, trailing a long, dark stain that was washed away almost as quickly as it bled out of him.

For a moment I stood, unable to move. More flashes of lightning broke the scene into still, hideous fragments. Pike's wide, staring eyes. The trickle of blood from his nose. His right arm, falling off the edge…

I was moving before I knew it. I grabbed him by an arm and a leg and hauled him back onto the solidity of the roof. Then, doing my best to ignore the dark smear and the damp, coppery smell, I pulled him back the way we'd come. Lowering him through the skylight took a bit of doing, but the logical part of my brain seemed to have locked the rest of me away, and it approached the problem with cold precision. Men think we are delicate creatures, but believe me, we can move a body if we must. I angled the ladder beneath the window, propping the end on my work table, and sort of slid him down it, like the ramp that bricklayers use sometimes for unloading their carts. It softened his landing somewhat, though the wet thump of him is something I will never forget.

I went down the ladder myself and arranged the sodden heap of humanity into something a bit more decorous. I laid him out on his back, his hands at his sides. His hands were blackened where he'd clutched the branch, and smoking faintly. Now that we were in a confined space, I could perceive that they smelled of charred meat. I had to put a hand to my mouth to avoid emptying my stomach. His face was frozen in a look of surprise. His eyes were wide and staring.

I fancied his mouth still carried a hint of his last gloating grin.

My candle still burned steady in the corner where I'd left it. I sat back on my haunches next to it and considered the body of Septimus Pike.

It wasn't like the night I revived my father. Pike was dead. His corpse was not unduly damaged—most of the blood appeared to issue from a wound on the scalp, but the skull seemed to be intact. However, the body was already growing cold. The blank, staring eyes held no spark of life.

I'm ashamed to admit that the cold, logical part of me that seemed to hold the reins asked: *Well, is that such a bad thing?*

Was it? Of course it was. In all my reading on morality, not one philosopher or man of God had proclaimed that if a young man stole your ideas you were allowed to kill him. And how was I to dispose of his body? At the point that one is asking that question, I realized, one may be certain that one is on the wrong path.

I thought of you then, Holzmann. We had of late been corresponding about the question of reanimation—do you remember? I am sure you thought it was all theoretical—I never told you about Cariad, for fear you would think me insane, but now that is the least of my worries—but it was you, you recall, who maintained that it was possible. And what was more, you suggested several revisions to the apparatus that I'd used on Papa.

In particular, you suggested the use of a great deal more electrical power…

There was no time to lose. Already the storm was starting to move away. I set to work. First I removed the fellow's clothes. It was the first time I'd seen a nude male up close.

Hard to see what all the fuss was about. Perhaps my sisters' husbands look more appealing, not being dead.

I took my formulae from his pockets. They were soaked with his blood and the ink was running. What a horrid man. Only the thought of how difficult it would be to get his corpse down three flights of stairs kept me going. At least he would not get to steal the formulae now.

Except, of course, for the one he'd already stolen. And what if he'd read them before I'd walked in on him? Probably he had. Probably he would quickly reconstruct them. And there was nothing I could do.

I pushed the thought away. That was *if* I could save his life, which was yet to be seen. I'd recently splurged on a lovely long roll of copper wire, and this I cut into lengths of around six to eight feet. I wrapped one end of each piece in damp wool and secured them to his temples, his chest, his tongue, and—well, you remember, Holzmann, we discussed the necessity of introducing the charge to certain orifices—and all the other necessary parts of his anatomy. When I was done, he lay on the table with a thicket of slender, shining wires protruding upward from his corpse.

The wires shone and twisted in the flickering candlelight. I had the eerie sensation that I was witnessing his soul leave his body. Then I shook off the unscientific thought. If all went well, I would see the opposite.

I gathered the copper strands, twisting them together like wool going into a spinning wheel. I wrapped them around the end of the wire on the spool, then, careful not to disturb my fragile framework, I unrolled it while climbing up the ladder.

The rain lashed me full in the face the moment I opened the skylight. The stinging assault was more than welcome, though. It meant the storm was still going strong.

I crawled up and across the roof to the tallest chimney. I wrapped the wire about it and thrust the end toward the sky. The spool was just long enough. The end of the wire was now the highest point of Longbourn.

Science had done what it could. Now it was up to Providence. Or, perhaps, Zeus.

I had not long to wait. I had scarcely settled back down inside next to my candle when there was another brilliant flash.

BZZAP!

In the flickering light, I saw the body twist and arch. The dead heels drummed on the table.

Then he fell still.

For a long moment, there was nothing. My ears were still ringing with the explosive sound, my eyes dazzled by the brightness of the lightning. I blinked and blinked. In the rain pouring through the ceiling, the candle fizzled out.

In the darkness, I heard a gasp.

Chapter 15

Bennet's Brights

I've got to be quick now, Holzmann. I've so much to tell you, and so little time to tell it in. How foolish I was to spend so much time writing about my little dreams and petty sadnesses, instead of sticking to the facts at hand. All I can say is that if I do not have time to conclude the story, I pray you will come here and we can discover the ending together.

Or perhaps you'll have to do it on your own.

It is so long now since I have had an answer from you. Am I pinning my hopes on a fantasy? It seems increasingly likely. But you are all I have to pin my hopes to.

There I go again, wittering on. Let us return to the matter at hand.

That long, broken gasp will live forever in my memory. It sounded desperate, like an animal struggling for breath. The next breath was deeper and louder, more of a groan.

Then it—he—sat up.

It was still almost pitch dark in the room. As my eyes adjusted, I saw the silhouette of his dark form rise to sitting on the table. There was something odd about the way he moved, as though the wrong muscles were drawing him upright. If I didn't know better, I was not sure I would have recognized that form as human at all.

Through dry lips, I croaked, "Pike?" That hulking shape turned toward me.

I remembered how Papa had been after the Procedure—confused but biddable. I took a step toward him, one trembling hand outstretched. "It's all right, Pike. You—you fell, but it's all right now, it's—"

He surged to his feet. The net of copper wires fell all around him with a discordant clatter.

He stepped into the square of dim moonlight under the skylight, and I gasped.

His face was deathly pale, but his irises had gone utterly black. Fine black veins traced at his temples and down his throat. Thicker ones traced down the powder-white insides of his wrists.

His expression was not blank, exactly. It was *empty*. As though it was not capable of human feeling at all.

Then he caught sight of the sheaf of papers in my hand.

Without thinking about it, I'd scooped up the formulae again. They were clutched in my right hand. When Pike saw them, he began to laugh.

The hairs on my arms stood up. "P-Pike? It's all right…"

He started toward me, still laughing that awful laugh. It was the same laugh I'd heard when he'd taunted me with the formulae—God, only half an hour earlier—exactly the same. And I do mean *exactly*. Same emotion, same intonation, even the same little falsetto *ha!* at the end. It was as though he was trapped in the frame of mind he'd been in just before his death.

And that was exactly right, I saw. For suddenly his jaw tightened and he lunged for the papers. I threw my hand out of his reach and stepped back. He stumbled a little but righted himself and came after me. That eerie chuckle still issued from his throat. His face was frozen in a version of his mocking sneer.

I did my best to stay out of his reach, but he was taller and stronger, and it was only a matter of seconds before he had me cornered. His hand shot out and gripped my wrist with brutal strength. I tried to shake him free, but he had a grip of iron.

"Pike, stop, please!"

He made no sign of hearing me. His grip only grew stronger, sending bolts of pain up my arm. Dear God, he was going to break my wrist. "You can have them," I gasped. "You can have them, just stop!"

He did not seem to understand me. His grip only tightened until I thought I would faint with the pain of it. His other hand came up to grasp my neck. He was going to kill me.

With my left hand, I groped behind me on the shelf for anything to fend him off with. My fingers closed around a small stoppered bottle. My vision and hope fading, I tried to strike him with it, but it only slapped weakly against his face. I felt the stopper come loose and liquid dribbled uselessly down his face. With my last breath, I whispered, "Stop!"

And Pike let me go.

I bent double, my head swimming as I gasped for air. When I raised my eyes again, I discovered something remarkable.

Pike stood there, a few respectable steps back from me. His sneer was gone. He wore instead a look of sweet amiability that struck me as somehow familiar.

Across his face, from forehead down to his nose and dripping into his mouth, was a damp splotch of cyan dye.

I was swaying on my feet, and he held out a hand in apparent concern. "Get away from me," I snapped, and he scrambled away to the far corner of the room.

I narrowed my eyes. "Sit down." He sat.

"Stand up." He stood.

I tossed him a rag. "Clean your face." He scrubbed off the dye as best he could. "Hop on one foot."

He hopped so vigorously I was afraid he would wake the household. "All right. Stop. Stop."

He stopped, and once more gave me that sweet, biddable smile that looked so peculiar on his face, when it belonged on—

Yes. It was Jane's smile.

Even as I watched, though, it was draining away, leaving that blankness behind. Soon, I supposed, Pike's own rage against me would return.

"Go to sleep," I said. "Right now. Do not wake until I say. Can you do that?"

Immediately he lay down, closed his eyes, and went still. A careful examination revealed he was still breathing, but all other signs of life were gone. I could even turn his head and peel his eyelids open without rousing him.

Right. To work.

Even in the dark, it was only a moment before I found the tinder and lit the lamp. After procuring a little tin bowl and a handful of bottles, I set to work.

It was all guesswork, of course. Somehow, though, I knew I was on the right track. Father had recovered from the Procedure on his own, but he'd been far less dead than Pike. It seemed that if the subject was really dead, the Procedure brought his body back, but not his personality—or only a tiny, terrible fraction of it.

But the dye had worked on him just as I'd long hoped. As a distilled facet of humanity. Perhaps if I gave him the right doses in the right proportions, he could find himself again.

A dim picture was growing in my mind: Cook, after Michaelmas, making us a cake. Every cake has a unique recipe—particular ingredients in particular proportions. Each human creature is made up of a unique "batter"—hence the unique color of each chromatic serum. But ingredients are not enough. You need the heat of the oven. Or, in this case, the heat of electrical fire. And adding foreign serum to a living creature had little effect and generally made them sick—a mixing bowl overflowing.

As it happened, I had a chroma serum derived from Pike himself. It was a deep black in color. Not very useful as a dye, but if it was the final step in revivification, it would be worth it. I unstoppered the bottle and held it to his lips.

Then I hesitated.

Suppose I succeeded. Suppose this Essence of Pike brought back the man I knew, exactly as he was. What then?

No doubt he would continue with his plans exactly as they'd been. He would exploit my formulae. He'd go on to success and fame, and humiliate me every chance he got. I could see a long, cold life stretching out before me, living in houses where I was barely welcome, with relatives who would rather I was gone. And all the while, he'd be getting rich off what was rightfully mine. *Mine.*

Why bring that man back at all? Why not bring back a better one? He'd wanted to steal my work.

Now, *he* was my work.

I stoppered the black bottle and set it aside. I fought the urge to dash things into the bowl haphazardly. The essence of science is precision. I forced myself to measure everything precisely, noting the quantities in my little notebook, under a heading marked *Pike batch 1*.

A generous dash of the cyan, and a few drops of the green. A little orange, some magenta, and a single drop of his own black.

"Wake up," I said. "Drink this."

After the dyes flowed down his throat, the effect was instantaneous. His expression stayed mild, but a spark of humanity returned to his eyes. He looked about the room, then widened when his gaze lit on me.

"Do you know me, Pike?" I whispered. "Do you remember me?"

He shook his head and made me a slight bow, as though to say "Pleased to make your acquaintance."

I fought the mad urge to giggle. "Can you speak, sir?"

He opened his mouth, but no sound emerged. He tried again—this time he gave a sort of strangled groan, which he cut off with an embarrassed cough.

Right. Manners but no speech. That would never do. Not for what I had in mind. "Sit down again, Pike. I'll be with you presently." He cocked his head for a moment and I thought he might refuse, but then he hopped back up on the table.

He was still naked, I realized. I'd have to do something about that soon. First, I turned back to my bowl.

What would bring back the power of speech? Cleverness, perhaps. And what had I extracted from someone clever?

This was no time for modesty. I tipped a generous spoonful of my own crimson dye into the bowl, passed it to him, and said, "Drink." He did so.

This time, it seemed to hit him harder. He closed his eyes and winced, shaking his head as though to clear it. Then he opened his mouth and said, "Blimey."

Triumph washed over me. "You can talk!"

He looked at me. "Who are you? Who am *I*?"

He stood up. I guided him back down to sit again with a hand on his shoulder. "You are Mr. Septimus Pike," I said. "You are a prosperous trader of dyes."

"Dyes?"

"Yes. That is one of your duties. To trade and grow rich."

"My...duties," he said slowly. "Have I others?"

My heart was pounding in my throat. "You have three," I said. "To love me, obey me, and marry me. You are to be my husband."

Chapter 16

Pike After Death

Holzmann, I knew the instant the words left my mouth that it was nonsense. Marry a dead man! Absurd. I was not even sure why I had said it.

Luckily, Pike gave no indication that he'd heard. He went to sleep, and I crept back downstairs and did the same.

Pike remained in the attic for some days. This gave him time to (1) regain his human faculties and (2) wear away the great blue splotch on his face.

He was very much changed.

"I am sorry, Miss Mary, that you must take such trouble over me," he said one day as I was reminding him how to use a fork. "You must find it exceedingly vexing."

"Not nearly so vexing as when you tried to steal my life's work," I said without thinking, then tensed.

But he only frowned. "Steal your life's work? How could I..." His brow cleared. He sighed. "Oh, you mean the other fellow."

"The other fellow?"

"Pike as was. The man before."

"Are you telling me you do not remember?"

"No, I do, at least some of it. But...the things from before, they happened to *him*, not to me. The things he did were his, not mine."

"Convenient," I grumbled and turned to clear the dishes away. But he caught my hand.

"He hurt you," he said. "He made you cry. I would not be him for all the world, Miss Bennet." He smiled. "You saved me. I shan't forget it. Or, since I do not feel that I am the same person...perhaps more apt to say that you created me."

I admitted to myself that I quite liked the sound of that.

At first, it seemed that my creation was a very fine one. He quickly regained his faculties, and soon he spoke and moved as a gentleman. He really did seem a new man. He looked at me with gentle fondness, always eager to please.

Pike improved greatly but rather unevenly. His memory continued to be rather spotty. He had to grope for details of his past and, even when he did remember, referred to them as happening to "the other fellow." His skills, however, returned intact no matter how obscure. He corrected a mistake in one of my account books—and I keep them in code, which I have never taught a soul. Yet he could not remember the names of his brothers and sisters. It was remarkable, really. Were it possible, I should write a monograph on the differences between narrative memory (remembering *that*) and functional memory (remembering *how*). My experience with Pike has left me quite convinced that they are stored in different areas of the brain. If things had worked out differently, it would have been fascinating to dissect Pike's; however, we've rather bigger fish to fry.

This "other fellow" business confounded me. I did, of course, consider that it might be a ruse. The "other fellow" was certainly capable of great deceit, and he and I had hardly parted on cordial terms. What if Pike was merely feigning this new innocence to gain my trust? I fretted about it constantly. Once I even caught the old look of cunning in his eye. When I whirled on him I found him swiftly slipping his hand out of his pocket.

"What's that you have? What are you about?" I demanded. Behind my back I grasped the poker. Had I been foolish to let my guard down?

With a look of supreme shame, he produced a currant bun. I'd brought us one each for an early breakfast.

"I am sorry," he said, with a face like a kicked dog. "I'm sorry, I'm sorry, I am!"

I loosened my grip on the poker. "It's quite all right. You had only to ask. I do not wish you to go hungry."

He gave me a sweet smile and wolfed it down in three bites. After that he stopped referring to himself in the third person, though I had the feeling this was only because he knew it upset me.

Pike came on so well that I soon felt it improper to conceal him in the attic, and late one night he climbed down the trellis and returned to his lodgings. (What they thought he was doing when he disappeared for three days, I've no idea—but rich young men are quickly forgiven their quirks.)

I'd another reason for getting him away. His affection was growing ever warmer, until I could barely meet his eyes because of the fondness there. Perhaps this was because of the foolish thing I'd blurted out.

For some weeks more I felt that my accidental experiment was not only a success but a triumph. Pike appeared at local balls, as charming and well liked as ever. He joked, rode to hunt, danced, ate with the correct fork, and was in every respect so gentlemanly and mild that I thought I ought to start a new factory turning out more Pikes. He was, perhaps, a bit more taciturn, but he had never been a man of many words, so no one took much notice of this. Not a soul but me knew that anything had happened. I was a bit worried that he might again broach the subject of marriage—but perhaps, with this Pike, that would not be so bad. I must marry someone, so why not a man I had constructed myself?

There was, however, the little matter of Pike's engagement.

His invitations to Miss Charing to dance became fewer. She watched him with fond puzzlement, then with hurt, then pointedly did not watch him at all. At one public ball she appeared with puffy, reddened eyes and fled as soon as he arrived.

I tried not to feel too bad about this. She had always been rather nasty to me, after all. Besides, with her lofty family name, she could get a new Pike in an instant. Still, it would not do. He mustn't jilt her. When I'd blurted out that Pike was to marry me, I hadn't been thinking of her. I hadn't been thinking of anything, really, except revenge.

"Pike, you cannot go on like this," I insisted to him at one party when he was turning for me at the piano as usual. "You are practically engaged to the girl. You must not ignore her this way."

"*He* was practically engaged to her," he muttered.

"*He* is you!"

"I am not so sure."

"Well, I am. Pike, if you jilt her, people will talk."

I felt his stare at the side of my face. "Do you not wish me to jilt her? How am I to avoid it? I am to love you, obey you, and marry you."

My face grew hot. Of course, *this* he could remember. "Pike...what I said when you awoke...it was...unfair."

"What you said when I awoke? I do not recall, I am afraid. That time is a blur."

"Then why do you say that you are to—" I choked on the words.

"To love you, honor you, and marry you?" He shrugged. "How does any man know who his great love is? It is inscribed upon his soul."

If it was, then I was the scribe. "I told you that at an impressionable moment. I ought never to have said it. I release you from it. You may marry Miss Charing as you planned."

"No, thank you," he said, flipping the last page. I hardly needed it—my fingers had been mechanically picking out the well-known Scotch reel even as my mind was, itself, reeling.

In my defense, I really did try to repair the damage. At every possible opportunity I urged him to resume his former life. In most respects he did so, but resume his courtship of Miss Charing he would not do. He ignored her most rudely, and it was me he always approached to ask for a dance first. And if I said no, he then offered to sit down with me for the rest of the night.

For a time I convinced myself that his behavior vis-à-vis Miss Charing was not a sign that something was amiss. Perhaps even before his resurrection Pike had been tiring of her. I myself had tired of her when we were four and she pushed me into a puddle. Surely the impression my first words had left to this new Pike would soon wear off. But there was worse to come.

CHAPTER 17

The Affair of the Netherfield Piano

It began, as so many calamities do, at a party. Jane and Bingley had gone to town for a few weeks, and Miss Bingley was to have accompanied them for part of the Season, but her sister was ill and she was obliged to stay with her. In order to cheer herself up, she held a small party at Netherfield. I was there, of course. She could not avoid inviting us, for we were family now. Pike was there, too. From the moment he arrived he danced attendance upon me, bringing me drinks, sitting at my card table, and, when the crowd separated us, staring at me from across the room. Miss Bingley was visibly displeased. Pike was of no interest to her—he had money, but as his fortune was even more recent than her own and smelled more strongly of commerce, there was nothing he could give her. However, she did not appear to like seeing a handsome, rich young man pay me attention, and under the guise of being an attentive hostess, she spent much of the evening addressing remarks to me that could not strictly be called insults.

"Oh, Miss Mary—I mean Miss Bennet!—Is it *very* strange to go from one of five to the only daughter yet at home? I hope you are not lonely! Do not be discouraged, things may soon change—the ladies of *your* family find husbands with such prodigious suddenness that you may wake up any day and find yourself a wife to someone or other."

"Miss Mary, what think you of this vase? Does it not remind you of the china vase in the portico of Pemberley? Oh, you have never been there? Well, I am sure no insult is intended in their overlooking you. There are so many Bennets, after all. Your turn will come."

"Miss Mary, that is such a becoming gown! It suits you much better than it did Miss Kitty last season."

I never know what to say when this sort of thing comes my way. It is not that I did not recognize the intent. I could hear loathing dripping off every sweet word. But nothing was ever overt enough to be countered, and I am no good at these poisoned verbal daggers, so I generally just stammered out some barely relevant quotation and then fell silent as everyone stared at me.

Mamma, of course, noticed none of this—she has no subtlety herself and never detects it in others, and in any case, she was so proud to have the Bingleys as relations that she assumed anything they said indicated a great fondness for all things Bennet. Papa did notice, and for once he was actually quite kind—he actually squeezed my hand after one swipe of her claws—but his attention was mainly focused on his attempts to persuade my mother to let us leave early.

Pike noticed, or at least he noticed that I was upset. I felt his eyes on us, saw his jaw tighten. He said nothing at the time. I hardly expected him to. A man who only recently relearned to talk can hardly be expected to engage in repartee.

I soldiered on, doing my best to ignore her insults. But she would not be ignored. When I happened to draw near the piano, she pounced.

"Oh, Miss Bennet, you must play for us! You are the most accomplished young lady in the neighborhood, and your taste accords so perfectly with mine."

I froze. Her smile put me in mind of a dog's snarl.

"Come, you will play for us?" she coaxed. "I know you will."

I sensed a trap. Of course I did. But I really do like to play before company if I can do it well. I always feel as though I can make up for the awkward things I've said and done over the course of the evening if I can at least play something nice. Then, perhaps, they will be glad they invited me instead of sorry. I allowed myself to be drawn to the instrument.

A mistake. As I arrived, she set a piece of music on the stand. "I know how you adore Herr Gluck. You must play this one, I've just got it."

I drew back. "Oh no, I have never played this piece before."

"Surely the most accomplished young lady in the neighborhood can give us a bit of sight reading? Come, we're all friends here."

I saw she would not give in. I am not a bad sight reader, in fact, so I thought it might be all right.

It was not. It was another aria, but far more complex even than the one I'd played that awful night, and worst of all the vocals tripped at the far high end of soprano. My rather husky voice could not reach the high notes, and I saw more than one face around me concealing a wince as my voice broke or fell flat. I tried as I went to transpose the vocals lower, but of course I could not do it on the fly. I sounded awful.

I stopped in the middle of the piece. "I beg your pardon. I will not make a hash of it any longer." My face flaming, I fled the instrument.

Pleading a headache, I joined forces with Papa and we prevailed upon Mamma to leave. Part of me wanted to stay, for leaving was such a clear admission of defeat—but the headache was no lie. Already I was seeing bright spots flashing before my left eye. Mamma, who has no ear for music, scolded me for not finishing the piece. I went to bed and put a pillow over my hot face. I told myself that I had much bigger problems than a little public humiliation, and eventually believed it enough to fall asleep.

The next morning Mamma shook me awake. "Cook says there is trouble at Netherfield," she said. "Come, Jane's sisters may want us, poor lambs."

It was early, but I allowed myself to be dressed and bundled into the carriage—"We are family; we needn't stand on ceremony," Mamma claimed—and we set off for Netherfield. I had serious doubts that either of the "poor lambs" would want us, but I was curious, too.

As we rounded the bend, a pillar of smoke rose beyond the hill. Mamma called for the coachman to go faster.

As we approached Netherfield, we found its elegant drive marred by a large, sooty bonfire. It was half on the gravel drive, blackening its elegant white-gray stones, and half on the lawn, scorching the normally impeccable grass. It was as though someone had taken the elegant painting that was Netherfield and deliberately slashed tar across it in the ugliest place possible.

"My!" said Mamma. "What on earth can have happened?"

I frowned. "Burning old furniture, perhaps?" That made little sense, but I could think of no other explanation.

But no, I saw, as we drew closer. This was not some pile of broken footstools. This was the piano from the east parlor of Netherfield. The one I'd played so disastrously the night before.

Miss Bingley stood outside, having hysterics. When she saw me, her eyes widened and her screams rose in volume and pitch so much that they could no longer be understood. She actually lunged toward me, but Mamma intercepted her with a motherly hug. Mamma has rather strong arms, and Miss Bingley's claws fell well short of my face. Mamma stroked her back and made soft maternal murmurings as Miss Bingley glared at me over her shoulder.

I turned and regarded the fire. The piano was the finest one at Netherfield—the finest in the neighborhood, really. I couldn't imagine how this had happened.

Eventually, against her will, Miss Bingley was calmed enough that she remembered her manners. She invited us in through gritted teeth, and

Mamma, never one to take a hint, immediately accepted. Soon we were sitting in the south parlor with tea.

"Now, my dear Miss Bingley, tell me everything," Mamma said, patting her hand. "We are the only family you ladies have in the neighborhood, you know." She ignored Caroline's flinch.

"I scarcely know more than you do," Miss Bingley said, drawing her hand away from Mamma's. "The butler awoke me before dawn this morning to say there had been a burglary."

"A burglary!" cried Mamma.

"So we thought. The french windows were smashed open." She smiled thinly. "That was before we realized that the piano only traveled as far as the front drive. It was already well alight by then, and efforts to extinguish the flames were in vain, so it was decided to let it burn itself out."

"How dreadful!" said Mamma. "Do you feel quite safe here, my dear Miss Bingley? You and the Hursts are quite welcome at Longbourn. Mary's room makes a very comfortable guest room. Why, Cousin Henry died there."

Miss Bingley's nostrils flared. "I thank you, but we will be quite well here. I have sent for my brother, and he will return today, I am sure."

Mamma shook her head in wonder. "Who on earth would want to do such a thing?"

Miss Bingley had, since regaining her faculties, behaved as if I was not there. Now her gaze swiveled to me. "I am sure I know no more than you," she said.

Presently we went to inspect the damage. Mamma, quivering with curiosity and the honor of being the first of the neighbors to see the disaster, soon outstripped us. Once she was out of earshot down the long hallway, Miss Bingley gripped my arm so tightly it hurt. "Your mother says we are family and we must not stand on ceremony," she hissed in my ear. "So I shall speak plain. I know this was you, Mary Bennet. I know not how you did it, for you would have needed at least three strong friends, and everyone knows you haven't a single one. But you did it, you horrid girl, and I hope you get what you deserve."

"I-I didn't," I stammered. "How could I—"

She scoffed. My weak protestations seemed to confirm my guilt. I pulled my arm away and ran out the front door. This could not have anything to do with me. Could it?

I looked at the smoldering piano. The fire was out now, doused by a light rain, and I drew close enough to examine it properly. The bench was on its side, its lid flipped open, and sheet music had blown over the lawn. However, there was one piece of music rolled up and shoved into the body of the instrument. Out-of-tune strings twanged and wailed as I reached inside and pulled out the half-burnt scroll. It looked as though someone had used it as kindling. I unrolled it. It was the aria I had butchered so badly the night before.

That settled it for me, with the feeling of a cold stone sinking into my chest. When Pike came to me the next day, panicked, to say he'd no memory of the previous night but had woken up smelling of smoke, it only confirmed what I already knew.

That is when I first wrote you, Holzmann, begging for your help.

I nearly despaired when I did not hear from you. Over the next few weeks Pike grew rapidly worse. Sometimes I had to hurry him out of a gathering when I saw his face beginning to go pale and his eyes feral. As it grew worse, the gentle side of Pike waned even when he was at his best. I tried to get him to take more chroma serum, but he would not drink it nor keep an appointment to get more. "I am not convinced your concoction had anything to do with my recovery," he said. "I can master this on my own."

There were more problems around Meryton. Some seemed connected with Pike's interests—fires on the properties of those who had slighted him when he was poor or who had laughed at me—while others were so random

I could not be sure he was at fault. He himself had only the dimmest flashes of memory of the events and could neither confirm nor deny his involvement. The one bright side in all this was that the Bingley sisters left Meryton for good, joining Mr. and Mrs. Bingley in town. Good riddance.

Yet what could I do? I could barely find time to speak to him at all. I rarely saw him in public. When I did, his temper was short, his eyes wild. He could not seem to maintain the façade of the suave young gentleman for more than a few minutes.

I needed time to speak to him, as privately as possible. I decided to do something truly unprecedented: give a party.

Not just any party. One that had never been heard of in Meryton: a Venus party.

My father owned a small but good telescope, and occasionally he took it out on the lawn to look at the moon's craters. I realized that we were near a time of unusual visibility for the planet Venus, and I begged him for days to let me invite a few young Merytonians to see it.

"On no account are a bunch of ignorant young dunces to get their grubby paws on my telescope," he said. "They'd likely break it."

"They won't. Even if they did, you would hardly notice. It has been gathering dust in your library these eighteen months. Please, I shall only invite a few friends."

"Wasn't aware you had any friends," he grumbled. I did not have to fake the scowl of hurt that flashed across my face at that, and he looked a little ashamed. "Oh, Mary, come now. Oh, bother." He heaved a heavy sigh. "How many guests?"

My mother, while utterly uninterested in astronomy, joined in on my side, as I knew she would at the first utterance of the word *party*. And so, a little after midnight, my parents and I met half a dozen young people and we set off to the top of a hill behind our property. Among the guests was Mr. Pike.

There was a walk of half a mile or so, and I managed to take Pike's arm and hang back a little. It was not difficult—at least two other couples were trying to do the same. Soon the whole party was strung out in a loose line of bobbing lanterns. Even taking into account the dim starlight, Pike's face looked pale. His arm gripped mine too tightly.

"I've more chroma serum for you," I murmured. My heart was pounding in my throat. How long before Pike's infirmity became obvious even in the dark?

"Don't need it." His voice was gravelly. Each word seemed jerked out of him unwillingly.

"I am quite sure you do. That fire last night at my uncle's house—"

"That wasn't me."

"Wasn't it?"

He just growled wordlessly. "Haven't you done enough damage? Shan't muck about with your nasty draughts."

"Oh, yes, you shall. *Pike.*"

"Why should I?"

"Do you want to be a monster?"

"Better a free monster than a man chained."

"*What?* Chains? It was my work, I'll remind you, that allowed you to regain your faculties and become yourself again."

"Myself," he snorted.

"Pike, you claimed to be devoted to me."

He made a sound that might be a laugh and gripped my arm even harder. "That does not make me a slave to your girlish whims."

"My girlish—!"

"Mary dear," Mamma called from up ahead, "come and help your father arrange the telescope."

"I don't *need* help, Mrs. Bennet. If you would just stop dropping the screws!"

I was out of time. I pulled Pike to the side of the path. "Listen to me," I said through gritted teeth. "What do you think will happen? You're getting worse. You know you are. Soon you will revert to the animalistic state you were in before I dosed you. You'll be caught, one of these nights, and then what? They'll hunt you down. Everything you've worked for—gone."

Pike drew up short. His eyes searched mine in the dim light.

Then he held out his hand.

With a sigh of relief, I dug out the stoppered phial and pressed it in his hand. He uncorked it, lifted it toward me in a toast, and drank it down. "Your health, Miss Bennet," he said.

I let out a breath in a whoosh. "All of our healths, really." He took my arm, gentler this time, and we went back up the hill. "What do you want, then? I said you could name your price."

"So you did," he said, with a pat of his gloved fingers. "And so I will."

I felt his body relax as we reached the summit. Within a few minutes Pike was laughing and joking with the others, helping my father to adjust the telescope with just the right note of deference.

After that I believed for almost two months that I could keep matters well controlled. As long as I dosed Pike twice a week, before his symptoms could recur, he remained presentable. His personality wavered somewhat, depending on what blend of serum I had available. I spent so much money on supplies that Miss Figg was seen wearing the second most expensive bonnet in the shop, but it was worth it.

This is when I wrote you most of the preceding narrative. I hoped I could conclude it on a note of triumph. This was not to be.

I have been worried, for some time now, that the serums were growing less effective. Pike tells me that the black and scarlet serums last the longest, but the others, especially the cyan, so useful in keeping him calm, wear off more and more quickly. A shame, for it is my impression that the scarlet and black leave him somewhat more aggressive, though he denies this. And then, this week, the worst happened. May God forgive me for the mistakes that have led this far.

Ever since Pike stopped courting Abigail Charing, all the Charings have snubbed him. They cut him dead in the street and glare at him at balls. Two nights ago I saw Lord William Charing pull Pike aside at a party. He was saying something in Pike's ear through gritted teeth. I was just able to catch "breach of promise suit." Abigail was watching from across the room, her sweet, pretty face set in lines of bitter triumph.

The next morning, the ghastly news raced all over town. Miss Abigail Charing had been found floating face down in the river. An accident, people said uneasily. Suicide, some whispered. But there was a stranger rumor. Abigail's tracks leading to the river were widely spaced, as if she'd been fleeing something. Fleeing for her life.

I don't know for certain that it was him. The man I have known since his resurrection is such a tangle of contradictions that I could not possibly be sure. But Pike has not been seen in public since her death. I will not lie to myself; the creature I made is very likely responsible for this. Her death is on my head, and I am left with no choice. Holzmann, if you get this letter, know that I did my best to stop him for good. Pray for me. Remember me. And, if necessary, avenge me.

Chapter 18

Holzmann Responds at Last

To Miss Mary Bennet, Longbourn, Hertfordshire

Good Lord, what a perfect rotter I am! You were right, I *was* ill, and then away from home for a bit—no time to explain all that now—but *then* my brother and I took the long way home and spent simply weeks gadding about the Lake District. I arrived home to find all your letters in a great pile on my desk (my old nurse collected them for me—she is my Miss Figg), and I've read through them with mounting horror. To think of all the weeks you spent surrounded by fire and death and dye fraud, longing for help from your dear friend Holzmann, and for so much of that time I was sleeping late in inns and attempting globby watercolors of interchangeable ponds.

You poor dear creature, I shudder to think what may have befallen you since your last letter. I shall keep you waiting no longer. I am throwing my things into a trunk as we speak. I shall be at Longbourn as soon as ever I can. Your mamma did entreat me to visit, so that's all right.

Isn't it remarkable that we had the same idea about pretending to be gentlemen?

I must fly. Please, *please* be careful until I get there.
In haste,
Georgiana Darcy

END OF PART ONE

PART 2
✦ ✦ ✦

CHAPTER 19

Miss Darcy Invades

18 July, 18--

~~Dear Holzmann~~ ~~Dear Diary~~ Dear Nobody,

I am in such disarray that I do not even know who to write to. I had grown used to addressing Herr Holzmann, but now I know he does not exist, and is in fact young Miss Georgiana Darcy, Lizzy's husband's sister, who as of this afternoon is our houseguest. I can hear her pacing above me as I write this. I have never been one to keep a diary for its own sake, but I feel I must write all this down in order to keep from losing my head. What am I to do?

It is two months since I wrote ~~him~~ her my last, desperate missive. Three days ago I received a letter from her—a few hastily scrawled lines admitting her true identity, and promising to fly to my aid. A few months ago I would have greeted such a missive with delight and relief; now it brought me only irritation. I had long since despaired of Holzmann's aid, or even his counsel, and had taken measures myself to stabilize the situation. And that was before I learned that Holzmann was, of all things, a Darcy. The thought of all I had poured into those letters, only for them to end up in the hands of a Darcy, made me feel as though my face might burst into flame. What if she told her brother? Lord, what if she told *my sister*?

I would have written back to Miss Darcy, telling her not to come, but her letter was quickly followed by one from Lizzy, saying that Miss Darcy was on her way to us. "As you know, my sister has developed an ailment over the past year that causes her great distress. She tells me that Hertfordshire air is quite healthful for those with her condition," Lizzy wrote. "I confess I had never heard such a thing, but I hope it will be true, and I know you will make her welcome. She will be with you tomorrow or the next day." And so she was. Her smart chaise rolled into our drive this morning, perfectly timed—Mamma had had enough time to make ready for such a great visitor, but not so much time that her anxiety forced her to invent more jobs for herself and abuse the servants.

She has lost some of her shyness since last I saw her. Indeed, I should hardly have known the bright-eyed creature who tumbled out of the coach. Her hat alone could have provided us with a month's gossip. I had seen ladies' hats trimmed with artificial fruit, flowers, birds, or feathers; never had I seen one with all four at once. Her gown, from what I could see of it, was the sort of plain dark dress we all wore to travel, but the pelisse she wore over it was of a brilliant shade of rose velvet with blue and gold trim. When I say gold I do not mean yellow—I speak of gold, the type of golden metallic embroidery that Bingley's sisters have on their ballgowns. It must be frightfully expensive, for I had heard Lydia and Kitty beg for such embellishments to their own gowns, but Mamma would not let them buy an inch of it.

All in all, she gave one the impression that a milliner's shop had exploded.

"Bennets, hurrah!" she said. "No, no need to hand me down—I am quite tall enough, and I like the leap." Ignoring the hand Papa held out to her, she leapt down, skirts billowing, shawl flying out behind her like wings. Oh yes, she had a shawl as well. It was purple. I thought I heard Papa suppress a snort. I could only stare.

I thought that, once the hubbub of her arrival died down, I could take Miss Darcy aside and explain matters a little and say that she was not needed. She was certainly very curious, for her quick dark eyes darted to me many times during luncheon. Of course I could hardly stop from staring myself.

I always pictured Holzmann as a stout, respectable foreigner of middle years, a man so outside my own sphere of life that even if we did meet no one could suspect us of a love affair. I suppose *that*, at least, will not be a problem. Still, in every other respect I am confounded. I feel as though my Holzmann has died, leaving this chic young lady usurping his place.

My hopes of stealing a quiet moment were dashed by Mamma's pride. Nothing would suit but that she must be seen immediately by the neighbors with a Darcy, and tell them that said glorious Darcy was actually staying in our house. After luncheon, she cajoled us both into the carriage on the pretext of asking Miss Darcy's advice about fabric ("for you are so well turned out, Miss Darcy, dear") and, with the cover folded all the way down, we drove into Meryton.

Meryton is rather more bustling these days. There are more people, the shops a little more prosperous. Mamma soon had her wish.

"How do you find our little village?" Mamma asked her, after parading her about in triumph for all our acquaintance to see. "It is a great deal changed, I suppose, since your last visit."

"It is," she owned. "Though…not quite as I had expected." Her eyes darted toward mine, then away again. "I had heard there was some trouble here…?"

"Oh! *That*," said Mamma. "Childish pranks, that was all. Too much was made of it. The Bingleys have replaced the piano, and"—she lowered her voice—"well, if the girl got herself into trouble...is it any wonder she would—"

"Mamma!" I said sharply. "She did *not*."

"Oh, well, there's no proof, of course. Still, that's always why, isn't it." She squeezed Miss Darcy's arm, then tugged her across the street when she caught sight of a tall, elegant figure. "Ah! Miss Darcy, you must meet our particular friend. This is Mr. Pike."

Miss Darcy gave a squeak of surprise and a flinch that she just managed to turn into a curtsy. "M-Mr. Pike?"

"Indeed." He bowed smoothly over her hand. "A delight to make your acquaintance. Any friend of Miss Bennet's is a friend of mine."

She pulled her hand away as soon as politely possible. She stared at him, her eyes round as dinner plates. "You look so—alive," she half whispered.

He coughed slightly. "Thank you."

"Mr. Pike is very alive indeed," Mamma cried. From the way she said it I knew she thought *alive* was some new faddish term. "He is putting Meryton on the map." She nodded to a column of smoke off in the distance. "That is thanks to Mr. Pike here. He is building his factory just down the river. He has managed it so cleverly, tucked away behind the hill there. Nothing to spoil the view."

"Has he indeed," Miss Darcy said faintly.

"Yes. The Brown mill, as was, and old Mr. Brown has always been very against selling, though he could not keep it up. Luckily, though, he died."

"*Mamma!*"

"Hush, dear, you sound like Lizzy. Well, it *was* lucky, was it not? If he had to die, and he *did*, for he was old as the hills, why should it not be at a time that benefits our particular friend, and indeed all of Meryton? I am sure that I would hope for such a death myself, if anyone gained anything by it. Mr. Pike, you must come for supper again," Mamma said, turning back to him. "Mr. Bennet delights in the company of so alive a man, you know, and Mary has a new concerto or some such. It is ever so clever. All the notes in the world."

"Name the date, madam," he said, and bowed. "Mrs. Bennet. Miss Bennet. Miss Darcy." With that he took his leave.

I could tell Miss Darcy was trying to catch my gaze. I avoided her eyes.

Later, it was her turn to surprise me. Mamma had insisted that I give my room to our guest—"For I remember Lizzy wrote that Miss Darcy was so fond of fresh air that she had taken over the highest bedroom at Pemberley." I had tried to dissuade her, but not very forcefully—Miss Darcy would surely beg off.

"And this is your room, Miss Darcy, dear," Mamma said, flinging the door open. "I do hope you will be comfortable here."

The room now contained every pillow, ruffle, quilt, and needlepoint Mamma could gather. It was as covered in frills as an abandoned sample becomes covered in mold. "It is quite charming," said Miss Darcy.

I gave her a significant look over Mamma's shoulder. "It is my room usually," I said.

"Is it?" She gave me a startled glance, then looked swiftly at the closet. Understanding crossed her face.

"Mary!" Mamma scolded. I ignored her. Alone of all souls in the world, Miss Darcy knew why I must not be exiled from my room or its closet. Surely she would insist on taking one of the empty bedrooms on the floor below instead.

Instead, she went to the large windows and flung them open. Cool air flooded in. The evening star was just visible in the sky. "Thank you," she said. "This will do very nicely for me."

"My cousin Harry died in that bed," I blurted.

Miss Darcy blinked at me. "Recently?"

"No," I admitted. "When I was eight."

For once I actually hoped to be disconcerting, but I was disappointed.

"Well," she said, "everyone has to die somewhere, I suppose." She sat on the mattress and gave a small experimental bounce. "Seems quite comfortable."

"*Mary!*" Mamma grabbed my arm and practically threw me out of the room.

So here I am, lying in Lizzy's old bed, waiting until I am sure Miss Darcy is asleep. I am too out of temper with her to explain to her what has passed, but I cannot stay away from my lab tonight of all nights.

This is not how I thought my first meeting with Holzmann would go.

No sound from above these three-quarters of an hour. She must be asleep. I am well used to stealth. I shall slip past her.

~

19 July, 18--, small hours of the morning

Well, that plan failed utterly. The moment I slipped into my room, Miss Darcy flung her covers off and sat up. "Finally," she said. "I've been waiting hours. I thought of going up to the lab on my own, but that seemed a bit rude." She bounced a little. "Please, please can't I see it now?"

I could think of no other option. "Very well," I said. "Come along."

The moment we entered the lab, she gave a besotted *oh* and ran to touch everything. Miss Darcy is different to what I expected. I remember her as rather a shy, self-effacing creature, made of quick, energetic movements and bright black eyes. Half the time she hovered on her toes as though about to take off into the air at the first sight of danger. She put me in mind of Cariad, the way she darted about. It has only been eight months or so, but she is nothing like that now. There is something almost indecent about a woman so confident. I am sure that Quindley would not approve. She is neither modest nor meek. When she looks at me I feel a bit like a dormouse must when the falcon's eye falls upon it.

She ran her fingers over my many-colored phials like they were jewels. I admit I enjoyed the *ooh*ing and *aah*ing. I have never had anyone to appreciate my little nest before.

"How cunning!" she said, regarding my collection of animal skulls, which adorned the sill. "Did you collect them yourself?"

I nodded. "Unfortunately, I cannot clean them easily. The process is foul-smelling and I fear I would be discovered. I have had to restrict myself to dry bones that will fit in my pocket."

She hummed a little in sympathy. "I shall bring you more if you like. I am always finding mouse skulls. Oh! Is that what I think?"

She dropped to her knees before the complicated apparatus that resides in the corner. It looks a bit like a chandelier, with a central column tied to a ring of glass vessels, only instead of candles, they hold leeches. She stroked her fingers reverently along the glass of one chamber.

"It is a tempest—"

"Tempest prognosticator," she finished with me. "I have read of the theory, but I did not know there was more than one ever built."

"So far as I know, mine is only the second. I had to begin to keep leeches, you know, for the apothecary's niece says I must replenish her stock. So I thought I may as well kill two birds with one stone. See, when the leeches climb above the marked line, it means there is a storm coming."

"Does it work?"

"Not perfectly, but there is a positive correlation."

She trailed her fingers over the glass. "It's beautiful. When you said you had put those glasses I sent to good use, I had no idea."

The glasses had, indeed, been a gift from Herr Holzmann, sent care of the apothecary and smuggled into my house one at a time. My whole brain seemed to lurch a little as I remembered that this girl *was* Holzmann.

"Thank you again for those."

"Not at all. I wish I'd sent twice as many." Her nose was almost pressed against one of the glasses now, home to one of the largest leeches. She tapped a fingernail on the glass. "What's this fine fellow's name?"

"I do not *name* them."

"Then I shall. He looks like a Barnabas to me." She sat back with a sigh. "Oh, Mary, this place. You are a lucky girl."

I stared. *I* was a lucky girl? When compared with this exotic creature, who wore what she liked and went where she liked and had a fortune all her own? "Would your brother not give you a laboratory?"

She sighed again. "I am afraid he would," she said. "But I think it would cause him pain, so I shan't ask. He does so wish I was more like other girls." Fancy being so rich you could not ask for things for fear you might get them.

"Are you not?" I asked.

"Not what?"

"Like other girls. To me, you seem…" *Ordinary* was not quite the right word. Not for that fine intellect, that extravagant wardrobe, those magnetic eyes. "Sufficient across all categories."

She looked wry. "Why, thank you. You ought to write love poems, Miss Mary. You have such a lovely way of speaking. What rhymes with *sufficient across all categories?*"

"I-I did not mean…I only meant…" My face was going hot. I was ruining things already. "Let us go back downstairs. It is late."

"No, wait." She grabbed my hand, anchoring me in place. "I'm sorry. This is what comes of trying to be ordinary. I was trying to be witty and bantery, but the truth is I *hate* bantering. Half the time it is just nastiness, anyhow."

"I hate it, too." Her hand felt just like I would have expected—soft skin, with strong, elegant fingers enclosing my own. I felt quite sure that her hand could span an octave or more on the piano.

"Good. Let's forswear it. No more social cleverness between us. All our cleverness shall be reserved for things that matter."

"Agreed," I said, and cleared my throat. I could not remember the last time someone had apologized for mocking me. My eyes actually swam for a moment. Absurd. I blinked the tears back hard. Most likely the dust in the attic merely caused some irritation of my internal ducts.

This discomfort was a good reminder. I had to get her out of here.

"Now go on, back to bed with you, please. I've work to do."

"I'll help you."

"No, thank you. Unless you wish to be in the company of a gentleman while wearing your nightclothes, I suggest you go."

"The company of a—?" She opened and closed her mouth. "To whom do you refer? Anyway, what about you? You're in your nightdress."

"Yes, well, I made him, which makes us as good as family, I think."

"Made him? You mean—Mary, what on earth is going on?"

Through the floor I heard the clock in the library strike two. "Go!"

It was too late. Above us, the window creaked open. Heavy boots thumped down the ladder. Pike dropped into the pool of lamplight.

"Good evening," he said. "Miss Darcy, this is a pleasant surprise."

"Miss Darcy is Holzmann," I explained.

Pike's jaw dropped, then he laughed. "What! Him too? A good joke, that! Like something from a stage comedy."

"You have heard of our correspondence, then," she said coldly.

"Oh, yes. Miss Bennet and I have had a great deal of time to converse this summer."

He bowed to her. Miss Darcy returned it automatically, her eyes never leaving him. She turned wordlessly to me.

How on earth to explain? I decided I would rather not. Ignoring her, I turned to Pike. "Good hunting?"

He smiled. "Yes, very. Wait till you see my catch." He reached into the sack over his shoulder. Behind me I felt Miss Darcy flinch.

He drew out a length of cloth. Even in the dim light of the lantern the colors made me gasp. He turned it this way and that, and the folds turned from deep purple to dark blue and back again. "Shot silk," he explained. "The better to display two of our dyes rather than one. What do you think?"

I took it and looked it over. "Rather gaudy for my taste, but it does display the colors well."

He nodded. "Old Jenkins of Manchester has a silk factory. He's offered to buy all we can make of these dyes. He believes they'll be a sensation."

"Good prices?"

"Very."

"I can do five of each per month."

"Eight would be better."

"Impossible."

"If you would let me make some of them—"

"I had rather do it myself."

"Yes, so I expected. I told Jenkins five."

"Excellent. No long-term contract, I hope?"

"No, month to month. We'll be dying our own fabrics soon enough."

Miss Darcy's eyes were darting back and forth between us, getting huger and huger. Pike turned to her with a slight bow. "I am sorry for all this dull business talk," he said. "I confess I did not expect to see you here."

"Nor I you, I assure you," she said. "Er—I thought the dyes had strong effects if exposed to heat? Suppose some dress or kerchief were to fall in the fire?"

"Miss Bennet has changed her process. The chromae no longer have that effect when in dye form."

"Ah," she said.

"Yes, well," I said. "As Pike said, our business is rather dull. Do not let us keep you from your bed."

"I am not easily bored."

They stared at each other. Each, I realized, was waiting for the other to withdraw.

Pike sighed. "Very well. Let's get on with it."

"Miss Darcy—"

"No, no, Miss Bennet, she can stay."

So I got out my notes and my mixing bowl, and I went to work.

Miss Darcy retreated into the corner between my cabinet and the tempest prognosticator. Away from the lamplight, she was little more than shadows on shadows and two glittering eyes. She watched as I interrogated Pike on his condition, noted down his answers, and then mixed a new batch. Cyan, magenta, red, black, and at Pike's suggestion a bit more red—I measured them all into the bowl carefully, noting down the proportions. Then I gave it to Pike.

"Your health, ladies," he said, raising the bowl to us. Then he drank deeply. When he'd drained the last dregs, he patted away the last few red-black droplets with a clean handkerchief.

He produced three stoppered bottles of blood, each neatly labeled in Miss Figg's crabbed writing. Then he bowed to us both, climbed the ladder, and vanished into the night.

The instant he was gone, Miss Darcy whirled to face me. "What on earth?" She grabbed my notes and rifled through them.

I swallowed. "Well, if you had just allowed me a little time to write you back, instead of flying here with practically no warning—"

"What on *earth*?"

"—I'd have told you not to come, I'd have *told* you that Pike is quite well now—"

"*Quite well?*" She seized a bit of marking chalk from the table and stalked to the wall. Notes in one hand, chalk in the other, and began to draw a graph. "Your first batch lasted fifteen days. The next, thirteen. The next thirteen as well, then fourteen, then twelve."

"Yes, we've been perfecting the recipe—"

"Perfecting the recipe!" she laughed. "Can you really be so blind? Look,

look at this." And she drew a great, swooping arc down through the marks on the wall.

I stared. "It's—no. It cannot be."

"It is. It's decaying. His medicine's effectiveness grows shorter and shorter."

I drew closer to the graph. Setting aside the slight variations as I altered the recipe, the trend was unmistakable. How had I not seen it?

"But if that continues—"

"Yes." She used a dotted line to draw it out into the future. "I estimate you've no more than two months before it stops working altogether." She glanced at me. "Don't feel bad. Fresh eyes, is all."

I put a hand to my mouth. God. It would all start again.

Miss Darcy blinked. "Oh. Your wall." She grabbed a rag and started to scrub away at the stains. "Do pardon me. I get carried away sometimes and forget about paper."

"That's all right," I said faintly. "This place is all soot and dust anyhow. What's a little more?"

She allowed me to lead her back downstairs after that. I stayed as she washed her sooty hands and face in the basin next to my bed. Her bed. She turned her damp face up to me. "Did I get it all?"

There was still a smudge on one cheek. I reached out and wiped it away with my thumb.

"Thank you."

"Of course." I dropped my hand to my side. "Well...good night."

"Mary, *wait*." Her hand shot out and grasped my wrist. "You owe me more of an explanation. Why are you acting as though nothing is wrong?"

My ears grew hot. I didn't want to tell her. She wouldn't understand. What would she think of me? "Nothing *is* wrong," I said. "I am medicating Mr. Pike. He is stable. You really needn't have come."

"Oh, needn't I? The last time you wrote me you *begged* me to come! You said he was a monster, that he killed someone! You sounded as though the world was ending!"

"Yes. I did. *Two months ago.* And you didn't come. So I fixed it all alone, like always, so what business is it of yours how!"

"I was ill! I'm *sorry*!"

And she truly was sorry. I could see it in her face. I turned away.

"Do you really want me to go, Mary?"

"Miss Darcy—"

"*Georgiana.*" When I said nothing, she said, "Holzmann, then."

I laughed a little at that. "Herr Holzmann."

"Ja, fräulein?"

I perched on the edge of the bed. She sat down beside me. In the cool night I could feel the heat of her through both our nightdresses.

"Come now, Sir Gregory," she said softly. "I read all your letters, you know. Every last one. Pike was an utter monster to you even before he died. How on earth did you wind up so friendly with that walking midden?"

"He's changed."

"How?"

"I-it was a difficult time."

"A proper lady would leave it at that, of course. But unfortunately, I am more scientist than lady."

Could I? Could I tell her?

I've never even written it down. I am not sure I can.

"I'll tell you," I said, "if you give me my bed back."

"Oh," she said. "I...that is, I am sorry, no."

She lay down, turning away from me. I felt a little better at that. No need to tell her all my secrets when she was clearly keeping some of her own.

"Is it true what you said before?" she asked. "Did your cousin really die here?"

"Yes. Shall I tell you about it?"

"If you do not mind."

I told her. I am not sure why I offered. I suppose I felt guilty. Or maybe I just wanted to. I have had no one to tell things to since Harry.

"At first I did not know that he was to die. I was excited, actually, that he was to stay with us. I hoped he would stay forever, even though I knew he was ill. Mamma was often ill, too, and it did not seem to prevent her from doing as she liked. He liked air and sunlight, so they cleaned up the little room on the third floor for him.

"After he arrived my spirits were damped a little—he seemed so very weak, and slept all the time. But he would smile when he saw me sitting at his side, and was always ready with an answer when I showed him a little creature I'd smuggled in and demanded to know family, genus, species.

"After the nurse changed his sheets one day and discovered a fat toad snuggled against the feverish warmth of his side, I was banned from the sickroom.

"For a time I appeared to respect my banishment. In truth I was only waiting for an opportunity. One night when I was meant to be asleep, I heard the nurse and the apothecary go down to the kitchen. Seizing my chance, I slipped out of bed, up the stairs, and into his room.

"What I saw made me freeze to the spot, a scream trapped in my throat.

"In the flickering light of the candle, there were patches of dark across his form that I had first taken for deep shadows. Then, as I stood and stared, I saw that one of the little shadows actually reflected the candle's light with a wet gleam. I screwed my eyes up, trying to understand.

"The shadow moved.

"My bare feet were pounding across the wood floor before I knew what I was about. 'Get off him!' I shrieked. 'Get off!'

"My shrieks had drawn the adults, and when my parents, the nurse, and the apothecary crowded in the doorway, they found me leaning over him, screaming, enraged, bloody, practically out of my senses with horror, and no doubt looking as though I myself was the monster draining his life away.

"Someone slapped me. Someone else seized my arm and shoved me from the sickroom. 'Hope you're happy, girl, for you've killed him,' someone snarled—that was the apothecary I think—and then the door slammed in my face, and I was sliding down the wall, too shocked to remember how to climb back down the stairs.

"Time passed. Ten minutes? An hour? An entire dark night? I could not say. I sat there in the dark, the cold seeping up through my nightgown, until the door opened again. It was my mother.

"She clucked in disgust when she saw me. 'Really, Mary, could you not even wash, you peculiar child?' She took my hand, pulled me to my feet, and led me into the room.

"Harry was awake now. He and his bedclothes had been cleaned. His face now, when he looked at me, had a hint of its old friendliness. I wanted to cry. He knew me.

"'May—I have—a moment with her?' he gasped out, the simple sentence seeming to take forever. The apothecary and nurse gave me scathing looks, but stepped outside. I found myself clutching Mamma's hand. I had not done so in years, but this shadow of my friend still frightened me.

"'It's all right,' he said. 'Your Mamma—can stay.'

"Still clutching her hand, I shuffled a little closer.

"'So,' he said, seeming to gather his strength. 'You have learned—a bit—of the anatomy of *Hirudo medicinalis* tonight, little cousin.' My frown deepened, and a smile twitched at one corner of his mouth. 'The leech.'

"'Nasty things,' I said.

"'I am sorry they frightened you,' he said. 'You were—' He stopped to cough. 'You were very brave to come to my aid. But look.'

"His eyes beckoned me closer, gesturing toward his loosely closed fist. I drew right next to the bed, my curiosity overcoming my fear. He uncurled his fist. There, cupped as gently as he'd held my hand on all our nature walks, was a leech.

"'There, you see,' he breathed, so quietly now I could barely hear him. 'Nothing to be frightened of. Just another of God's creatures, doing as He made it to do.'

"Very gently, I reached out a finger and touched it. Its slimy surface twitched, and I fancied I could feel the movement of tiny alimentary muscles. 'Oh,' I murmured, ignoring my mother's shudder. 'How marvelous.'

"'Indeed,' he said. 'Have you any questions, cousin?'

"I see now he meant questions about the leech. But I looked at him and said, 'What is it like to die?'

"His breathless laugh was a shadow of itself. My mother gasped. 'Mary! How could you!' She started to pull me away, but he shook his head a little.

"'I do not know,' he whispered. 'And when I do know…I shan't…be able to tell you. But standing…on the threshold…is not so bad. I, too… have been…as I was made.' He drew a deep breath. 'He made rainbows and ponies, but He made leeches and crickets, too. He made me and you, Mary. He *meant* to. Never…never…'

"But his speech had taken the last of his strength. With a sigh—the same sigh with which he greeted a comfortable chair after one of our walks—he died."

By the end of the tale I found I had lain down across from Miss Darcy. With her hair spread out on the pillow, her dark eyes gleaming in the moonlight, she looked like some sort of spirit out of a folktale. The kind that leads you into the river and leaves you to drown. She really has grown into her looks.

"No wonder you love this bed," she said. "He sounds lovely."

"He was." I waited for her to say *Of course you must have it back, then; let us swap directly.*

"Goodnight, then," she said.

"Goodnight."

I went down to my new room. Sleep eluded me, however, so I have taken up my pen once more. I think I know who to write these pages to now.

Dear Harry,

Holzmann is here. I cannot get rid of her. Worse, I do not want to. Having her here may upset all my plans, and I am so close to being the kind of woman that you and Quindley could esteem. But the thought of losing her again so soon makes me feel like I am being sliced open. Surely, a little more time will not hurt. I needn't tell her all. Anyhow she did catch me in a serious statistical error. She could be useful.

I cannot shake the feeling, though, that associating with her will only lead me into more dangerous waters.

I wish you could tell me what to do. Perhaps writing to you will keep me on the right path. I will write to you, and read my *Quindley's*, and all shall be well.

I wish Pike had smelled as good as she does. We could have avoided a great deal of trouble.

CHAPTER 20

The Venus Kiss

19 July, 18--

I awoke this morning to find Miss Darcy sitting on the end of my bed, staring at me.

"You really do not want me here?" she asked. "Say the word, and I will go home."

I opened my mouth to reply.

"Up, up, up, Mary, up!" my mother came bursting in. "You must get dressed and come down, so you may entertain—" She stopped at the sight of her quarry. "Oh! Miss Darcy dear!"

"Good morning, Mrs. Bennet," she said. "I was just stopping in to ask if Miss Bennet might like a walk with me today."

"A walk! I hope we can entertain you better than *that*," cried Mamma. "Not to worry, Miss Darcy, I've a hundred things to show you today, and none of them as dull as a *walk*."

And so it fell out, for as soon as we arrived at breakfast, Mamma had filled every hour of the day. Our house was crammed with visitors from the moment it was proper for morning visits till the last possible second, and after that there was a card party at the Longs', an assortment of Lucases to supper, and from then until bed an unbroken monologue from Mamma about every conceivable topic—her elder daughters' mighty marriages (Mamma seemed to forget that Miss Darcy knew both daughters well), her distress at Miss Darcy's illness, her insistence that Miss Darcy must have rest and quiet on this visit, and her intention to make all rest and quiet impossible with a schedule so ambitious that a hardened soldier would have quaked at it. I have often wondered if Mamma is capable of having a thought without voicing it. The possibility remains wholly theoretical.

The result of all this bustle was that Miss Darcy and I were together the entire day but could hardly speak a word to each other. However, our eyes often met and held. Every time I felt the burn of that gaze, I knew she was waiting for an answer to her question.

You really do not want me here? Say the word, and I will go home.

I should, of course. There were excellent reasons to do so. If she stayed, I might have to explain about Pike, and—no. I could not. Miss Darcy must go.

And yet—

Another pair of hands *would* be welcome. There was so much to do just to make enough serum for Pike's current regime, and as she'd pointed out, that wouldn't be sufficient for long. Dash it all, I was *sick* of doing everything by myself. And the way she'd lit up in my laboratory—she could understand it. She could understand *me*.

I was not sure if it was a point for or against her.

Back and forth all day, the argument raged silently in my head. I avoided her gaze and came to no firm conclusion.

Then I remembered how she'd stolen my room and, with it, the gate to my little sanctum. No. She could not stay.

That night after bedtime I slipped up to her room and scratched at the door. She threw it open immediately. I walked past her, stopping in the center of the rug.

"Well?" she said.

"I am sorry," I replied. "It was terribly kind to come all this way, but I think it's best if you go."

She nodded. "I was afraid you'd say that."

"I really think it's—"

"No."

I blinked.

"No?"

"No. I am staying here."

"But you said say the word—"

"I've changed my mind."

"You can't!"

"I do not see how you can prevent me."

"Why?!"

She took a quick step toward me. "I think you need me, Mary," she said. "Oh, I know you're brilliant, but you've blind spots like anyone else. What's more, I think you're exhausted. You have got to let someone else shoulder your pack awhile."

"I've managed so far."

"Debatable. Regardless, it is no guarantee for the future. A horse that has just run fifty miles cannot run fifty more."

When one has been alone for a very long time, it can be rather overwhelming just to be perceived. I found myself trembling under her appraising gaze.

I *was* tired. Why hadn't I realized it?

Shadows flickered wildly across the room from the way the candlestick shook in my grasp. Then she was there, her hand wrapped around my own.

"Steady," she said. "Let's not burn the place down."

"Thank you."

We stood there for a moment, hands locked together around the candlestick. Her hand was soft and warm on mine. I wondered how many young men had bent over that hand and kissed it after a dance. Of course, she would have been wearing gloves then. He would not know, as I now did, how warm that hand was, how soft, despite its slender strength.

"If you won't do it for yourself," she said, so close, "do it for me. I've not seen half of all you have in that glorious workshop of yours. Won't you give me the full tour, at least?"

I shook off my odd musings. "That at least I can do."

I soon showed her the rest of my meager store of equipment. The pièce de résistance was, of course, my electrostatic rig. It was covered in a sheet, which I whipped off with a bit more pride than Quindley would approve—but given all it took to get it, I think I can be forgiven.

"Oh, my," she cried, grabbing my arm. "Mary, she's *beautiful*. I am dead with jealousy."

"No need to be jealous," I said. "She—er, it is at your disposal." In fact I had intended to stipulate a rule that only I was to operate my precious rig, and I cannot say why I gave way immediately, except that her grip on my arm was rather nice.

"Oh! May I really?" She scrambled over to it and ran those long, clever fingers over the polished wood, the shining brass. After years of use it was a bit burnt in places, but I took pride in keeping it in peak condition.

"Gorgeous," she proclaimed, carefully wiping a fingerprint away with the edge of her sleeve. "You know, I've not been near one of those since I was a little girl. Papa took me to an electrical salon. The fool who presented it gave us a far stronger shock than he was meant to." She chuckled. "Papa was quite cross."

An electrical salon.

No. It could not be. But I compared my memory of the little girl at the electrician's show with the woman in front of me and felt a lurch of possibility. I despise hunches, but I was having one now. "The salon," I said. "Where was it?"

"West Hertfordshire," she said absently. "Not far from here, I believe." She had climbed atop the grounding stool and was at present absorbed in observing her distorted reflection in the glass bulb.

"There was another little girl there. You held her hand."

"Mm. I wanted to play with her, but there was measles about so Father said no. How did you know? Did Fitzwilliam—" She paused, then turned. "No. Were you, really?"

I nodded. "My father and Harry brought me."

"I read your account, of course, but I gave it no thought. I never thought we had seen the very same show. But now I come to look at you…" Her quick eyes darted over my features. I felt it almost like the touch of a hand. Or, perhaps, the race of a spark.

"Then you were the one who…" Her hand rose. Her other still rested on the metal rod of the apparatus, but as it stood idle, I allowed my own hand to rise to meet hers.

We both jumped at the moment of contact.

"A residual charge," I said as briskly as I could. The little shock I'd felt from her fingers was still shivering through my insides. My fingers were tingling. "That is all. I should have warned you. Sometimes it builds a little even when the machine is idle."

She cleared her throat. "Of course." Then she grinned. "You know, there is one common electrical trick that that shabby little show did not display. I suppose it was because of our presence. May I show you?"

"By all means."

"Then charge her up."

I obliged, turning the globe against the cloth only a few revolutions until it had begun to crackle. Miss Darcy, still standing on the grounding stool, said, "Now then. It is called electrical Venus. I am a beautiful young lady."

"Yes," I agreed.

"I *mean*," she said, "I am a beautiful young lady attending an electrical salon. The electrician has bade me stand upon the stool. Now he bids one of the gentlemen"—she pointed at me—"to come forward."

I stepped forward just as she leaned down. "And now," she said, "the young man gives the young lady a kiss."

I knew, of course, that it was a foolish thing to do—knew the consequences—and yet I leaned in closer, standing on my toes. She leaned down and just as our lips were about to touch—

Zzzzt.

Even behind my closed eyelids the spark was visible. My head was thrown backward a few inches. Sharp pain stung my lips. I stared at the slant of the ceiling boards until the stars faded from my eyes.

"The electrical Venus," she said, blinking. Her free hand was pressed to her lips. "Also known as the Venus kiss. I have read numerous accounts of it."

I cast about for something to say. "I suppose Quindley would say that this shows how even nature rebels against a young man and woman taking such liberties."

"Perhaps, but neither of us is a young man."

I was quite sure that Quindley would not approve of my current sensations, either. My heart was racing, and I have given myself enough shocks to know I cannot wholly blame the apparatus. It is all right, isn't it, Harry? I am sure it must be, for the kiss was quite innocent—we are both ladies after all, and friendly kisses between ladies are quite usual. Yes, I am sure it is all right. Just the excitement of having someone to share my studies with.

Georgiana put her hand on my shoulder to help herself down from the stool. It was trembling slightly. I am glad to see that her excitement about this field of study matches my own. You would be happy for me, I am sure.

Harry, I have decided she should stay.

CHAPTER 21

To Work

25 July, 18--

Dear Harry,

 A week now of Miss Darcy and our research proceeds. However, only in such hours as we can steal late at night, for our days are fully occupied. Her second morning here we arrived at the breakfast table to an unexpected problem. There was a perfect mountain of letters and notes at each of our plates. Upon opening them I found that they were all invitations. Card parties, walking parties, tête-à-têtes—overnight I had become overwhelmingly in demand.

 "You shall accept them all," my beaming mother proclaimed. "I am sure that Miss Darcy will relish the opportunity to get to know the neighborhood."

 "Can't you take her, Mamma?" I asked. "I've got that new concerto to study, and I'm right in the middle of the most fascinating chapter on—"

 "No," said Mamma. "They have invited you both."

 "They don't really want me, though. They only said so to be polite. It's a Darcy they want."

Miss Darcy looked a bit awkward at that, and I felt bad. I do not suppose being in demand for one's name and fortune alone is very pleasant.

"Oh, very well," I said.

"Good," said my mother. "Now, Mary, mind you smile upon that clubfooted nephew of Mrs. Long's. I have always maintained that he has a fondness for you, and he is doing quite well as a curate, and does not drink so *very* much. I know Mr. P's attentions have been marked, but you must cast a wide net. Miss Darcy, you need not trouble yourself. There are no single men here worth *your* having."

And so we are to spend our days ensnared in the social whorl, which will leave us little time to talk. Luckily there is one window of daylight we have managed to reserve for ourselves: our daily walk.

Conveniently for Miss Darcy's cover story, there really is a spring in Meryton. I took her there this afternoon. Its reputation for healthfulness is only local, but perhaps it will spread in time, and at least it comes out of the ground cold and pure and sweet.

"Good lord," Miss Darcy said, when I first took her there. She peered into the tin cup, then took another sip. "That's actually good! The water at Bath tastes like one is swilling gravel. How is it that it is not better known?"

I was sitting on the bank, hugging my knees. "It is only the last few years that it's been drinkable." I pointed across the spring to the nearby field. "The Johnson farm used to have a privy just there. I was at the time rather interested in the transmission of disease and found that proximity to such foulness leads to an increase in cholera and typhus for those nearby. It seemed a shame to ruin an otherwise pure spring."

"So you...What? Persuaded the town to remove it?"

"Of course not!" I said. "I, a young lady, speak to a gentleman on such a subject? It would be most improper."

"Right," she said. "Sorry."

"No," I continued. "I blew it up."

She froze in the act of scooping up another glass of water. "I beg your pardon?"

"I blew it up," I explained. "As you know I am a dab hand at crafting gunpowder, so it was a fairly simple matter to build a tidy little bomb and to leave it under the privy."

She was staring at me. "What if someone had gone *in* the privy?"

"Unlikely. I chose a cold, wet day just after harvest so no one would be about. But even if they had been, I believe I had calculated the power of the bomb carefully enough that such a person would have got a fright and a singed underside at worst."

"Right," she said. "Then what?"

"Well, then they rebuilt it. So I waited till they were done and blew it up again."

"Quite proper."

"Thank you. Then I wrote to Mr. Johnson anonymously and suggested that the location of the privy was causing a buildup of hazardous vapors and that he had better move it. He did. Thus—" I gestured to the water burbling before us. "Spring."

"Meryton really doesn't know what it has in you."

I scanned her face. Was she mocking me? No, she looked sincere. "They are quite certain that they do know."

"They're blind then," she said. "Clubfooted drunken curate, indeed."

"Perhaps," I said. My face felt hot.

We use our walks to discuss the problem of Pike. Miss Darcy continues to treat the matter as an emergency, though I maintain it is no such thing.

"I agree that we must have a more permanent solution," I said this morning, "but at the moment he is a model citizen."

"Is he?" Miss Darcy was striding ahead of me, as she does when her emotions get excited. For a girl who is supposed to be in delicate health, she has the stride of a dragoon.

"Yes. You've seen him. He is everything charming."

"Hmph," she said. "How did Mr. Smith die?"

"In his bed, of old age."

"Did anyone see it happen?"

"No, but—"

"Perhaps it was Pike, then."

I laughed. "Do not be ridiculous."

"Why ridiculous? He killed once already."

I flinched. "We don't know that. Anyway, that was before I made him better."

"Right." She shook her head. "I do not *understand* you, Mary. I know you must keep him under control, but you act as though you are *friends* now. Have you forgot how horrid he was to you?"

"Well, it is my fault he died."

"More's the pity he did not stay that way. Have you never thought of repeating the application of lightning till he stops moving for good?"

"Miss Darcy!"

She sighed. "Yes, all right, murder is inadvisable. But how can you trust him? Do you not remember what he was like to you, even *before* he died?"

I swallowed. The trouble was, I did.

I remembered how his eyes had followed me when I was invisible to everyone else. How we had had each other to talk to. I remembered the Meryton game.

Miss Darcy is pretty and rich, and anything but invisible. She could never need the Meryton game, nor even understand it. I knew if I attempted to explain she might revile me.

And yet I found myself explaining it to her anyway. I shall do so in these pages as well.

The Meryton game was a pastime Pike and I used to indulge in years ago, before his first proposal. It started at a card party at Netherfield.

Netherfield was at the time let to an admiral and his family, and Mamma had been very eager that my sisters and I should befriend his daughters. Unfortunately for all concerned, Lizzy and Jane were away on a visit, and my little sisters were ill, which left only me to try to form the acquaintance.

Henrietta Hogarth loathed me. There is something about the particular ways I am deficient that fills some people with a sort of rage. She could not escape inviting me to things, but she made no secret of her disdain. Pike, too, was often at her parties to make up the numbers. She did not actively hate him, but she treated him as part of the furniture.

Once when I was about fifteen I arrived at a card party to find that instead of the intended twelve guests, there were only nine of us. Miss Henrietta immediately formed her particular friends into two groups of four for bridge. "Miss Mary will not mind," she announced in my general direction. "She dislikes cards."

True enough that I disliked cards, but this was a card party. She could have chosen a different game, one that allowed more players at a table. My cheeks heated. I hovered next to one game, then another. I tried to participate in the conversation, but my voice seemed inaudible to the players.

My head began to ache. I could, of course, have claimed illness and gone home. It would have been quite true, really. However, I was quite sure that if I fled, I would be the topic of conversation the rest of the afternoon. I would see it through if it killed me. It felt as though it might.

Then a footman entered to announce a late arrival.

Miss Henrietta rose and greeted Pike quite politely. As he bowed, I saw his sharp eyes take in the situation at a glance. She promised to rearrange the tables more inclusively "after this game"; then sat again and was soon reabsorbed in her hand of bridge.

I felt a touch at my elbow. "Miss Bennet," Pike said, "will you take a turn about the room?"

It was something to do, at least. I took his elbow. We walked. He was wearing his best clothes, but his sleeve was cold and damp. He had walked here. It was snowing.

We had made two circuits of the room at least before either of us spoke. "A charming hostess is Miss Henrietta," he said.

"Mmm," I said. We were at the far end of the room from the players. He needn't bother flattering our hostess, for she could not hear us.

"A shame about the pox."

I looked at him in alarm. "The pox?"

"Didn't you know? Died of smallpox, poor thing. Long and slow. First it spoilt that lovely complexion of hers. She became quite a hermit."

Had he gone quite mad?

There was a titter of high-pitched laughter. Miss Henrietta was whispering behind her hand to her cousin, an arch young man called Thompson. He looked in our direction, caught my gaze on him, and guffawed. I looked away.

"Mr. Thompson, too," he said. "Rest in peace. Torn apart by lions."

Surprise tore a laugh from me. "You speak nonsense."

"The pox spread to Miss Henrietta's mouth, eventually," he said. "Her beautiful laugh became a torture to her."

"At least she could still play cards," I offered.

"Yes, thank God she had that comfort. At least until her fingernails fell off."

The laugh I tried to suppress came out as a snort. The headache that had begun to blur my vision receded a little.

"Quite a shame," he said. "I do not know how they will make up their card games with those two dead."

"Do not despair. They will still have a perfect four for bridge, since the Misses Charing drove their barouche into a volcano last week."

His laugh was loud enough to draw the eyes of the players. We scorned to look at them. By the end of that afternoon, no one had made room for Pike or me at the tables, and we had killed each of them many times over. And that was the Meryton game.

Oh, Harry, I can imagine how you'd look at me if you could really read this. I know it's odious. You were always so kind, so desirous of thinking the best of everyone. We only played it, I assure you, when we had been so aggressively ignored that it felt like the only respite. It was always Pike who began it, but I admit I played, too.

Do you see? I cannot abandon him. Whatever awful things Pike may have done to me—deep inside, I am just as bad.

I could not look Georgiana in the eye after telling her all this. Well, telling her a softened version. I may have been vague about how vicious and frequent the deaths I assigned were. It may be selfish, but by some miracle she likes me, and if she knew what I was really like that would be quite impossible. "I daresay it sounds strange," I said.

We had reached the spring by then. She was sitting on the bench, plucking dandelions. "I do not think it at all strange, Mary, if you should want to burn Meryton to the ground," she said softly. "I read your letters. They do not deserve you."

My face went hot again. Why must she *say* things like that? "Well, still. I spend too much time thinking about death, I suppose. Perhaps it comes of sleeping in a bed that—"

I froze midsentence as an idea sliced through me like a thunderbolt.

"Yes?" Miss Darcy said. "A bed that what?"

"I think I know what to do," I said. "We will need something more substantial than blood, though."

Her eyes gleamed. "What do you have in mind?"

I told her, but I hardly dare set it down here—not till I know if it works. It is an audacious idea to be sure. I am not at all certain that Quindley would approve—but I hope that you would, Harry. You were always so kind, even to those, like me, who do not deserve it. I hope that very much, for you shall have rather a large part to play in it.

Chapter 22

I Develop a Fixation

7 August, 18--

Dear Harry,

Do you suppose there is something wrong with me?

Of course you do. Everyone with sense does. Why, you very gave me a whole book with which to repair it. But I mean something else. Something new.

It is nothing to do with my research. *That* is proceeding quite well. I have never had a partner before—well, Pike, I suppose, but not one who could really work with me. Georgiana is *brilliant*. I thought myself passable at mathematics, but to her numbers are like playthings. One glance at a table of figures and she not only commits them to memory but spots trends and anomalies that I might not see even with hours of calculation.

We have been making a more precise study of the effects of various serums. Miss Darcy was unexpectedly missish about inhaling the chromae ourselves, for she reminds me that she is in delicate health, and she worries it would interfere with her medicines. Instead, we feed the chromae to Cariad. Rather difficult to extrapolate, since our only research subject is a long-dead bird, but still the results have been illuminating. A few key examples:

Color: Canary yellow
Donor: Sir William Lucas
Effect on Cariad: Becomes extremely social. Clings to my shoulder for as long as he can. Sings a mournful dirge if I put him away. Even becomes affable toward G. Once, after giving him a dose, I put him to bed in his cage and awoke the next day to find him asleep next to me on my pillow, making a nest of my braid. He is lucky I am fond of him.

Color: Cyan
Donor: Jane; Emma the milkmaid on Johnson's farm
Effect on Cariad: He goes to sleep

Color: Apple green
Donor: Miss Figg
Effect on Cariad: Loud complaining, and a bit of intestinal distress

Color: Red
Donor: Me
Effect on Cariad: G and I disagree on this, but I insist that he becomes cleverer. I devised a little test whereby he must choose which cloth I have hidden a grape under. He is markedly better at it when dosed with my red. G says this is because if he cannot find it he simply tears the cloth to bits with his sharp little beak. G says I am looking at him with too much of a proud mamma's eye and not enough as a scientist, which is absurd, because he is a dead bird,

not my child, even if it is **rather ador**able how he hops about when he finds his treat.

Color: Beige, threaded through with brown
Donor: Georgiana
Effect: Seems to make Cariad develop a taste for raw meat

Color: Black
Donor: Pike, before his death
Effect: Difficult to pin down. Sometimes Cariad seems quite himself; other times his mood alters. More analysis needed. That is, needed but unlikely—one common thread of a black dose is that it seems to upset him greatly. I shan't give him any more, I think. It is weakness on my part, but there it is. I hate his little cheeps of distress.

We've a great deal still to do, of course. However, we progress admirably. Her research is not the problem. No, it is G herself.

Georgiana is here three weeks now, and I fear I am becoming a bit unbalanced regarding her. I think of her all the time. If I am not careful, my notes become crowded with sketches of her hair and hands and eyes. My lips are ever tingling with the memory of that electrical almost-kiss.

It is just having a friend, I suppose. I have never had a proper one before (yourself excluded), and I'd no idea it would feel like this. She has become so dear to me that when she leaves I sometimes feel I will cease to exist. When other young ladies monopolize her at parties (which they do, of course, for she is clever and pretty and kind), I find myself scowling at them. I declare it is even affecting my bookkeeping. I have three tubes less of blue serum and two less of red than I expected. No great surprise when I spend more time imagining saving her from a fire than I do on taking inventory.

I keep waiting for her to tire of my nonsense, but remarkably she has not. Indeed just last night she threw an arm about my shoulders and said, "Mary, you are my best friend in the world, you know, but if you do not hurry up with that sodium solution, I shall wallop you." I blushed and stammered and dropped the saline so we had to start all over.

I suppose it is not me, so much as my lab, and the chance to use it for something that matters. She never looks so alive as she does when we are huddled up there together.

I am not at all sure that my own feelings are so simple.

You know, there is a passage in *Fanny Hill* where two young ladies ~~[redacted]~~

No. That is absurd. It is friendship, that is all. And Papa ought never to have kept *Fanny Hill* where an impressionable young girl might read it. I believe Quindley would go into apoplexy.

It only stands to reason, I suppose—I have always been excessive, so of course my friendship would burn as hot as the rest of me. Still, I must strive to control it. I mustn't let her see how often I think of her. She would be frightened away, and I *mustn't* frighten her away. I need her. Not merely to satisfy the howling maw that is my affection, but because she was right. Pike is getting worse.

He runs out of serum much more quickly these days. The effectiveness is collapsing toward zero, as Georgiana predicted. Even at the height of its effectiveness, there have been incidents, such as that of my uncle's house.

Uncle Phillips was Pike's master in the old days, you will recall. He treats Pike now as an old friend, almost a son; he seems to believe that Pike regards him in the same light, and he is very familiar and fond whenever they meet. Pike is by no means as warm in his affections, but he is polite enough to both my aunt and uncle.

Some part of him, perhaps, feels differently.

One night while Georgiana and I were working we heard the clang of bells off in Meryton. Cariad, too, was agitated, shrieking about the room before settling on my shoulder. There was a smell of smoke in the air. Looking out the window toward Meryton, we could just see an orange glow in the distance.

"It will be the Longs, I suppose," I said. "They never get their chimneys cleaned properly, and it has been colder lately."

But it was not the Longs, nor their chimneys.

Half an hour later my aunt's carriage pulled up outside Longbourn. She soon had the house in an uproar. Disheveled, hairpiece askew, smelling of smoke, she had mild hysterics on her sister's shoulder as my mother, unused to being the one comforting hysterics instead of having them, patted her hopelessly, and Georgiana and I looked on.

"It was some brigand," my aunt said. "Mr. Phillips said the house will be all right, for I happened to be awake, and I saw the villain take a torch to our back door, and I shrieked and frightened him away, but the front of the house is horribly singed, and the parlor is all over soot, and all the furniture quite ruined."

"A brigand!" said Mamma. "Why on earth would a brigand want to burn down your house?"

"There's many who dislike a keen man of business." Aunt sniffed. "Or perhaps it is one of my old swains. I'd many, you know. No doubt they still pine."

"You did?" asked Mamma with interest. "I'd no idea you ever had more than one! Who were they?"

My aunt glared at her and asked if we were going to offer her a place to sleep, or if she would have to go home and sleep in the embers. Mamma made up Lydia and Kitty's old room for her.

A few days later we saw Pike at a ball. He looked a bit shaken, but his manners were still good, and his bow was very smooth when he asked Georgiana for a dance.

"Thank you, but—" she began. I stepped on her foot.

"She would adore to," I said.

"Why must I dance with him?" she hissed at me after he'd moved away.

"You can talk to him on the floor," I pointed out. "He's engaged you for a waltz. Find out what he knows."

"Why not you?"

I laughed. "You are the jewel of Meryton these days. It would cause comment if he asked me before you."

"Stuff," she said. "You are much prettier than I am."

I did not know what to say to that and merely wandered about arm in arm with her until Pike came to collect her.

I watched them whirl about the dance floor, deep in conversation. When he returned Georgiana to me she looked grim.

"He says it was most likely his doing," she said. "He woke with no memory of what happened, but his clothes smelled of smoke."

"Oh dear," I said. "I suppose we'd better augment the dose again."

"Yes, that's what he requested," she said. "Specifically the red and black portions of it. Don't you think that's a bit odd?"

"What?"

"He wants more red and black. The serums *you* believe make him more aggressive."

"He believes otherwise."

"Well, Pike claims he has no memory of the event, and no idea why he chose your uncle's house. But he had to walk by half a dozen other houses to get to it."

"What do you mean?"

"I mean this seems less like a random act of madness than calculated revenge. And if he really was out of his senses, he ought to be glad of any medicine you care to provide that will keep him in them."

I watched Pike across the room, bowing to Uncle Phillips. He said something, and my uncle laughed and clapped him on the shoulder.

"He's not like that anymore," I said. "Not when he's in his right senses."

"And what if you're wrong? What if he is 'like that'?"

She was gripping my arm. I turned my eyes to hers and forgot what we had been talking of. Her face was much closer than I expected. My stomach swooped as though I'd just leapt from the hayloft.

Why is this happening to me? Is not Pike enough for one girl to deal with?

I cleared my throat. "If I am wrong," I said, "all the more reason to advance our project."

Harry, if your spirit would care to visit me in a dream with any advice on how to make my friendship more calm and proportionate, I would be most grateful.

Chapter 23

Insufficient Blood

21 August, 18--

Setbacks, Harry. Setbacks.

We have, of late, been experimenting with bones. It is a promising line of inquiry—we've found that they can, if submitted to an altered version of chromatic decoction, sometimes produce a stream of chroma serum—much more than blood. When people say *It's in my bones*, they have no idea how right they are.

But the effects remain temporary, uneven, and insufficient. To be any use, either for dye production or for Pike's medicinal needs, we would need much, much more from them. And we are at our wits' end to do so. More electrical power means more serum, but I am already taxing my rig to the utmost.

Our research has slowed to a crawl. For one thing, we cannot get blood so easily as in times past. Miss Figg did not respond to my last three orders, so I went and visited her shop.

"Uncle is selling his practice," she told me, her hands occupied with mixing some remedy. "I must seek a new situation. Sorry, Miss Bennet, no more blood for you."

"Oh," I said in dismay. "Oh dear. I am sorry to hear it."

She laughed a little. "I'm sure you are. You know, it couldn't have lasted much longer anyhow. More and more blood you wanted, more and more and more, and even our stupidest patients began to ask why we bled them so much these days. You've sucked this town dry."

She has always been an odd, rude little thing, but I am in no position to complain.

"What sort of situation do you seek? Perhaps I can help."

"Nay." She grinned. "I know your father's income. He couldn't afford me, even if you and your mother *are* half our practice. Not to worry, I shall soon find something *very* suitable."

"Right. Well. I certainly hope so." And I left her.

Pike was alarmed when I pulled him aside at the next ball and told him of the shortage. After thinking on it for a few minutes, he told me, "Leave it to me, Miss Bennet. Perhaps I can obtain what you require."

"What *we* require," I pointed out.

"Well, quite."

"How can you? There is no other apothecary."

"Not here, but I am often in London upon business. I shall speak to medical students of my acquaintance. They are always hard up."

Thus far he has not produced more blood, but it hardly matters, for I cannot access my laboratory in any case. Georgiana's illness has laid her low at last. I thought, given how close we have become, I might now be admitted to nurse her, but she refuses. She only tells me through the door that she will be better in a few days. Perhaps that closeness, as I have sometimes conjectured, exists only in my head.

So I have found myself with something I have not had since I was eleven or so: free time. It is fine, amber late summer weather, and I have been wandering the country lanes.

It was on one such wander that I formed a new acquaintance of a kind.

I was traversing the road through the woods near the river when I spotted a young woman standing in the lane.

"Good day," I said.

"Dia duit."

She must be Irish, I realized, for my feet had taken me near Pike's factory. It was soon to begin production, and he had imported several dozen young Irishwomen to work it.

It sounded like *dia daitch*. Pretty. I am, of course, fluent in Latin, and my French and German are quite good, but this was a language I had never heard a word of before. If my mind had a stomach, it would have growled. "Dia duit," I repeated carefully.

The girl burst out laughing, then quickly covered her mouth. "I suppose my pronunciation is terrible," I said, and tried again. "Dia duit."

"Dia duit," she repeated slowly, and I copied her. We went back and forth a few times.

The tight, pinched look on her face relaxed a little. She almost smiled. I suppose it must be awfully difficult, starting over somewhere no one speaks your language.

She taught me a few more words of her tongue—it was hard going, for it is a lovely but strange language, with a slow, dreamy rhythm and vowels that sound different to me every time she repeats a word. You would love it, I think, Harry, for it is very musical, though not on my tongue. She did her best not to laugh at my attempts. In return, I taught her a few words of English. *Hello. Goodbye. My name is Mairead.*

Is that not funny? Her name, in English, is Mary, too. That is not so extraordinary of course—every fifth girl here in Meryton is another Mary. Still. It echoes in my mind.

Then a bell rang.

Instantly, Mairead's smile vanished. "Slan," she said, and darted back down the lane, quickly swallowed up by the trees.

Since that day I have gone back several times, hoping to see her again. Something about her tugs at my mind. Boredom, I suppose—with no new books and no Georgiana, my mind has seized this new language like a dog chews a bone. In any case she's a good sign. Pike's factory plans proceed briskly, which means he is still in possession of his faculties. Hopefully he can source us some more blood as he promised.

(Next morning)

Had a gift from Pike. A hamper of pheasant and fine fruits of the season. Mamma does not know whether to be indignant at being treated like poor relations who must be sent hampers or hopeful that this means that Pike is sweet on me.

As soon as she'd emptied the hamper, I left her and Cook to their surmises and took the basket up to my room. Sure enough, it had a false bottom.

Blood. Phials and phials. No names, but he's labeled them *Subject A*, *Subject B*, *Subject C*, et cetera, so I ought to do all right. Pike must know an awful lot of medical students. And I can hear G stirring upstairs. Back to work.

Slan, Harry. That means goodbye.

CHAPTER 24

Lightning Hill

4 October, 18--

We have had a breakthrough.

For weeks now, Georgiana and I have been feverishly pursuing a promising line of inquiry I previously mentioned re: bones. However, we ran up against a wall, eventually: insufficient power. Finally, though, we realized, more was in fact available. All we had to do was wait and watch the leeches.

"Look," said Georgiana last evening, kneeling down next to the tempest prognosticator. "St. John has a message for us."

I leaned down next to her. Indeed, St. John had crawled nearly to the top of his glass, well past the tempest line, ignoring the lovely puddle of fresh offal in the bottom.

I frowned. "Just because he is your favorite, it does not mean you should abide by his counsel only."

"Just you watch," said Georgiana. "The others will soon follow him."

Sure enough, as we watched, Barnaby, Andrew, Lily ("She's too pretty to be a boy," said Georgiana), and all the others began oozing up the sides of their glasses. Within fifteen minutes every leech in our instrument had passed the tempest line.

We looked at each other. Then I went and opened the window.

It was not raining—yet. But the air felt thick and close. The sky had gone a yellowish gray. A restless breeze chased down the skylight, ruffling my hair. I might not be a leech, but I knew what that feeling meant.

"Right," I said. "It had better be tonight."

We were able to sneak out a little before midnight. We waited for the rest of the house to quiet, packed our rucksacks, and went out into the tempest.

At this juncture, Harry, I must remind you that all we did that night was in service to the public safety. Surely you understand that I meant no immodesty. We simply could not go about the countryside dressed as young ladies. I assure you I took no pleasure from the exercise. Well. Very little pleasure. Trousers do allow one more freedom of movement.

I always thought it was absurd in stories and plays when girls donned boys' clothes and went about in disguise. I still do not believe it would serve at, say, a public ball, or the court of Illyria (come, Olivia, you are cleverer than that!), but on a stormy night, when no one is about, two young ladies may don trousers and homespun shirts and tuck their hair up in their caps and pass without remark. More than one lamp shone out from the farmhouses as we passed; but the only gossip I heard about it the next day was a little head-shaking over some farmer who had sent his farm boys out on some errand despite the foul weather.

The rain stung our faces, and the wind howled around us. I kept my head down and my eyes on my hobnail boots as I tried to keep from losing my footing in the rivers of mud that had formed. I had never been out in a storm like this—not for any longer than the distance from a carriage to our front door, at any rate.

I ought, perhaps, to be frightened. It was a five mile walk to our destination, and a hard one even in good weather. Jane had once nearly caught her death making the journey. The roads were swamped, the stiles were slippery, and more than once the thunder roared so loud that my ears rang afterward.

My heart pounded. But not with fright.

I do not know what Quindley would say about young ladies who, instead of staying quietly inside, go out into storms and fall in love with them. Young ladies who long to fly up with the lightning, to sheet down with the rain. To be *wild*. I suspect he would not approve.

However, *Quindley's* does not actually *say* anything on the subject, so I felt myself at liberty to enjoy it.

It took us some time, but at last we arrived at our destination. Netherfield looked very fine, silhouetted against the sky whenever the lightning flashed.

"Are you sure about this?" I yelled over the rain.

Georgiana nodded. Laying a hand on my shoulder, she put her lips near my ear and said, "The Bingleys are permanently installed in Derbyshire. However, Bingley still holds the lease to Netherfield for some months yet. The place is quite empty."

Even *quite empty* houses of that size usually have a servant or two who stays with the property to keep it from falling to ruin. However, it was true I could see no light in any of its windows, so we hurried on.

It is not only Netherfield's emptiness that suits it to our purpose, Harry. Its park has certain peculiarities. There is a large artificial hill to the rear of the house, which quite blocks the view; no doubt this is why the house is never let for long.

It was to this hill that we now made with all haste. It is surmounted by a little ornamental pond, with a garishly tall fountain at the center. At the very top is an ugly little cherub pointing at the sky. The artist had not the skill to accurately portray a child, and his face was strangely old. He put me in mind of a miniature nude Mr. Collins.

Georgiana gave me a boost up, and I wound a coil of copper wire round that chubby little finger, then down around the body, and so to the base. From there we unwound it down to a stone bench near the side. On the bench resided the third member of our little party tonight.

"He looks a bit pale," Georgiana said. "I hope he is not taking ill."

"Ha-ha." I placed phials on either side of him. "Must you talk of it as though it were a person?"

"He *is* a person." Georgiana patted the yellowed skull. "Not just a person—a *Darcy*. Show some respect."

"If you had any respect, you would not have secreted him out of your family catacombs and into your trunk."

"Yes, well, good thing I did, is it not? I had a feeling he might be needed."

"Right." I put the ancient Darcy skull in a soup tureen I had borrowed from the kitchen. Then Georgiana and I wrapped the filaments of wire around the screws we had earlier secured to Sir Guy D'Arcy.

"Hopefully no one will ever look closely at him when he is returned," I yelled over the rain. "They might wonder how a thirteenth-century knight had acquired skull holes from a steel drill."

"Nonsense," G called. "Submitting the skull to the procedure left it far less dingy. I am sure he's not looked so well in centuries."

Sir Guy certainly looked better for all the acid baths, electrocution, and other treatments we had subjected him to. But the most radical step was yet to come.

There was a small pavilion near the pond. To this we repaired, shivering, to wait. We were soaked through, so we pressed together to avoid catching our death. Beneath her sodden clothing her flesh still glowed with heat against my own. I had a momentary vision of how much more efficiently we might share body heat without clothing between us. Cold does strange things to a person.

"Are you sure about this?" she asked. "It seems a matter of chance."

I nodded my head with more confidence than I felt. "Sir Thomas's estate has had to replace the fountain three times. It has been struck again and again."

"Very well. I hope it goes before I do. Brr-r-r." Georgiana clung to my arm.

An eternity seemed to pass. I suppose it was only about twenty minutes really, but when one is soaked to the skin, that *is* an eternity. Even pressing closer to Georgiana brought no relief, for her skin was now as icy as the lashing rain. I could hear her teeth chattering almost as loudly as my own. I was just toying with the idea of tying a kite to the cherub's finger—something I read about in a report from the Colonies—when it happened.

BRRRRROOOOMMMM.

The brightest light I had ever seen in my life flashed before my eyes. With a shower of sparks and a *CRAAA-AACKKK*, the fountain broke in two. Half a cherub listed crazily for a moment, pointing this way and that in the sky, then toppled to the fountain.

I seized Georgiana's hand and ran forward.

Before the afterimages had even cleared, I was kneeling by the tureen. There was certainly liquid in the basin—but was it just rain?

I raised the lantern high, holding my breath.

Black, thick liquid was dripping from each of the holes in the skull. The volume was tiny, but steady. As we watched, the black serum made tracks down the skeleton's face, pooling in the bottom of the basin.

We must have watched for an hour. The stream remained utterly steady.

I heard a loud *whoop* of joy. So unused to the sound was I that at first I thought it was Georgiana. But no. It was me.

Not that she was far behind. Her scream of delight was so loud it drowned out the rain. We threw our arms around each other and jumped in circles, crushing an embrace, screaming in one another's ears.

"We did it! We did it!"

The cold was forgotten. We had a new source of serum, and provided we could pour enough electricity into it, it seemed it could provide endlessly.

At last we pulled back. Georgiana was still grinning, still gripping my hands in hers. In the darkness, I could just barely make out her features.

Her smile faded a little. She was still looking at me. Her face was so close to mine.

Harry, do you remember when I was small and I told you I looked forward to being a ghost? No need, no sensation, just pure, drifting brain?

I do not think I want that anymore.

Georgiana's chest was heaving against mine. There were damp blades of hair stuck to her face. I could brush them back. A friend might do that. We had forgotten ourselves in our moment of triumph. What if I forgot a moment longer?

BOOM.

A crash of thunder made us start and jump apart. Just as well, of course. We had work to do.

Georgiana raised the lantern so I could examine the ichor in the bowl more closely. "Too bad it's black," I said.

"No great surprise there," Georgiana said. "He was an absolute rotter. All we need to do is find bones from someone nicer."

"Yes," I said. "Still, it is greatly heartening to see that our hypothesis was correct."

What happened next was, I admit, my own fault. A serious scholar must be more careful.

But I was still dizzy with triumph and from spinning with Georgiana, and I was not being as cautious as I ought. As I peered down at the fruits of Sir D'Arcy's labor, my braid slipped free of its pins, fell out of the cap, and slithered over my shoulder until the end rested in the black liquid.

Before I could move—*BOOM.*

I thought I heard Georgiana scream. I had the feeling I was flying. Then everything went dark.

"Mary!"

Ouch.

"Mary, my dear, please!"

Ouch!

I awoke with a pounding headache to find myself sprawled out on my back. Georgiana was kneeling astride my chest, slapping my cheeks.

"Ouch," I finally managed to say aloud, and she sat back with a sob of relief.

"Oh, Mary, I thought we'd killed you!"

"Not entirely," I managed. With a groan, I sat up. I felt as though a herd of cattle had trod over every inch of me. My ears were buzzing, my eyes still dazzled with the flash of light. As I turned my head, it felt strangely off-balance. I shook it, trying to clear it, but it only made the uneven, rubbery feeling in my neck feel worse. "What happened?"

"Another stroke of lightning," she said breathlessly, pulling me to my feet. "The wire was still secured to Sir Guy, and your hair was…"

Here she trailed off. Her hand half-lifted toward my head.

My eyes followed hers. My hand found the end of my braid nearly a foot above where it ought to have been. It felt coarse and frizzy, and there was a strange burnt smell, like when one of my sisters left a curling iron in for too long.

"It appears that Sir Guy's essence is quite combustible," said Georgiana apologetically. "I'm sorry, I ought to have brought his daughter. She was a nun."

A snort of laughter escaped me.

Georgiana's lips twitched, and soon we were both convulsed with hysterical giggles. "Ah well," I gasped at last. "Sir Isaac Newton lost his senses to mercury poisoning. A little hair is a comparatively light price for advancing the sum of human knowledge."

Advancing the sum of human knowledge. We really had done that. We might not be able to tell the rest of humanity, but we had done it.

We packed up our equipment—Sorry, Mr. and Mrs. Bingley, you may have to replace a very ugly cherub to escape the Netherfield lease—and poured out Sir Guy's serum. (It hissed a little—the Bingleys may have to pay for some emergency gardening as well.) If anything, the conditions were worse when we headed for home than when we set out, but the knowledge of our success kept me warm and my feet light all the way home.

More soon, Harry. I thought Georgiana asleep, but she has called me to her (my) room. Something about "the problem of my hair."

CHAPTER 25

The Problem of My Hair

8 October, 18--

We have found a solution to my poor burnt hair. Well, after a fashion. We've done something, anyway.

After she summoned me, Georgiana and I sat in front of the glass for hours, trying to conceal it. Since my hair is so thick, I thought perhaps I could just twist it up as usual and conceal that two-thirds of it was now gone. But it was no good. My braid had not come off cleanly or evenly—on the left side it still hung past my shoulders, but then it slanted upward and the right side barely covered my ear. No amount of pinning or adorning would keep the mutilated lock from springing free—and even if it could, what would people think if I started wearing a large bunch of silk flowers over my right ear all the time?

It was singed, too. Nothing we could do got the smell—a combination of smoke and rotten eggs—out.

"It's no good," Georgiana announced suddenly, letting my hair fall out of the complicated twist she'd been attempting. "It will have to come off." And without waiting for a response, she gathered what remained of my hair at the nape of my neck, squared it up, and chopped it off.

For a moment I could not breathe. I do not think I am terribly vain, but I do think I have nice hair—it is very thick and shiny, and unless it is about to rain, it lies elegantly—and now it was gone.

"Georgiana!" I croaked. "What on earth are you doing?"

"Hush." She had narrowed her eyes and was kneeling in front of me, the tip of her tongue poking out of the side of her mouth. "It's terribly fashionable, you know. All the most daring ladies of the *ton* have it."

"Have what?"

"The Lady Caro crop." Snip. Another four-inch piece of hair drifted into my lap. "The French call it *à la guillotine*."

An apt name, since the guillotine was where Mamma would probably send me when she saw it.

Why did I let her do it? I am still not sure. My whole life I have hated it when people fussed with my hair. Georgiana, clumsy as a bear cub and hardly reliable in matters of taste, was the last person I ought to let near it. But she did know about the *ton*—if she said that the finest women in the nation were going about this way, she must be right.

Besides, I rather liked the feeling of her fingers threading through my hair. Little tingles seemed to burst across my scalp whenever she touched me, cascading down the back of my neck, loosening that place between my shoulder blades that is always tight and sore. I would have let her do anything to me, as long as she did not stop. I suppose she has a natural talent for scalp massage. I ought to study its relaxing properties further.

After about twenty minutes, she blew out a breath and said, "There." She stepped back and examined her work critically, then snapped her fingers, dived into the depths of her trunk, and came up with a little pot.

"Bingley's man's favorite hair pomade comes from the Meryton chemist," she explained. "I promised I'd buy him some." She was doing something to the hair on top of my head—brushing it forward, twisting the pomade into it. The spicy smell of the pomade mixed with Georgiana's own smell—fine Italian soap and rain and a little bit of sweat.

Finally she stopped, raised my chin, and looked at me. She blinked. "Good heavens. That's extraordinary."

"What's extraordinary?"

"You are. Do you want to see?"

She sounded a bit nervous. I wondered if she'd made a mess of it. I nodded, and went over to the glass. When I saw what she had done I thought my heart might stop.

My hair was shorter than any woman's I'd ever seen. Almost as short as a man's. It was cropped very close in the back, longer on the top and sides, and brushed forward in a mop of wild curls that crested over my forehead.

I'd seen young men with this look before. Byronic, they called it. As I was a girl, apparently it was the Lady Caro crop.

"Do you like it?" Georgiana said. She was standing just behind me, and I met her eyes in the mirror.

Did I like it?

My features are stronger than my sisters'. Strong nose, strong jaw, dark slashing brows that tend toward frowning. Every coiffure I have ever had thrust upon me has been an attempt, in some way or another, to apologize for this. Bunches of round curls to soften the jaw, bright sprigs of girlish ribbon to distract from the brows. None of it worked very well.

There was nothing apologetic about the way I looked now. I scarcely recognized myself. The face in the glass was proud and elegant and a little wild. Still not a beautiful face, but—striking. I felt, suddenly, that to be striking was all I had ever wanted.

"You hate it," Georgiana said, and put down the scissors with a glum thump. "I am sorry, Mary—"

"No," I cut her off. "I don't hate it. It is—well, it may strike Mamma dead when she sees it, but…" I blew out a breath. "But it will be worth it."

She gave a little squeak of glee. "Oh good! For an instant there I thought you were going to murder me."

"No," I said. "I mean it. Thank you." And on some strange impulse, I stood up and kissed her on the cheek.

I regretted it immediately. It obviously discomfited her. I was close enough to hear the little *tck* of her swallowing. When I pulled back, she pressed her hand to her cheek.

"How Continental," she whispered.

"Yes, well," I said, "I need sophisticated new manners to go with my new hair."

She jerked a nod. "Well…good night, Mary."

"Good night, Georgiana."

I tried to read a little *Quindley's* before going to sleep, but my mind kept drifting to the feeling of Georgiana's cheek against my lips. I shoved the book in a drawer.

Mamma did faint when she saw me at the breakfast table the next morning. But once she woke up, Georgiana told her about the *ton* and the Caro crop and Mamma was at least partially convinced. There has never been a Caro crop before in Meryton, but Mamma is so in awe of the Darcys that she would believe Georgiana if she told us to shave ourselves bald and tattoo our scalps.

At the next assembly, my only hair ornament was a wide velvet ribbon, wrapped over the tumble of my curls. As I am a young unmarried girl it ought to have been in some pale shade, but it was deep crimson, dyed with my own dyes. Striking was absolutely the word for me—the conversation actually stopped when we came in. I'm sure two thirds of Meryton thought I'd gone mad, but I didn't care. I felt like a new person. Besides, not everyone was unappreciative. Four young men came up and asked me to dance—a record for me—and two of them asked twice. I told them all no. I preferred to sit and talk with Georgiana. Sorry to Mr. Quindley. At least I am still obeying his maxim to avoid flirtatiously courting male attentions.

Chapter 26

No Title for This One

11 October 18--

~~Harr~~

I will not even address this page to the ghost of Harry. The thought even of that nonexistent gentleman knowing about what transpired this morning makes me squirm. Yet I *must* write it down. I feel if I do not pin the memory down it will disappear.

Well. Perhaps it would be best, but…

Last night, after a particularly long session of serum-making, even my powers of sleeplessness were taxed. Georgiana and I were deep in a discussion—a question of whether Leyden jars could be made to discharge their electricity over time, instead of in one big shock—and I was so tired and distracted that I forgot my room was now Miss Darcy's and, instead of making my way downstairs, I collapsed into bed alongside her.

I awoke slowly, comfortably, feeling a sort of gentle tired ache around my heart. Georgiana was a lump in the bed next to me, only visible as a tangle of locks. I ought to be embarrassed by this, but I could not be. I was too warm, too comfortable.

Before I could slip away down the stairs, Georgiana stirred and stretched. Blinking awake, she turned, saw me, and smiled.

"Morning," she said in a gravelly voice.

"Good morning."

"We ought to be more careful of the hour, I s'pose," she said, still in her sleep-roughened tones. "We did not even wash our faces last night."

"Did we not?" I struggled to remember through an unaccustomed haze of drowsiness.

"Mm, no indeed." With a yawn and a wormlike wriggle, she inched closer to me till her head shared my pillow. She reached out a hand and touched my face. "Oop, jam."

"Jam?"

"From the sandwiches last night. You've still jam on your chin." Gripping said chin, she wiped at it with her thumb.

"Well, so too have you." I mirrored her actions, wiping at her bottom lip. Without thinking, I popped my thumb in my mouth, sucking away the morsel of sweetness.

The sleepy smile vanished. She was looking at me, quite awake. She, too, licked the jam from her thumb.

"You've…a bit more," I said.

"Have I."

"Yes. Here, let me…"

I tugged a little at the neck of her sleep shift. The collar was tight; I undid the knot that held it closed. Her breathing stopped when I folded it aside, exposing a little more of her skin. There, perhaps two inches below her collarbone, lay another blackcurrant splotch.

"Shameful," she murmured. I could feel her voice through my hand. "I must have eaten like a child. No more jam sandwiches while we work, I think."

"No more jam sandwiches," I echoed. I scarcely heard myself.

I suppose I was still half-asleep. That is the only explanation for how I came to do it. I leaned down close, and, instead of wiping the jam away with a finger, I closed my lips over it and sucked it away. Blackcurrant jam, and pear soap, and the lab, and recent sleep.

Georgiana gasped. But she was not pushing me away. Both her hands threaded through my hair, pulling me closer, almost crushing me against her. Then she was pulling my head up to hers, lining our bodies up, one of her knees sliding between mine, and I could feel her breath on mine, and something bright and warm seemed to have cracked open in my chest, and oh God, we were going to—

"Mary?"

We had just time to jerk apart before the door opened and Mamma came bustling in. "Ah, there you are," she said. "You gave me quite a turn, child. I found your bed empty and thought we had another runaway elopement on our hands. But of course, *you* would never do such a thing. I am glad to see you just came up here in the night. I suppose you got cold?"

"Yes'm. What? Yes. Cold. I was cold."

"Well, you must ask Betsy for a bed warmer tonight. I'll not have you crowding our guest."

"She did not crowd me, madam," said Georgiana. "I…er, was also… cold."

"A bed warmer for you, too, then. No—for you, *two* bed warmers, my dear Miss Darcy." She threw back the covers on my side. "Now come, Mary, we're to have a morning visit from the Longs, and you know how they are—their morning visits are *actually* before noon."

I followed her down the stairs, washed, dressed, had my breakfast, and made appropriate noises to the Longs. It was a bit like trying to politely go about your business whilst on fire, but I did it. Georgiana, with the excuse of her illness, avoided the morning visit and spent the next few hours "in bed" (actually in the attic working on a batch of promising purple serum).

When next I saw her, she said nothing of our morning activities, so I did not, either. Soon I wondered if the incident had simply been a dream, after all.

I rather hope it was. Heaven knows what she must think of me otherwise. And we've more important things to think of.

No. I don't hope that. I ought to do. But I cannot.

CHAPTER 27

Great Lengths Are Sometimes Necessary

13 October, 18--

Dear Harry,

I am well served for my unspeakable conduct the other morning. I am sure as a clergyman you will be glad to hear that it torments me as though I was on the rack. G and I can hardly look at each other. Every time I think of it, guilt slashes through me like a knife, and yet I cannot stop thinking of it.

Perhaps I have mortally offended her. And yet—surely my memory is not mistaken? Surely she is the one who ~~reached out to ki~~

Harry, I know we are not papists and you are dead, but what would you say to setting me a bit of penance? I feel it would ease my mind. I do not know their catechism, but perhaps I could recite the times tables.

There is little to distract us, for we can take no further action till the leeches climb the glass again. Today I set out alone to meet Pike. On my way I once more came upon Pike's Mairead. She looked rather different—not

The Shocking Experiments of MISS MARY BENNET

ill; in fact, she had more bloom than before—but her color was rather high, almost feverish. But she smiled when she saw me.

We exchanged a few more words—I can now proudly say *green* and *nose* and *eyes* and something that is either *dirt* or *brown*—and then Pike himself strolled up.

"Miss Mary," he said with a bow. "I should have known that the lure of an unfamiliar tongue would draw you." He turned to Mairead and said something in her tongue that made her smile.

"You know me well, then. Can you ask her if we might meet regularly? I could pay for an hour or so of her time."

Pike frowned a little, then shrugged and turned to the girl and spoke again. The girl laughed and gave a smiling reply. Pike turned back to me. "She says she is sorry but she is very busy here, and she doubts you can afford such good wages as Mr. Pike. You may go now, Mairead."

"Slan," said the girl. She bobbed a curtsy and headed back toward the factory.

Pike offered his arm to me. "Shall we walk?"

I took it and we set off down the lane. "Why did you bring factory girls who spoke no English?" I asked him.

He patted my hand. "The factories in the north always import workers from the east coast of Ireland, where the people speak English already. That leaves the Irish speakers to the west unemployable. I felt sorry for them." He shrugged. "My mother's people were from near Derry. She brought an old nurse with her when she married Father, so I speak a little of the Irish tongue. I thought I could make a good bargain and do a good turn at the same time."

"That makes sense," I admitted.

"Good." He patted my hand again. "Where is your friend today?"

"At home, I believe. She did not care to walk. She is probably making more serum. We always need more."

"Hmm."

"Hmm what?"

"I am glad you've such affection for her," he said. "You deserve to be surrounded by worthy friends."

"But?"

"But is she worthy?"

"Sir!"

He held up his hands. "I intend no rudeness, but surely we have been through enough not to stand on ceremony?"

"I suppose," I said reluctantly.

"Do you not think she has secrets from you?"

I could not deny it. "We all have secrets."

"True. All I mean is that when you return home you should make sure that her afternoon alone in your lab has left you with more serum, not less."

"What?!"

"I could be wrong," he said hastily. "I mean no offense. Only—Miss Bennet, I could swear I saw her secreting phials away in her apron pocket last time I was there."

"I am sure she was not 'secreting' anything! That is what pockets are for!"

"Brilliant people often have those around them who would take advantage."

I thought of her strange behavior regarding her illness. "Why don't you trust her?"

"I have tried, for your sake. But she is too different. You and I, Miss Bennet—we know what it is to be seated farthest from the fire and expected to hide our shivers."

"What are you saying?"

"Put not too much trust in the rich. They will never really understand the cost of things."

I tried to suppress it, but an image rose up in my head: Georgiana, on a trip to the village dressmaker's last week, holding a bit of deep blue ribbon up to my cheek. "It complements your complexion," she'd announced. "You must buy it."

It *was* pretty. "I cannot afford it. My pocket money for the month is nearly gone."

She shrugged. "I shall buy it for you, then."

"No!"

My voice was louder than I intended. Several patrons turned to look at us. I modulated my voice. "No, thank you. I've plenty of ornaments."

She looked rather hurt. I took her arm and dragged her to the sweet shop as a distraction, but there was a bit of a bruised feeling between us the rest of the day.

Now, I tightened my hand on Pike's elbow. I turned us down the lane toward the churchyard. "It is not her fault she is rich."

"No indeed," he agreed. "I am being silly, no doubt. Why is it you wished to see me today?"

"Right." I drew a deep breath. "Miss Darcy and I believe we have found a way to reduce or even eliminate your dependence upon our serums."

"That's wonderful."

"Yes, but we need something from you."

"If it is in my power, it is yours."

We were in the churchyard now. Red and brown leaves drifted down and whirled around us in the wind. I led him toward the back, to a modest but well-kept grave.

"This is what we need," I said. "Human bones. Ribs, to be exact. Two of them ought to be enough."

He frowned down at the gravestone. "Who is Henry Bennet?"

Forgive me, Harry. I know it is ghoulish. But you were a man of both science and faith; as the former, you will understand that sometimes sacrifices must be made for progress; and as the latter you will agree that great lengths are sometimes necessary to save a soul.

CHAPTER 28

We Add the Bones

25 October, 18--

We have taken the leap, Harry. Pray that it will be enough. It *must* be enough.

It was midnight last night when we set to work. A very dark, moonless night. For some reason those seem to be better for Georgiana's illness. She was by my side, and quite strong and lively as ever. (Actually I have never seen her otherwise than strong and lively. She takes great care to guard her illness from view. The Darcy pride at work again, I suppose. Never mind Pike's suspicions.) It was storming, as well—a good thing we are having a stormy autumn!

A rapping at the window alerted us that Pike had arrived. I opened the window to him and let him climb down from the roof, sodden from head to foot. By the time he reached the floor there was a puddle beneath him.

"You're late," I said to him.

"There was a line of carriages waiting to go home from the Lucases' card party. I had to go through the woods so as not to be seen." He examined his feet and growled. "Quite ruined my new boots, too. Why all this rigmarole, pray?" He offered a brusque bow to Georgiana. "Miss Darcy."

"Mr. Pike." She nodded.

"If this 'rigmarole,' as you call it, succeeds," I said, "your dependence on me will be permanently at an end."

That got his attention. "Then let us get on with it."

I waved a cup at him. It was a muddy blue color—the last of the blue extract, mixed with a few drops of the ruddy orange I got from Papa—that seemed to make Pike sleepy. "Medicine first."

He took the cup and peered down into it. Then he made his way to the shelf and helped himself to several phials each of red and black. "For later," he said.

Georgiana and I exchanged glances. "As you will," I said at last. After all, if this went well, he would soon be free of both the need and the inclination for the stuff.

"Are you sure about all this?" he asked, eyeing the array of instruments gleaming on the table.

"Hush," I told him. "We're going to make you better."

"By cutting me open."

"You already agreed," said Georgiana. "You brought us the bones. Lost your nerve?"

He smiled faintly. "I would never disoblige a lady as charming as yourself, Miss Darcy."

"Good."

Pike toasted us. "Your health, ladies." Then he drank it down.

We bade him lie down. He did not actually fall asleep, but lay quite calmly on the table and watched us as we made our final preparations. The neat twist of copper wire hung above him, flickering in the lamplight. I saw the peace of the blue serum steal over him. If only he could always be this biddable.

"Will it take long?" he asked me.

"Not if you hold still."

"I shall hold still, then."

He was humming when we made the first incision. In the moonlight, his already pale chest looked as white as a snow-covered field, with two little purple-black smudges for the nipples. Consulting the anatomy book, I cut along the sternum. I flinched when the scalpel sank into his flesh. He did not.

"Are you all right, Pike?"

Silence.

"Pike?"

"You told me to be still."

I blew out a breath. "You may answer me."

"I'm well enough. A bit bored."

"We'll soon have you up."

His eyes, still compliant and uninterested, rolled away from mine, and stared at the ceiling. He began to hum softly, then to sing.

"A fox went out on a chilly night / Prayed to the moon to give him light / He'd many a mile to go that night, / before he reached the town-oh, town-oh, / He'd many a mile to go that night / before he reached the town-oh."

Geo and I exchanged glances. "Should we make him stop?" I whispered.

She knelt down by the table until her eyes were level with his sternum. "We needn't," she said. "Look."

She took my leather-clad hand in her own and laid it on his chest. It ought to have risen and fallen with the rhythm of his song. It was perfectly still.

"He'd many a mile to go that night, before he reached the town-oh…"

I swallowed. "R-right. Onward?"

I could feel a slight tremor in G's hand, but she nodded crisply. "Onward."

The long cut I opened from collarbone to stomach ought to have bled horrendously. There was little blood, however. Just a thick dark red fluid that welled up almost decorously at the edges, and was easily wiped away by Georgiana. I opened a second cut along the bottom of his ribs in an upside-down T shape, and then carefully peeled back the flesh.

"He grabbed a gray goose by the neck, / Threw the goose across his back, / He didn't mind their quack, quack, quack, / With their legs all dangling down-oh…"

Slowly, slowly, I peeled back the flesh, the only sounds Pike's singing and a faint whispering, as of cloth against cloth. At last I had him pinned open, and I stopped and stared.

I am a farmer's daughter. I have seen the insides of animals before. Once, with a sharp blade and a book of anatomy, I even cut open my own thigh to see if it looked the same as beast meat; it did. Pike did not.

There was no scent of life, nor of death, either. His organs were all there, just as the diagrams had said, but they were a dusty gray-black instead of the colors the book said they ought to be. There was none of the dampness of the inside of a living thing, nor any shriveled desiccation. All was plump and smooth and dry as a bone. His scent was something between gunpowder and charcoal. A calm, inorganic smell. His heart was pumping, but it whispered instead of thudding. His lungs seemed to be working out of sync, rippling rather than pumping in and out together.

I knew then that I was seeing something no living creature had seen before. And I had made it. I had done it.

Georgiana made a slight sound, and I started out of my fascinated reverie. I worried she must be disgusted with it and disgusted with me. Perhaps I was as dry and dead on the inside as Pike was.

When I raised my eyes to her face, though, she was not looking at me, but down into the whispering pit of his abdomen.

"Fascinating," she murmured. "Do you think all the organs are in such a state? What about the liver?"

I bit my lip, then blurted, "Let's see." Carefully, I lifted up a corner of the right lung and peered beneath it. "It's too dark."

"Here, let me help you." With one hand, Georgiana lifted her lamp a foot above the incision; her other hand joined mine beneath the lung. I could feel her fingers next to mine, deft and seeking. A little delicate probing, and then, without needing to discuss it, we lifted the organ together.

"There it is," whispered Georgiana. Very gently, I palpated it. Most creatures' livers are fatty, of course; his felt as though it was full of a fine powder.

"Here," I said. "Feel this." I moved her fingers where mine had been and gently squeezed them. I felt as much as I heard her gasp. Our fingers still tangled together, her eyes were glued on the cavity, but mine were on her face. Her eyes sparkled in the lantern light.

Then she lifted her eyes to mine and smiled.

"This is the most captivating thing I have ever seen in my life," she said. She understood. I felt as though my heart would burst.

Not dry and dead, after all.

I was aware of every place her gloved fingers touched mine. I could have stood there all night, entwined with her. But—

"...The legs all dangling down-oh..."

I jerked away. Georgiana flinched and withdrew as well. We had work to do.

Harry, your ribs were not free of flesh when Pike brought them to us, but after many decoctions they were as shining and white as a freshly scrubbed floor. You'd be proud, I hope. We'd thought, from our readings on anatomy, that we might have to cut or even saw Pike's own ribs away; we'd prepared by abstracting a set of garden shears and even, in case of greatest need, a saw. Here again his peculiar form surprised us. His lowest rib on the right side worked out of its socket with nothing more than two soft pops.

When I turned my attention to the left side, I frowned. "That's odd."

"What?"

"He's got fewer on this side." Quickly I counted. "Yes, thirteen on the right but only twelve here."

"I've heard about this," said Georgiana. "Apparently it's not unusual for someone to have an extra rib on one side. The body is not so uniform as might be wished."

"Really!" I wished I could spend hours inspecting the rest of his internal organs, but that seemed a bit rude, so I set Pike's rib aside and took up Harry's ribs. "Well, after this he will be properly symmetrical."

"Then the fox and his wife without any strife / cut up the goose with a fork and knife. / They never had such a supper in their life / and the little ones chewed on the bones-o, bones-o, bones-o…"

For a moment I held them in my hand. The smooth, curved weight of them. They rolled end-down in my palm.

These were your ribs.

What would Mr. Henry Bennet, rector of Longbourn and Meryton, think of what I was doing now?

You would not be angry, I hope? You were never angry with me. You believed, so strongly, that natural research was a way to grow closer to God. But what I was doing was hardly godly.

But what choice did I have, Harry? I was all that stood between Longbourn and a monster, and God had shown no inclination to step in. Pray forgive me. I only chose your bones to desecrate because you are the best man I ever knew.

"…they never had such a supper in their life / and the little ones chewed on the bones-o."

One at a time, I carefully slid the new ribs into place. They shone bright white against the gray of his other bones. The right-hand one was a little bigger than Pike's own—you were a tall man, cousin—and we had to push some viscera aside to make room for the left-hand one, but we managed.

Finally, I reached for the two pieces of copper wire hanging down above the table. I wrapped each one several times around a rib. Then Georgiana stepped back several paces and I cranked up my electrical apparatus. Once, twice, three times, until the very air crackled with power, and then—

Zzzap.

We had been hoping that, as your bones are fresher, you would not require a full lightning strike to perform. Peering into Pike's chest cavity, we found we were quite correct. Your ribs were already dotted with tiny beads of dark liquid, like beads of sweat on a hot day. I blew out a breath. "We did it." I swiped a bit onto my thumb and forefinger and held it up to the lamp. A perfect cyan blue.

"Can we conclude then?" asked Pike. "I am developing the urge to sneeze."

Georgiana and I exchanged glances of alarm. "On *no account* must you sneeze, Pike," I said. "You would expel your new ribs and Lord knows what else."

"Sew me up, then."

"Very well."

Pike sang his fox song three times over by the time we had him sewn up. When we were done, we bade him sit up.

"How do you feel, Pike?" I asked.

His hands traced slowly over the stitches that now crisscrossed his chest and abdomen. "Like a chimney that wants cleaning," he said.

"What?"

"Itchy," he said, "but on the inside."

"It will go away," I said with as much confidence as I could manage. "You go to sleep now. We'll wake you when you're needed."

We'd poured every drop of blue serum that I had down his throat. We wouldn't know if the ribs were working until that had worn off. Approximately thirteen hours, I estimated.

Georgiana's heavy smocks had been a stroke of genius—once we removed them, there was no trace of our late-night project on our hands and clothes beneath. We slipped into bed and fell asleep as innocently as ever two girls had. That afternoon, we slipped back up to the laboratory and shook him awake.

"What will you do now, Pike?" Geo whispered.

He gave us the sweetest, most obedient smile I had ever seen from him. "What would you like me to do?"

I blew out a breath. It had worked.

CHAPTER 29

The Fight

27 October, 18--

How quickly things change, Harry.

Monday was one of the best days of my life. Pike was under control. Georgiana and I had succeeded. Our partnership had exceeded every expectation. There seemed no limit to what we might accomplish together.

Now, Harry, it is Wednesday, and everything is dust.

But I shall not let it stop me. You are still my friend at least, Harry, and you cannot betray me as Miss Darcy has.

Anyhow, she is gone, and I daresay we will never speak again. I shall have to think carefully about how to avoid future invitations to Pemberley. I do not think it will be too hard. Nobody wants me there.

Dash it all, why couldn't she understand?

It comes of being rich, I suppose. And beautiful, and personable. Miss Darcy has never had to regard herself with the harsh glare of honesty and admit that nearly every part of what she saw needed alteration to make it tolerable.

She has never had to worry about her future. About her family's future.

It all came to a head yesterday. I was walking in the garden, enjoying the sunshine, when Miss Darcy came pelting up to me at a pace that Quindley would certainly not approve in a lady.

"Trouble," she panted.

My heart plummeted. "Oh no. What is it?"

"He's here."

"Who?"

"Pike. He says he wishes to see you. It must not have worked after all."

Oh, no.

I raced inside. I could hear his voice from the parlor. If he was alone with my mother—I rounded the corner and there he was.

Not the monster I had expected to see. No black veins or black eyes.

Instead, here was Pike the young gentleman. As I entered, he laughed softly at something my mother said. She looked utterly gratified at his attention.

When he saw me, he rose to his feet. "Miss Bennet. Would you do me the honor of a walk up to the hill?" His eyes flicked over my shoulder. "And your companion, of course."

At that I became aware of Georgiana standing at my shoulder. A glance back showed her staring unsmiling at Pike.

I curtsied. After a moment, Georgiana did the same. "As for a walk," she said, "I am sorry, but we—"

I trod on her foot. "We would be delighted."

I ignored her wide, staring eyes all through our walk to the hill and back. His smile was as sweet as ever the blue serum could make it. Really, she was being intolerable. She was barely civil, hardly deigning to converse with Pike. Luckily, he had enough manners for both of them. He managed to converse quite comfortably with us both, while still distinguishing me with special attentions.

I reveled in it. This new man, this well-bred, soft-spoken, kind Pike—we had done it! We had made him! Why did Georgiana not share in my triumph?

She also ignored several broad hints on my part to fall back a ways and let me and Pike walk alone together. *What is the matter with the girl*, I thought in irritation. Was she jealous? She could have a hundred Pikes with the snap of her fingers.

After my mother went to bed, I slipped up to the laboratory. I was not surprised to find Georgiana already there, pacing like a caged tiger.

"What on earth are you about?" she demanded before I could speak.

"What do you mean?"

"What do you think?" She wrinkled her nose. "You and *Pike*."

I felt a prickle of sweat breaking out across my nose. It was hard to meet her scornful gaze. "He—We were successful. The ribs worked. He is better now."

"Better!" She gave a hysterical laugh. "Successful! That is not what I mean, and you know it."

"I do not know what you—"

"You're letting him court you!"

My mind whirled with confusion. Why did she look so surprised? What did she think all this was for?

You never told her the whole story, my conscience whispered.

"I cannot imagine what has come over you, Miss Bennet," she hissed. "A week ago you were elbow-deep in his entrails! Three days ago we were holding our breath to see if he'd hurt anyone else!"

"Yes, but he hasn't," I pointed out. "We fixed him. He has goodness inside of him now. Literally."

Georgiana made as though to tear her hair out. "He's dead!"

"No, he isn't. He died because of me, and now he lives because of me. And we've made a splendid fellow of him. Who better for me to marry?"

She laughed, a harsh sound in a minor key. "I suppose you are right. He is handsome and rich, and half the girls in town are setting their caps for him. You will have pin money to rival your sisters', and the finest gowns and carriages."

"You sound jealous," I said. I did not like the jeering tone in my voice, but I could not seem to help it. I felt as little control as the night I was struck by lightning. "Have you lost your heart to him?"

"Ha! Have *you*?"

"Perhaps I have."

"Oh, stuff." Her face was very white. It had a stricken expression I had never seen before. "I am not jealous," she said. "Not of—I am just worried about you. You cannot mean to marry a dead man."

"I really do not see what difference it makes. I have to marry someone, and at least his faults will be more easily managed than another man's."

"If he lets you."

"He will. Harry will see to that."

"This is absurd, Mary. You cannot expect to make up your husband's character to your liking all your life. You are playing God, and it will end ill for you."

"Why shouldn't I manage his character, as you put it? Is it not the kindest thing anyone could do? Unlike the rest of us, he will never be tortured by faults that make him appear awkward, or lazy, or stupid before his fellows! He will never be lonely, for I will craft him into a man everyone can like! My God, I wish someone would do that for me!"

She stepped toward me, one hand half raised as though to touch my cheek. "I thank God no one can," she said in a shaking voice.

It was too much. Her big, tear-filled eyes, the soft brush of fingers on my cheek. Soft, soft, all of it soft, and my mind screamed against receiving it. Such tenderness was not for me. Pike, at least, understood that.

I pushed her hand away with more violence than I felt. "What would you have me do? Not marry?"

"Yes!" She grabbed my hand and held it between both of hers. The pleading look on her face made my eyes sting. "Come with me. Stay with me. We don't need husbands, we can live out our days together, please, Mary, please."

I tried to pull away, but my hand would not obey my commands. Her fingers were as cold as they'd been that rainy night on the hill. "Easy for you to say, you—you *Darcy*!"

"You could be my companion," she persisted, clutching my hand to her. "You will want for nothing. Stay with me. Let us be together."

"And when you marry?"

"I shan't. Not ever. My illness."

"Ah yes, your mysterious illness." I choked back something that was almost a sob. I wanted to stumble into her arms so badly—to say yes, to let her manage everything. But a moment's reflection made me see how it would be. "So I will follow you about, and nurse you, and flatter you, and do your mending, and mind the house when you are ill—until you meet a young man who does not care about your illness, and then you will fall in love, and I will have given up my only chance at a home of my own for *nothing*."

She shook her head. There were tears pouring down her cheeks. "How can you talk like that?"

"Because I know the world." Again I heard myself give that jagged laugh, like a hole in the universe. "You know nothing of it, really. You have never been poor, or ignored, or pitied! You have never been frightened of being *dependent* all your life!"

She drew a deep breath. "Perhaps not. But I know what it is to be frightened." Another deep, shaky sigh, like she could not get enough air. "I am frightened now."

"Don't be," I said, as coldly and rudely as I could. "It is really no affair of yours."

"You stupid girl!" She grabbed me by the shoulders and shook me. "This will get you killed!"

"You insult my abilities."

"No, I insult your intelligence if you go through with this!" Her eyes narrowed, peering into mine. "No, you are not stupid. There is something you are not telling me."

"What? No."

"Tell me."

Should I? Should I tell her about that night before she came? Even now I could not. "You are mistaken."

"I am not," she said desperately. "Mary, it's me. I have never had a friend I loved like you. You can tell me anything. You *must*."

"Must I? And will you tell me your secrets, then?"

"What secrets?"

"Oh, how about the truth about that mysterious illness of yours?" She flinched, and I pressed the weak spot. "The one I have never witnessed? Or how about your theft of my phials of serum? Yes, I know about that. I can count, you know."

Her eyes dropped from mine. "I-I didn't—"

"You *did*." I snarled a laugh. "You never trusted me. You *stole* from me. And you would have me throw over a good match and put myself in your hands."

Her throat worked for a moment. Then, to my astonishment, she put both hands up to cup my cheeks. Around my nearly soundless gasp, she stroked my cheeks. My pulse thundered in my ears. If I just leaned forward a little—

No. I was going to marry Pike. I was going to live correctly. All the outrages I had committed against God's creatures were only justified if I became the woman He wanted me to be.

"You are right," she said softly. "I did steal from you. I was too ashamed—I am too ashamed. I was trying to cure myself. I could not explain." She drew a deep breath. "It is true. I do not deserve you. But Mary, neither does he. I fear for you if you put yourself in his power. Please, I'll do anything."

One of my hands crept up to cover hers. "There is nothing you can do. Nor I, nor anyone. Pike is the only chance I will ever have. *Look* at me."

"I am looking at you," she said softly. And she leaned forward and kissed me. Oh, Lord. How am I to explain?

My favorite dish is duck confit. If I had never tasted it, I would not know that I liked it. Perhaps that would be better. Papa prefers to sell our ducks, not eat them, so we have it rarely. If I had never had it, I would not daydream about it when I was hungry, or long for it when something less delightful graces my plate. My mouth would not water to the point of pain, thinking about it during the long days without it.

She should not have kissed me. I should have pulled away.

I did not. That first taste wiped my mind clear like a sponge on a slate. It went through me like the lightning on the hill, but sweeter, oh, sweeter. A vise I did not even know was around my heart seemed to loosen and then unfold inside my chest into a thousand flutters of warmth. At the first touch, I had stepped back in surprise, but she followed me, her lips moving over mine, and then I was surging forward, against her, voracious, my hands wrapping around her waist, clutching the soft fabric of her nightdress. Oh, glory. I knew I would be hungry all my life.

The tinkle of broken glass awoke us. I pulled back and opened my eyes to find that we had careened against the laboratory table. We had knocked a phial over, and a pool of golden-beige liquid was dripping onto the floor. With a guilty start, I took my hands off her and stepped back.

Georgiana made a broken little sound. "There I go, making a mess as usual," she said. "You go on downstairs. I'll clean it up."

I made to step forward. "I'll help. It was—"

"I *said*, I'll do it," she said. "Wouldn't want to get any of me on you." And she grabbed a rag from the counter and began to clean. Her tears were wet on my cheeks.

My throat was too tight to respond, so I just nodded and stepped back. "Be careful," I ground out. "Don't hurt yourself." She nodded without turning around.

I went down the stairs and sat on her bed. I only meant to give her a moment to recover—but I was so upset that my brain seemed to simply shut down, and I fell into a half-sitting, troubled sleep.

As ought to be clear, I was by this time extremely overwrought. What happened next—what I thought happened next—was surely no more than a freak of my anguished brain. I believe in elemental particles, and calculus, and Linnean classification. I do *not* believe in mag whatever this was.

I awoke to a sound from above. Miss Darcy gave a yelp, as though in pain. Forgetting our quarrel, I rose immediately. "Georgiana? Did you cut yourself?" There was no response. I hurried up the stairs.

She was kneeling in a pool of moonlight and looked up at my reappearance. From Cariad's cage came a low keen of dread. Georgiana's eyes went wide and she stumbled to her feet. A hand came to my shoulder, urgently guiding me back toward the door. "I am quite well. Go on."

"But what was—"

"Nothing! Go, I say!" She practically snarled the words. She had never spoken so to me, even in the midst of our recent, vicious fight. I flinched, but did not let go.

"Not until you tell me what is wrong."

"Tell you?" She laughed hysterically. "You have made it quite clear you do not wish to know what I really am."

My mind was whirling. "I have no idea what you are referring to."

"And that is for the best, for both of us. Go, for God's sake! Leave me to my shame!"

"No!" I said. There were strange shivers passing under her skin, like the tremors of a frightened horse. The rippling seemed to grow deeper, deeper than anyone's muscles really could. Georgiana wrenched herself away from me.

"Very well," she said. "You shall regret it." She laughed a high, despairing laugh. "You wanted to know the secret of my illness? You shall. Never say I failed to warn you."

Her tremors were so deep now that they were visible to the naked eye. In their wake, she looked—*different*. Her skin, dappled with moonlight, looked suddenly covered with a fine, downy coat.

Not a coat. *Feathers.* "Georgiana?"

"It used to happen every night," she whispered. "I have been able to restrict it to a few days a month. The moon makes it worse. Your potions have been of some help there." She gulped a sob. "Goodbye, Mary. Good luck with whatever your own secret may be."

Another high, desperate sob turned into a keening cry. Cariad screamed in counterpoint.

Where Miss Darcy had crouched, there was now a large, tawny-white owl. Before I could do more than gasp, it spread its wings and was out the window.

I am asleep, I thought. *I am asleep and this is a dream.*

Mechanically, I went to Cariad and comforted him. I finished cleaning the broken phial; the liquid it had spilled was the same creamy, brown-threaded beige-white as the owl's feathers.

I am asleep. I am asleep. I am asleep.

I went downstairs and went to bed. Sleep seemed a long time coming.

I know it was a dream. It had to be. The alternative is that I am going mad, and that I refuse to do, no matter how richly I deserve it. A strange dream, a sort of metaphor for our sudden and shocking rupture. Now I have written it down, I shall put that strange vision out of my head.

Today I told my mother I felt ill and stayed in bed. I lay, staring at the wall, trying to separate which parts of that strange night I had dreamt and which were real. The whole thing was so painful that in the end I gave it up and soothed myself with an hour or so of calculating Fibonacci numbers, which I always find to be a balm to the spirit. I had got to around the forty-fourth one (701,408,733—a personal favorite) when I heard a clatter of wheels outside. That was all the notification I had that Miss Darcy had gone.

She was right, of course. When she said I was keeping something back from her. I could not stand to tell it—not even to you, Harry. But I suppose the time has come. Once I can get out of bed without trembling, I will finally put pen to paper and relate the story of that night.

Chapter 30

The Events of the Night of 21 May, 18--

3 November, 18--

It was some months ago, now. May. The days were lengthening, and the nights growing too short for my purposes.

Ostensibly, things went on as usual in Meryton. There was the occasional ball and far too many garden parties. People gossiped and flirted and gossiped about the flirtations. Morning visits, afternoon cards, evening parties.

Beneath it all, though, there was a current of fear.

No one talked of it except in hushed tones. Not in our circles, anyway. How could they, when they had no idea what was going on? This was the Home Counties in the nineteenth century, not some medieval forest teeming with savage beasts.

However, it did seem that there was a savage beast about.

Farm animals were found mauled to death. There were the fires, the beatings. The mothers of young men begged them not to go out alone at night, and I suspected that most young men, however they might protest, were secretly relieved to oblige.

Gossip strove to account for it. It was a bear, escaped from its owner. No, a wolf. No, a mad dog—how could a bear or wolf hide itself in the scant, genteel woods that Meryton had to offer? No, a highwayman—how could a dog have done that to the pay wagon? No, a gang of highwaymen… no, an ape…no, the devil himself.

It was at that point that the conversation usually fell still. Meryton folk were good, respectable people, who thought no more about God and the devil than was decent.

And over everything hung Miss Charing's strange death, a reminder of just how little we knew about what roamed our countryside at night.

Mr. Pike was often applied to for his opinion. He had traveled, seen much of the world, come back rich—his opinion was now greatly valued. (Besides, it gave them an excuse to talk to him.) He was now a more sought-after guest than ever—a demonstration of the maxim that absence makes the heart grow fonder, for he accepted no more than one invitation in four, and then only appeared for an hour or so. If any other young man had come to a ball for only an hour, he would have been considered abominably poor spirited—but in Mr. Pike's case it seemed only to add to his mystique. Appearing rarely, saying little, and being rich seemed enough to raise him to demigod status.

Hence their turning to him for his opinion on the beast. The first time this happened in my hearing, I nearly choked on my biscuit. Imagine applying to the monster himself for solutions to its brutality.

He was well able, though, to dispel such inquiries with soft-spoken civilities about nothing.

I had to stop him. I knew it was only a matter of time before he killed again. Before *I* killed again, really. He was my creation.

His eyes were always on me in public, but I could never steal a moment to speak to him alone, not now that he was *the* bachelor of Meryton. Even when I danced with him, someone was always watching and listening. In the old days the piano would have been safe, but now there was always some young lady or other draping herself across the instrument in an artistic attitude, attempting to catch his eye. Silently, I cursed my looks. If I had been beautiful, they might have regarded him as my property, given the marked partiality he showed. However, because I was just plain, awkward Mary Bennet, most ambitious young ladies chose not to believe in his attachment and threw themselves in his path.

Of course, if I had been beautiful, none of this would have happened at all.

Just once, he managed to speak of it. A servant on the other side of the ballroom dropped a platter with an immense crash; while the whole room turned its attention to the luckless fellow, Pike leaned toward my ear and whispered, "It's getting worse. *Help.*"

"*How?*" I whispered back.

"Red," he whispered. "Black. *Please,*" and then the young Miss Long, who'd attached herself to him, resumed fluttering her fingers against his arm and giggling, and he was forced to turn away.

Red. Black. I began to make my preparations.

That is when I wrote the first letter, Harry, that was so full of despair. I meant it when I said I was prepared to kill him if it came to that—even if it meant losing my own life.

Here is something, Harry, that I believe I am the sole inventor of. Perhaps it will be my legacy. (I have invented other things, I know, such as the resurrection of the dead, but I am not sure I will be eager to claim those.) We have long used leeches to extract blood; I have discovered that we can also use them to do the reverse—to insert blood into a subject.

Blood or, in fact, another substance.

I knew that Pike had been hunting near our house. Dead animals had been found in the woods, and one of our lambs got its throat torn out. On the next clear night, I set about to lure him closer yet.

The woods do not look like much by day. Just a few acres of trees and a few winding paths. You can scarcely lose sight of the road behind you before you are glimpsing it on the other side. But the trees are ancient and close, and what seems quite tame and manageable by day is far more frightening at night. The trees closed over my head, blocking out the moon and stars. I had too much to carry to bring a lantern, so I had to trust my feet to stay on the path, though the well-known way seemed utterly foreign now.

My heart was pounding in my ears. I adjusted the sack over my shoulders, ignoring the protesting squawk from within. My other hand trembled around the handle of the large knife I'd borrowed from the kitchen. I'd have to clean it well. I knew well, now, the power of other people's blood.

I reached what I judged to be the center of the forest. I drew out the trembling little bundle from the sack. The poor little thing scrambled to get away. I had certainly put her through enough already—the bald patches in her feathers attested to that. Grimly I ignored her scratches and pecks and tied a string around her neck. The other end went securely around a low branch. Then I climbed the tree and settled down to wait.

It could have been five minutes or an hour, I've no idea. Time does funny things out in the wild. I became nothing but a set of eyes and ears, watching, waiting, waiting—

And he came.

The little chicken's complaints became frantic, then hysterical. Then the rustling and crying ceased. I crept down.

Pike hardly looked human now. His hair and beard were long and unkempt, his clothes muddy and torn. The black streaks had taken over half his face—or maybe that was the chicken's blood, smeared across his mouth and jaw, black in the moonlight.

I stared, willing my eyes to use every scrap of moonlight as I strained to see the truth. I'd fed three leeches on serum. When they were gorged and fat and tight as drums, I'd attached them to the little chicken, squeezing gently, forcing them to regurgitate the serum back into her veins.

Pike ought to have received a massive dose.

He raised his face. His veins were as black as ever.

I closed my eyes in disappointment. I had failed. Nothing for it. I clutched the knife. Before I could make a move, Pike saw me.

Faster than ought to be possible, he came swarming up the tree. I tried to get away, but he grabbed my ankle. I choked out a scream as my body scraped helplessly down the trunk, my fingernails scrabbling uselessly for purchase, the bark scraping against my cheek.

Somehow, my hand managed to keep hold of the knife.

I twisted so that I landed on top of Pike and drove the knife into his shoulder. He roared, and I pulled it back to strike again, but he was too fast. He grabbed my wrist and twisted the knife away. Good lord, he was *strong*. Luckily he was too far gone to think of picking it up—I seized his moment of distraction to scrabble backward. Before I could get far he lunged after me, grabbing my left leg. I tried to kick him away, but he ignored my blows. He sank his teeth into my calf, and a scream ripped out of me.

The agony was like nothing I had ever known. There was none of the pinprick precision of the leech—he was *worrying* at me. The teakettle scream he elicited would have seemed to come from a stranger, but that I felt it tearing at my own throat. Surely my leg would never be the same. He bit down harder, clamping it in place against the ground to still my struggles, and I sobbed in pain and despair.

Still, my hands were questing for the knife. I did not find it, but my fingers closed over a large stone. With a roar of my own, I swung it as hard as I could at his skull.

He fell back. Not dead, but stunned, momentarily. Ignoring the bloody mess of my leg, I patted at the ground until I finally managed to find the knife. I clamped both hands over the handle and lunged.

He was still disoriented, shaking his head, and I was able to drive him onto his back.

Looking into his pale face, I raised the blade—

"Miss Bennet?"

I gave a little jerk—opposing impulses screaming *Hold on, something's happening* and *Finish him off!* in my head, not to mention *Oh, the world's gone wobbly*—and he managed to roll me off him. I scrambled to my feet, holding the knife in front of me.

He stood up, too—slowly now, wincing. When his face hit a patch of moonlight, I saw that the black lines were receding.

"Good heavens, Miss Bennet," he said. "I declare you practically dashed my brains out."

"P-Pike?"

"Yes, it's me." He made a face, and then spat. "Though I don't imagine I look the gentleman at the moment. Good Lord, what have I been eating?"

"Chicken," I managed. "Serum…and…" It was no good. The world began to swim before my eyes, and then everything went dim.

I saw Pike take a step toward me. *Oh well,* I thought. *At least if he kills me I won't have to be anyone's poor relation.* And then I knew no more.

Somewhere beyond the red-black darkness that swirled up to consume me, I felt myself being caught and moved. My stomach tried to lurch, but my body was too weak. I fell deeper under the black, pulsing waves.

I awoke to the scent of dust and hay and animals. I opened my eyes. I lay in our hayloft. Something was tied tightly around my leg.

"Apologize to your mother from me for the loss of her drawers," said

Pike. "Actually, don't. Rather difficult to explain." He was lounging about five feet away, leaning against a haystack. "You will live, I trust?"

I winced and sat up. "I-I believe so. Assuming you carry no communicable diseases."

Pike looked grim. "So that was me, then?" he said, gesturing to my leg. I nodded. He held up the knife, and I flinched. "And this was for me?"

"If it came to that," I croaked.

He put the knife down, shaking his head. "Oh, Miss Bennet," he said. "What a mess we've made."

"I-I tried to—"

"You *killed* me." He surged forward, his hands caging me in. "And then you tried to do it again. Do not try a third time, if you please."

I swallowed. It was very loud in the silence.

He sat back. "Don't look like that, please. You know I do not wish to hurt you."

"You d-d-don't?"

"Of course not." He looked rueful. "Oh, I have been an ass, haven't I. Pray accept my apologies."

These changes in mood were too much for me to follow. My blood-starved head pounded. "Pike—what do you want of me?"

"What do I want? If you do not know that, I am even more of an ass than I realized." He picked up my hand. I flinched, but he held on and raised it to his lips.

"Wh-when I told you to marry me—"

"You were only speaking the desire of my own heart. Ever since you gave it voice, it rings like a perfect chord through me. I want what I have always wanted, Miss Mary. You, body and soul." Another kiss, this time to the inner part of my wrist. His lips were cold. I jerked my hand away.

"Always?"

He grimaced. "As I said, an ass. You wounded my pride. I convinced myself that what I felt for you was hate. I can see now how foolish I was." He peered into my face, then sat back, hands raised. "I humbly beg your pardon. I could not have chosen a worse moment to speak. Leave it."

"Pike—"

"Leave it," he said, a little louder. "Let us speak only of the problem at hand."

My head was clearing a little. "The serum worked."

He tilted his head. "Eventually."

"It was—more than I gave you before. A great deal more. Much more concentrated."

"Diluted with chicken, though." He sighed. "Or perhaps that was not the problem."

"Habituation."

From hanging about the apothecary's shop so often, I had grown to know a little of their art. Often had I heard Miss Figg complain of the price of treating a longtime invalid—"For," she said, "the dose that would have eased their pain four times over at the beginning now leaves them still whining for more, saying their pain is not one drop less. Uncle's books call it ha-bit-yoo-ay-shun. *I* call it a waste of good poppy juice."

Pike, it seemed, was already growing habituated to the effects of the serum. "It will take more and more to keep you safe and sane—unless I can devise some other treatment."

He gave me a remarkably sweet smile. It looked strange on his blood-stained face. "The different serums have different effects, is that right? I suppose that perhaps some combination of them might stretch its effects for longer."

"I hope so," I said. "In the meantime—"

"Yes, in the meantime I will be quite at your mercy, I am afraid." He spread his arms. "Cheer up, Miss Bennet. I have the utmost faith in your ability to solve the problem. I will await word on where and when to obtain my next dose. Don't look so frightened, dearest. If I must be locked in such a conundrum with anyone, I'm glad it's you, and I shall do my utmost to help you to feel the same." He started down the ladder. "Er, if a simpleton like me may utter one word of advice on the subject—the serum in the chicken was blue, wasn't it?"

I nodded.

"Yes, I thought you were partial to that one. Well, do as you think best, but I feel in my bones that we'll find the red and the black have the most staying power. The black is my own self, is it not? And the red—well, I will not embarrass you with theories about why it nourishes me so well."

The red was me. I'd have blushed, had I blood enough.

He began to descend again, then paused. He wasn't looking at me. "I will see to it that you get the life you deserve, Miss Bennet," he said softly. "Pardon my speaking when I promised silence on the subject, but I must say a few words. I see how they all ignore you, talk over you, take you for granted. I need you to know that I see you for the magnificent creature that you are." His eyes flashed to mine, then away again. "I always will. No flavor of serum will change that." He smiled. "Even death itself could not stop my loving you. No, do not say anything yet. Take your time. Just know that I am here. Longing for you. I always will be. This dance of ours will continue until we give in to it."

He vanished down the ladder, and I heard him slip out into the night. I leaned my trembling head on my knees.

He was right. In the end, this night had been a success. A famous one. Not only had he proven that his condition was treatable, but he would let me give him the formula I thought best. I could do it. I could.

And then…and then…

And then he would ask me to marry him. And I would say yes. If the worst happened, I would be nearby, and my dreadful mistake and I could destroy one another. But I was filled suddenly with a wild hope that it would not be so. It was as he said. I could find a solution. I could make him good. Make him *right*.

Make him into the one thing I never thought I'd find—the thing I desperately needed: a man I could bear to marry.

I told my parents I'd gone for an early morning walk and stumbled on a sick fox that had attacked me, and then I'd fallen in the ravine. It is the sort of unglamorous thing that *does* happen to me, so no one thought much of it, except to worry when I was almost out of hearing that the wounds would scar and leave me uglier than ever. And if the wound on my leg looked nothing like a fox's bite—well, only the apothecary's nurse looked very closely at *that*, and she knew better than to tell my secrets.

I was tired, and everything hurt, and I had to pretend otherwise. The worst of the attacks ceased, and Meryton soon forgot them—the wolf, in the telling, became a fox, then a weasel, then ceased to be mentioned at all.

And Pike? He was…good. Mostly.

Quiet, and gentlemanly. There was no overt attachment between us, and he was busy much of the time, making arrangements for his factory. When he was there, I could feel his eyes on me.

The situation remained precarious, however. He consumed serum as fast as I could produce it; I had to dip into my small savings to get the right blood from Miss Figg. Her sharp little eyes pierced me like needles whenever I asked for more blood from a particular cook or doctor, but she asked no questions.

Conveniently, the serum of Miss Figg's blood was as raven black as Pike's own. As he had predicted, the red and the black had the most staying power, and it was those and the blue that I relied upon the most. The blue was a constant worry to me, for I did not have an easy source of it at hand. Still, I insisted on feeding him blue always, despite his claim that it did him less good.

My leg took a long time to heal. I learned to ignore the pain and walk without a limp. Pike acquired Brown's mill; construction on his factory began.

We found a treatment regime that kept him stable. Still, I realized that regulating Pike's treatment was likely to be a lifelong endeavor. He would always need me. I would always owe him. There is a word for that arrangement: *marriage*.

It was then that Miss Darcy came.

This…this is what I could not tell her. The events of that dreadful night—well, I never wanted anyone to picture me that way, least of all her. That night—and my intention that, once he was finally stabilized, I would marry him.

How could I? How could I possibly explain?

If Pike is a monster, I made him that way. If he can be made a good man, that too must be my doing. It is not love. It is something deeper and stranger that binds us. He is a dark, broken creature, and so am I. We deserve one another. We may even be happy. That is not the most important thing, however. What is important is that we will prevent each other from causing any more damage.

And really, why *shouldn't* we be as happy as any other marriage? He is rich; I am clever. I will give him new dyes to sell, and we will get richer. My foolish little foray into business showed me that no lady can earn her own fortune. My brains do not matter on their own; if I do not intend to sink into poverty and dependence, I will need *some* man, and it may as well be Pike. Perhaps someday the Pike family will be spoken of with the same awe as the Darcys.

No, I do not love him. I will not love any man, though, so in that respect one is as good as another.

It is for the best, I think, that Georgiana has gone. She made me too soft. Parts of me melt like butter around her, parts that need to be hard as steel. The world is not the laughing, warm place it has seemed since she came. Not for me. Georgiana makes me enjoy my own company, but Pike makes me see myself for what I truly am. I will keep my distance from her in future.

Better for us both.

But oh, I can still feel her kiss on my lips. Quindley, Pike, Lord in heaven—*someone* please teach me to forget.

Chapter 31

In Which All Is Well

14 November, 18--

Almost three weeks since G left. All is well. *Exceedingly* well. Could not be better.

Pike is a perfect gentleman and no longer seems to require regular serums at all. I have cured him, it seems, permanently. All Meryton speaks of him as my beau, and why should they not? In the last few weeks:

- Pike and I danced three times at a public ball.
- We have gone for walks every day that the weather is fine.
- Mamma took me into town to have a dress made—the first new dress from town I had ever had. I heard her murmur the word *wedding* to the dressmaker.
- Old Reverend Halcombe, our retired rector, complained to me of the factory plans. "Not right for a genteel town like this to be stuffed with dirty, vulgar factories," he said to me the other day, after accosting me in the street. "Keep that business to London

and the North." Of course, he will not stop the plans going forward, but can there be any greater proof of how Meryton views us than the fact that even a bad-tempered old man considers Pike my responsibility?

One moment. I hear a horse approaching.

(Later)

It was Pike. He brought a bit of sad news. "The old rector was found dead in his bed by his housekeeper," he said.

"No great surprise there," said Mamma. "He was eighty if he was a day."

"Quite. I wonder...Mr. Bennet, may I speak with you?"

My father gave me a long look, then led Pike into his library. After fifteen minutes' conference, they emerged, and Pike asked if he might speak with me alone. Five minutes after that, we were engaged.

CHAPTER 32

I Am Engaged

28 November, 18--

Do I like being engaged to Pike? Do I, in fact, like Pike? Well…Think of it this way.

Consider Pike himself. Did he enjoy being dependent on my serums? Was his situation, in which I could play upon his character as upon the harp, absolutely what he would choose?

Perhaps not. However, it was his best choice, as the only alternative was death.

My situation is not dissimilar. In my case, the alternative is not death, but something rather worse: spinsterhood. Dependence. No laboratory. Whatever free time I had would be at the disposal of whichever sister deigned to shelter me. I could foresee a life of no more value than providing a fourth at bridge.

Pike's smell has grown no more attractive than it ever was formerly. He no longer smells of paste and ink, but like a fine gentleman: pomade and fine cloth and a hint of scent. Underneath all his luxuries, though, there is still a thread of a scent of the Pike of old.

Something that, when it hits my nose, makes me go cold inside. Just a hint of sterile, dusty death.

However, what does it matter? Once we are married, I will hardly ever have to come within smelling distance of the man. I hold the reins in our relationship, and will continue to hold them once we are married. I shall induce Pike to build a large house, and we can each occupy an end of it. Perhaps we will go north after all. If we lived somewhere out on the moors, no one would wonder that we kept no company and rarely came within shouting distance of one another.

Of course, I know I would be sinning by denying him his husbandly rights. However, Pike is so pliable at present to my whims that I foresee no protest from him. Perhaps I could perform the act just once, and get it out of the way. Or perhaps, once we were married, I would become like other girls at last, and find the thought of the act less repulsive.

And other than Pike himself, I rather like being engaged to Pike. People smile now when they see me. Mamma speaks of me with pride. She and I have spent hours making my trousseau, and I am surprised at how nice it is to have her all to myself.

I am Mamma's last daughter to be married, and the least urgent one. Kitty is well settled, Jane and Lizzy are spectacularly settled, and Lydia is at least disposed of. Now that I am marrying, too, and marrying much better than anyone had expected, Mamma views my upcoming nuptials as a sort of finish line to her long, grueling matrimonial race. She is taking more time over my trousseau than she did with any of the others. Mamma gives me advice and tells me stories about when I was a baby, and we show each other how to do stitches we did not know, and all the while we are covering my trousseau in a perfect cloud of flowers and fruits and birds and clovers and hearts. I know I have stated my preference for simple, dark clothing, and it is true, but my preference for wearing simple clothing is matched if not outstripped by my enjoyment of making the most difficult, complex clothing possible. In this case I decided that the sacrifice is worth it. It is silly, perhaps, for a grown woman to care so much that her mother loves her at last—but I must own I find it enjoyable.

Any time I regret my engagement, I think of the words from *Quindley's*: "A young lady who breaks off an engagement, for any but the gravest misconduct on the part of her future spouse, shows herself to be frivolous and flighty, and does as much damage to her honor, and gives as much pain to her family, as if she had abandoned her husband after marriage."

If, after rereading that passage, I still have doubts, I think of the relief on my mother's face.

I am ready—eager, even—to stop being Mary Bennet. Becoming Mrs. Pike is a prospect I look forward to with relief, like the oblivion of sleep at the end of a long day. At last, the future holds no fear, and the past no shame. Pike is acceptable. Poverty is avoidable. I have, for the first time in my life, a solid place to stand.

There is of course the trifling business of Pike's factory but

Dropped my pen. Bother. Hands shaking rather for some reason.

No matter. It is nothing. It must be nothing. Everything is all right. It is just that

To tell the truth, the idea of writing to "Harry" grows stale. He died when I was eight. It is not Harry to whom I wish to unburden myself, from whom I need advice; it is

No!

She is gone. That is for the best. We can only hurt each other.

Tomorrow, Harry. Tomorrow, I shall gather my strength, and tell you—only you—what has arisen. Then I will see that there is nothing to worry about.

I pray she does not come to my wedding.

29 November, 18--

Pike's factory opened at last two weeks ago. Meryton does not know what to make of having a factory so near at hand. It is so unusual that even the most judgmental scolds scarcely knew what to judge them *for*.

Men like Bingley proved that it was entirely possible to make one's fortune in trade and still be welcomed by good society—even, if the fortune was big enough, celebrated. All good society asked in return was that the family in question hide away the source of their wealth like something shameful. The Bingleys of the world must be separated from their factories by several hundred miles and, ideally, several generations. My uncle Gardiner, a prosperous and genteel man, would never be a truly sought-after guest, for he lived within sight of his London factories.

However, Pike was by now such a favorite that Meryton carved out an uncomfortable exception for him. And the Brown mill was a few miles downriver from Meryton proper, so at first it was easy enough to ignore.

There would have been grumbling, I expect, had Pike hired local people. No one would have liked it if he'd poached their servants or raised the cost of a gardener or milkmaid. But, as I have mentioned, he did no such thing. Instead he imported his workforce.

The young Irish women became a common enough sight on the road to Pike's factory. Those who have encountered them reported that they spoke no English.

Otherwise, they kept to themselves. For the most part, this suited everyone, for no one knew what to make of Meryton as a factory town. There were about twenty of them, and they did all their eating and sleeping at the factory, not even coming to church on Sunday.

"Well, no doubt they're papists," Papa said. "The smoke ceases on those days, so I am sure he gives them the day off."

Why, Harry, do you suppose we converse so easily about money but so haltingly about where it comes from? I once met a baron's son with a gorgeous country house and, everyone said, ten thousand a year. This information was conveyed quite stridently, but they all dropped their voices to convey that all that money came not from centuries of wise and benevolent landlordhood, but rather from sugar plantations in the Indies.

In any case, it worked to Pike's advantage, which I suppose means it is to mine as well. Everyone determinedly ignores his factory, just as surely as they would if he had properly placed it hundreds of miles to the north. And he makes it easy for them, for most days the only sign of its presence among us is a plume of smoke above the trees.

As for me, though, I have always had trouble not noticing the things I am meant not to notice.

I have been walking a great deal lately. Since Miss Darcy left, I have a great deal more free time. The other day—early in the morning, well before most well-bred people stir—I was walking on the winding lane north of Meryton. I did not consciously set out to pass my intended husband's factory, but my feet turned in that direction.

That is when I met the Irish girl again.

She looked different now. Her color higher, her eyes brighter. When she saw me, she flinched and turned to run back toward the factory, but when she saw it was me, she slowed and gave me a smile.

"Dia duit," she said softly.

And with that, my Irish lessons resumed.

Every morning, I go for an early walk and find her there. She looks more tired than she did when I first met her, so I am surprised she makes the time for me, but I am exceedingly grateful for the distraction.

It is difficult, with no shared language, but I believe I get on well. I can now say complete sentences, like *My dress is green* and *I have four sisters,* and though she often laughs at my grammar or my accent or both, she seems as determined as I am that I should progress.

There is no reason on earth for me to keep such a thing a secret. No reason at all. Her master is my fiancé. I could quite properly tell him. I ought to tell him.

I have not told anyone.

Why, Harry? Why do I keep this commonplace interaction a secret?

Perhaps it is her feet. Every time I meet her, she is standing outside in the lane. Her feet are always pointed away, as if she means to set out away from the factory and never return.

When the bell rings, she seems to have to drag herself back inside.

I am making too much of that. Everyone drags their feet going back to work, I suppose. Perhaps it is the look on her face. I see no sign that she is being mistreated—if anything, she looks better fed than some of the milkmaids hereabouts—but she seems…frightened.

Oh, perhaps I am imagining it. It is not long now until I shall be Mary Pike, and the thought is itself a bit frightening, after all. I am, to be strictly accurate, marrying a dead man. Who knows what the future will hold? I am sure the spark of fear I imagine I see in her eyes is nothing but the fear of my own heart.

Courage, Mary. You have arranged everything. Your husband-to-be is impeccably gentlemanlike. Do not upset the life of a girl well outside your sphere merely for the sake of your own boredom. Attempt that new loop stitch that Mamma showed you and let the girl be.

Oh, Harry. I used to find it so restorative to write to you. Now it feels like a pale imitation of what—who—I really want.

What would Georgiana say, if I were writing all this to her?

No. She abandoned me. Her opinion is *quite* irrelevant. If I ever see her again—and I hope I shall not—I shall merely bow coldly and turn away.

(Later)

I am back. Pike's man came to the door, laden with gifts for us all. An amber cross for my mother—she is in paroxysms of joy over it. For my father, a new gun, with which he gruffly allows himself to be pleased. For me…

A telescope. My very own. Far finer than the one that Father rarely lets me touch.

I am so close. So close to the life I am meant to have. I must not let my courage fail now. Quindley, what say you? Here we are: "It is quite right for a young lady to be fond of her home, of her mother and father, but it is her duty to overcome these maidenly scruples once she marries, to set aside her homesickness and devote herself to her new lord and master. He cannot guide and protect her if she does not joyfully give herself to him."

Maidenly scruples. That is all it is.

(Later)

Pike dined with us tonight. I blush to reread what I wrote before. Everything is as it should be.

Pike is the mildest, kindest, most considerate gentleman I have ever known. He even listens with infinite patience to Mamma. If I can ever grow to love any man—and why should I not?—it can only be Septimus Pike. Occasionally, when Mamma is being extraordinarily tiresome, or Papa is teasing her to distraction, I see Pike lightly touch his right rib—and then he takes a deep breath, lets it out, and finds my eyes with a sweet smile just for me.

We walked in the garden a little before we ate. We talked of what our lives will be. He is to let Netherfield when Bingley's lease is up, and he hopes to buy it in time. I shall be the mistress of the grandest house in the neighborhood. I shall have the finest library, and the largest gardens, and the only ballroom that can really compare to the greatest ones in London. I shall have, too, my own laboratory, for Pike, with no prompting from me at all, is already planning to set aside an attic room for me. It is large and airy, he says, and I need not hide anymore, for I shall be his wife, and no one may tell me nay.

"Are you sure?" I asked. "Even owning Netherfield will not save us from gossip. Will it not hurt you to hear whispers of Mr. Pike's eccentric wife?"

He turned to me and took both my hands. "Mary, your eccentricity, as you called it, saved my life," he said. "I have not forgotten that, I promise. Nothing anyone could say could stop me from holding you in the very highest esteem." He pressed one of my hands to his heart—no, not his heart, his left lower rib. "You have waded through darkness and horror and blood," he said, "and that is why I stand before you. You have made me a good man. I shall spend all my days repaying you for it." A teasing glint. "Although I confess I also propose this space for your laboratory in part because it is so well-ventilated. Some of those chemicals you use are quite pungent."

I laughed and threaded my arm back through his. He really will make an excellent husband. I must learn not to be so ungrateful.

I *will* burn that hair ribbon Georgiana left here.

I will *at least* stop sleeping with it under my pillow.

I write this down only to exorcise the fixation from my brain so I can sleep. Mamma and I are to go to Netherfield tomorrow afternoon to meet the housekeeper.

(Next day)

Oh, Harry. What am I to do?

Met Mairead again this morning. I intended this time to bid her farewell. I believe our linguistic studies have proceeded as far as they may. In any case, I must prepare for my wedding.

I tried, when we met, to convey this to the girl. "Slan," I said.

She frowned. "Good-bye?"

"Yes. Goodbye. I am to be married." Her frown deepened. I pointed to my ring finger, still bare as yet. "Married," I said.

She smiled and spoke. I could not understand her, but from the look on her face, she understood. I suppose no matter your station or tongue, a wedding is a joyous occasion.

"Yes," I said. "Thank you. I am to marry your master. Mr. Pike." I pointed down the lane from which she had come.

An extraordinary change came over her. Her black eyes went wide, her face went white. "Miss Bennet—married Mr. Pike!"

"Well, not yet." I held up two fingers. "Two days."

She placed her hands over her mouth. She backed away, starting back down the lane, then turned back. She seized my hands—a far greater liberty than we had yet taken with each other—and began to speak in her own tongue so fast that I could not catch a word. I squeezed her hands.

"What is it? I cannot understand you."

She only spoke faster and higher, her voice rising with panic. It struck me how hard and bony her hands were. "I'm sorry, I can't—"

The bell rang.

I expected her to drop my hands and turn to go, as usual. This time, though, she sank to her knees. She gripped my skirt in clear supplication and spoke one of the few phrases that I did know. "Le do thoil. Le do thoil. Le do thoil!"

Please, please, please!

I cannot ignore it any longer. Something is wrong.

30 November, 18--

Dear ~~Georgiana~~ Miss Darcy,

I know you are not planning to attend my wedding. Indeed, I have not encouraged anyone to come in from out of town. I prefer to ~~get it over with~~ celebrate my nuptials quietly, with none of the fanfare that Mamma insisted upon for Mrs. Darcy and Mrs. Bingley.

However...

I am uneasy. I need your counsel. I need *you*. I feel as though I cannot even *think* without you here. Food has no taste. Sleep grants no relief. I cannot seem to properly *want* anything at all ~~except y~~

Apologies. My pen ran away with me. Please just come.

Yours,
Mary.

[This letter was never sent.]

―

30 November, 18--

Pike has an answer for everything. An excellent quality in a husband for a lady who always has questions.

We went for a long walk today, and he patiently answered everything I asked, even questions that were not exactly ladylike. He was so unruffled that my fears were quite nearly allayed.

"You told me your reasons for hiring the Irish girls," I said, "but why bring them all the way here?"

He looked surprised. "To be near you, of course. I could have much more easily established myself in the North, but after everything we have been through, I had no wish to take you far away from your people."

"Oh." I felt a twinge of shame at my inquisitiveness. But Mairead's huge, dark eyes rose in my mind.

"And how goes the factory?"

"Oh, splendidly. We're just beginning, of course, and I must keep things small so as not to upset life in Meryton too much. Perhaps one day, when I am more established, a larger factory in the North may be in order. Rest assured, though, I will not spend too much time away from here. Would you like to see it?"

"See what?"

"The factory, of course."

I had been working up my nerve to make that very request. I had little expected him to agree, let alone suggest it himself. Pike laughed a bit at my surprise. "You look shocked."

"Well...even Uncle Gardiner never let me see his factories. He says they are no place for a lady."

"Hmm. Even Uncle Gardiner, who has led a far more blameless life than I."

"I didn't—"

"No, no, you are quite right." He patted my hand again, then squeezed it closer to his side. "To my knowledge, your uncle has never died even once, nor has his wife ever been forced to save him from descending into animal savagery. You have every reason to doubt me, Mary, and I shall do all I can to prove to you that I really am worthy of your trust now."

"It's just—well, you were—quite terrifying," I said.

"I know. I'm sorry. My memory of those...episodes...is spotty, but I assure you I have not had the shadow of an attack since your little... intervention." He rubbed his ribs absently.

"Mmm," I said.

"You do believe me, do you not?"

"Yes." It was true. I listen hard for rumors, and there has been no sign of the return of the man-beast. Chickens sleep quietly in their hutches; fires remain unlit. Ever since your gift of the rib, I have had no reason to believe that Pike is anything less than an ideal man.

"Perhaps," he suggested, "your fears are not really fears, but an excuse."

"An excuse?"

He smiled sadly. "Not to marry me."

I looked down at my feet. Was he right? Now it was Georgiana's face that rose before my mind's eye, Georgiana's scent of expensive soap and chalk that filled my senses. I swallowed, ashamed.

"Come," he said. "Let us go there right now."

I tried to stop. "Oh no, you needn't—"

"Come." He pulled me on, gently but inexorably. "No time like the present. I *will* answer every qualm of yours, dearest. I will remove every obstacle to your loving me."

And he took me to his factory.

I believe I am the only member of Meryton society who has been inside since it began operation. Perhaps that ought to change. If, say, Papa and Sir William Lucas were to tour the facility, it might dispel comment.

Pike's factory looks little different to how it did when it was a mill. He has added a few windows and a coat of whitewash. Outside, the wheel creaks around sedately, turning the shaft as it always has. Inside, it is bright and clean, lined with looms and more complicated machinery that I could not name.

He introduced me to the women. They were as bright and clean as the factory. Some smiled and chatted with Pike; others merely bobbed a curtsy, too busy with their work to stop, even when Pike told them (he translated for me) that they might have a rest.

Mairead's hands were busy at a loom when we found her. Her eyes grew wide when she saw me, but she bobbed a curtsy to Pike with the utmost respect and laughed at something he said. There was no sign of the terror I had fancied in her eyes.

He let me have a closer look at the wheel, which I admit I have been itching to do all my life. It hangs out over the water in a small room attached to the main structure. You can actually open a trapdoor and look at the water rushing beneath you! He showed me how the wheel could be raised or lowered, the sluice gate opened or closed, and laughed fondly when I was as entranced as a child.

He pointed out the dormitory he had had installed in the old barn, including the addition of a wood stove for their comfort when the weather turned. He showed me the copse of trees that he intended to cut down to construct a sort of small village green where the girls might spend their leisure hours, and the small kitchen where his staff prepared meals, provided free of charge to the workers. All of it was so thoughtful, so kind, so far above what any other master would have thought necessary, that I felt quite ashamed of my qualms.

"Well, love?" he said when we left.

"It is wonderful," I admitted.

He smiled. "It could all be much cheaper, but my cloth is good enough to fetch a high price, and I would rather my workers look up to me as a kindly father than fear me as a tyrant. That is better, don't you think?"

"Absolutely. I do not believe one factory master in a thousand would agree with you, however."

"Perhaps they will when they see what excellent work happy, healthy workers are capable of."

"Let us hope so," I said, "dearest."

His glance down at me was so full of surprise and fondness that I could not help but smile back. Pike walked me home, then said he must return to work.

There you have it. Pike has answered every question. Shown every card. He has, as he said, removed every obstacle to my loving him.

And once I have slipped into his factory on my own tomorrow night and satisfied the last of my curiosity, I will do so.

Chapter 33

The Factory

6 December, 18--

I know the truth at last. May God have mercy, I almost wish I had not found it out. But I did. How blind I have been!

The night before their wedding, I believe most ladies stay in. They finish the last stitches of their trousseaux, dine with their families one last time, and go to bed early so that they might be fresh as rosebuds when they go to church in the morning.

They do *not* do as I did, which was to stay up until the small hours, teaching tricks to a small dead bird to stay awake. They do not don boys' clothing and a pair of heavy hobnailed boots, nor tuck their hair into a flat cap. They do not set out alone into the dark night.

It was clouded over heavily. I wondered, as I tramped along the road, what clouds meant for Miss Darcy's affliction—would she transform anyway, if the moon was full behind the clouds?

I cut off that thought ruthlessly. There was no transformation; just a silly dream that I had been too upset to tell from reality. I felt a spike of rage for Miss Darcy, as though she had deliberately tricked me into thinking her some sort of magical were-owl.

I had trouble banishing her from my thoughts now. I had been so busy these last few weeks, preparing to wed and move to Netherfield, I'd scarcely had a moment to dwell on any Miss Darcy–related sorrows. But now I was alone on the road, clad in boys' clothes, and I was inevitably reminded of my last nighttime adventure when another "lad" had tramped beside me.

An owl hooted somewhere in the woods. A strange, lonely sound. My foul mood got fouler.

I had felt so *free* last time. This time I just wished I was back in bed, that I had never met Mairead, that I felt no call to investigate Pike's doings any further. Surely I would find nothing, and what a fool I would feel then—what a fool I would *be* then.

The trees around the lane grew so high and thick that I could barely make out my hand in front of my face. Only having walked this path a thousand times before gave me confidence that I had not wandered from it. I almost missed the turnoff for the factory, but the faint sigh of rushing water off to my left told me I was near the river and thus near Pike's factory.

The water grew louder as I picked my way down the drive. My heart did, too. I stood outside the front door, uncertain, my hand poised over the handle.

What am I even looking for? I wondered. *What will I say if I am caught?*

My leg throbbed. The marks of Pike's teeth had never entirely faded.

Enough. *Do not be insolent or inquisitive,* Quindley said. He also said, *Be guided by your husband.*

Though the lines all but screamed in my mind, I knew myself well enough to be sure that the only way to stop myself from asking questions was to find out the answers. I tugged at the latch. Locked.

That was a bit odd. There were no near neighbors, so why bar the door?

There were lights lit within—I could see them spill out of the high windows—but the *chunk-chunk-chunk* sound was absent. The wheel was not running. Still, I could hear sounds from within—rustlings, scrapings. Voices? Hard to tell. It was well after midnight. What could they possibly be doing? If Pike was as kind a master as he claimed, his workers ought to have gone to sleep hours ago.

I crept around to the rear, but the entrance to the dormitory was locked, too. I thought about knocking—I meant the girls no harm, after all—but I doubted my ability to make that clear, and they might alert whoever was within.

That was it, then. The windows were too high to peer through, and the doors were locked. I had tried, and I had failed. All I could do now was go home and sleep. I was not going to be Meryton's most beautiful bride in any case, so I ought to at least ensure I did not appear at the altar with dark circles under my eyes. Quindley would surely say—

Oh, do not be such a wet stocking, Sir Gregory.

I shook the stray voice from my head. Quindley would say—

You got struck by lightning, and that did not stop you. What is a little lock?

It was the clothing, I suppose. Wearing boys' clothes reminded me so powerfully of that night that I felt as if she was by my side.

Right. There must be another way in.

The *chunk-chunk-chunk* was still absent. My heart sank. I knew the way in, and wished I did not. Before I could change my mind, I waded into the icy waters of the river.

The cold of the water was like a slap. I could only hope the sound of it had covered my ragged gasp. Grimly, I half-walked, half-swam against the current, toward the sluice gate. The water was high and fast. It had rained much of late. This would be a very silly way to die. Deeper and deeper. I had never been taught to swim. I understood the theory, though, which was good, for my toes were about to leave the ground.

"Who's there?"

Pike's voice broke the silence just as my feet left the bank. He leaned his head out the window. I must have made some noise. Luckily he did not expect his intruder to be in the river—he turned first toward the road. Before he could look at me, I scrabbled at the brick wall beneath the lane and pulled my head underwater.

As it was the first time putting my head entirely under the surface, I cannot claim I made a great success of it. I ought to have taken a breath before doing it, for one thing, for my lungs quickly screamed for air. Next time I am at leisure, I must do some practicing. One never realizes what a luxury air is until one must go without. I would also advise a first-time submerger to avoid my mistake and close her mouth. If she does not do so, she may find that she swallows half the river, then tries to cough it out, then consequently breathes in the other half.

How I managed to keep from bursting to the surface, I shall never know. I managed to creep along by feel, using the submerged barge rings as tethers, until I was sure I was under the wheel shed and out of Pike's sight.

Then, finally, I allowed myself to break the surface. Hacking up about a hundred gallons of river without making a sound ought not to be possible, but I am nothing if not determined. I let my frustration grant me strength. Honestly, all those years growing up on the bank of this creek, and not *one* swimming lesson? It is as though they *want* us to drown.

At last, I managed to quell my desperate gasps. My throat was still raw and my hands shook, but there was no more time to lose.

What if Pike came into the wheel shed? That was a chance I would just have to take. Wedging one elbow in the crook of a support beam, I pulled myself up and groped with my other hand until I felt a plank move. I had found the trapdoor.

With muscles that, I believe, had never been taxed before, I managed to pull myself up through the gap. Thank goodness it wasn't locked! Apparently even Pike had not expected so determined an invasion.

My bridegroom ought to know his bride better than that. But I was glad he didn't.

The room I emerged into was small and nearly pitch dark, except for one high window. I eased the plank back into place. I winced at its creak, but the rush of the water would surely cover it. I opened the door and crept down the small, dark corridor. I squelched and dripped with every step. If anyone cared to shine a lantern this way, there would be no doubt that a damp intruder had passed through.

Luckily, this seemed unlikely. The floor was painted a deep black—a practical color for a working factory, I supposed—and as I emerged into the main structure, I found it only dimly lit. Crowded, too, with crates piled high—they must be shipping their first batches of fabric soon.

Keeping toward the outer wall, I crept among the maze of crates and machinery. Toward the north wall, the light was a little brighter. Someone had a lamp there. I could hear voices, one of them Pike's, the other a woman's.

"This one's almost dry, dash it. Almost the last of that variety, too."

"Would sir like another?"

"No, no, I shall get by with the dregs. For the moment, at least."

Over the sound of the river, I could now hear something else: a faint trickling sound.

Sticking to the shadows, I eased a little closer. If Pike's great secret was that he liked a drink of wine in the evenings, then I had been very silly indeed.

Pike's servant approached, and I froze. Luckily she passed by me with no apparent notice. I peered around a large weaving apparatus and felt my body grow cold.

Near the northern end of the factory, where sacks of flour had been stacked in the old mill days, an empty space was now cleared. In the middle were two things: a large table, and a large apparatus of some kind. It had been covered with tarps on my last visit, and I had taken it for unused looms or something. It was no loom. No, it was a tangled mass of jugs and phials, of small gas lamps heating delicate copper pots. I ought to have understood at once—I, who take such pride in my cleverness!—but I was too mesmerized by the ghastly sight before me.

On the table lay a young woman. She was dead.

I had taken her at first for a pile of old clothes, so rumpled and discarded and inhuman did she appear. But no. It was a human body that had been so carelessly left there. I saw, to my relief, that it was not Mairead, then scolded myself for my partiality. This young lady was fair, with wide, staring blue eyes. Even for a dead woman, her pallor was shocking. After a moment to master my horror, I could see why. One white, white arm was stretched out, forced into a kind of metal tube that led down into Pike's machine. A trickle of her blood ran down her arm, through the tube, dripping into a funnel.

Oh, no, no. It couldn't be. It was.

Over my brain's screams of horror, I began to pick out the different parts of Pike's apparatus. There was the lye mixer, and that lamp must be for the reduction in the third stage. Pike had reverse engineered my entire process—except I had never worked with more than a few drops of blood at a time, had never, with the exception of Sir D'Arcy, produced serum in any great volume, and this machine was orders of magnitude bigger. I had never taken more blood than would fit in a leech's stomach, and Pike—

Pike was shaking the girl's arm, tapping and flicking at it, like a man might tip his glass back to catch the last dregs of a drink. After a moment he gave it up with a sigh. "I told you," he said. "I told you and *told* you, my good woman, not to take too much, did I not? This one has a truly remarkable ruby color at the moment. Quite delightful, and if you had not drained her so, we could have another batch of her in a fortnight."

"Sorry, sir, I'm sure. 'Pon my honor, I took no more than the last time."

The woman's voice was placid and unshocked by the grisly scene. It was also familiar.

Not to worry, I shall soon find something very suitable.

This Miss Figg had certainly done.

Pike sighed and released the girl's arm. "Never mind. Take more care next time. If you had a good layer, you would not wring her neck for Sunday dinner, would you?"

"S'pose not, sir."

"Quite. There's enough here for one more batch, at least. That will be all."

Miss Figg bobbed a curtsy and withdrew. My mind was whirling. I watched Pike titrate, and pour, and time the steps on his pocket watch. He had deduced every part of my process, and seemed to have introduced a few new ones. As the servant picked up the girl's body and walked off with it, Pike poured off the fruits of his labors into a glass and raised it to the light, tilting it critically back and forth. It was, as he said, a deep, rather pretty ruby red, and translucent, looking now more like a good claret than someone's lifeblood.

As if it was claret indeed, he took a connoisseur's sniff, but instead of savoring the contents, he tossed them back in one long gulp. With a sigh and a shiver of satisfaction, he put his glass back on the table, straightened his cuffs, and said, "You can come out now, and stop skulking about in the shadows."

Horror flooded me anew. How had he—

He nodded at the floor. "There is a puddle spreading from behind those boxes. Come, do you think me stupid? I suppose you thought it would go unseen in the dark, but my senses are quite keen, thanks to my little medicines. Come on, out with you." I tensed to run—could I make it to the trapdoor again? Perhaps I could lose him in the water—but before I could try, he shot forward with inhuman speed and seized my wrist. "Come, lad, stop struggling. The jig is up, so you may as well—" He pulled me fully into the pool of light and froze. "Mary?"

"Pike," I gritted out.

He hissed a sigh between his teeth. "Oh, Mary. I had hoped to postpone this day as long as possible."

"What day? Pike, what on earth is going on here?"

He laughed ruefully and smoothed a spike of damp hair back from my face. "Oh, surely you are cleverer than that, love. I know you recognize your own innovations when you see them."

"All these women," I said. "You brought them here for…for their blood?"

"Well, not just for that," he said. "I really did need workers. This apparatus cost a pretty penny."

"You're draining them," I said. "You're killing them."

"Not the latter. Not intentionally." He sighed. "I always knew you would find out in the end—you are too clever not to—but I hoped it would not be for some time, and not on a night like this. I suppose that dratted girl was too short. Her blood volume must be correspondingly lower." He smiled the same sweet, gentlemanly smile I had grown used to these last weeks. "I shall soon learn how to avoid such things. The road to progress is not without bumps, you know."

So he intended to force more women to give up their blood—perhaps their lives. A sour pain rose up in my stomach. Stupid, Mary! Stupid! Stupider than Newton drinking mercury, than Mr. Davy blowing himself up with chlorine—their hubris had harmed only them, at least. My arrogant certainty that Pike was under my control had killed at least one woman already, probably more, and who knew how far he would take it. Oh, Georgiana, you did try to warn me, and I would not listen.

"Why?" I asked. "Why do this? You had everything. I gave you everything you needed."

He scowled. "You mean you forced me to be what *you* needed." His grip on my wrist tightened. Under his unnatural strength, I feared the bones would break, but my heart was racing so fast I could scarcely feel the pain. "My God, girl, you have no idea—" His free hand drifted to his ribs. "You were wrong, you know."

"Wrong? About—"

"You said it would stop itching. It never has. Every thrice-damned second. And that is not the worst of it. Oh, Miss Mary. All these years, I have bowed and scraped to men a thousand times my inferiors. That hurt far worse than the hunger and the cold. All…*all* I wanted was to be free—to speak my mind without fear, to say the things I knew to be true without being called insolent or a liar. And then…then I had money, and position, and I ought to have been as free as any man—but instead I was more a slave than ever." He shook my wrist. "*Your* slave, my darling."

"I was trying to *help* you," I said, fighting to keep the tremor from my voice. Lord, how had I forgotten how *tall* he was? He had been so gentle these last few weeks that I had quite forgotten how much strength hid in his frame. I was trying to dig my heels in, but without Pike paying my resistance the slightest mind, I was being inexorably drawn farther from my hiding place. "I don't understand," I managed. "Harry's ribs ought to have made you good."

He gave a *tch* of exasperation. "Good, asleep, is there a difference? I daresay they would have, had I not replaced one of them with a more suitable donation." He patted his right chest. "A bit tricky to remove my *own* rib, but I managed. Being dead is actually superior in many ways."

My throat seemed to close in horror. That strange unevenness of his rib cage. "We—you made us treat and reinsert your own rib?"

"Indeed. I had my right rib out the night after you asked me to obtain your cousin's. There are some benefits to the half-dead state you've left me in. I hardly ever feel pain. A few minutes with a scalpel and a mirror and the thing was done."

"But why?"

"Why do you think? Had I not replaced one, I am sure that your friend's ribs would have dulled me into the sheep you wished for. Indeed, it almost did. All that *blue*," he said. "Bad enough when you were pouring it down my throat, but now it is inside me. Smothering all the vital parts of me. After the insertion I was as docile as a cow being led to the slaughter." He made a sound of disgust. "I was *happy*, even."

"But that's good—"

"Is it?" He shook me a little. "Is that what you would like? To have your most vital parts excised, to be hollowed out like a rotten tree, filled with what proper society deems *good* and *useful*?"

"Of course," I blurted. "That's what all this was *for*."

His eyes widened. "What?"

My shock almost overcame my fear. Was my aim not obvious? Seeking words, I found none, but inevitably someone else's rose to my lips. "Quindley says, 'Ladies, make of yourselves empty vessels, to be filled with g-good precepts and useful h-habits—'"

"And blue serum, and pink, and a dash of orange?" He looked disgusted. "My God, girl, I thought you'd made a monster of me, but what you've done to yourself may be far worse."

"It doesn't matter. I never made it work on living people for more than a few minutes."

"Ah. Just another area where my genius has outstripped yours." He began tugging me forward again. "Not only have I solved *that* little problem, but I have done so in a form that the market will actually take to. I shall introduce you to it presently. A pity, really—I had hoped to enjoy the full force of all your bad precepts and unuseful habits for at least a little while. But needs must. I hope you enjoy the blue more than I did."

He was tugging me toward the apparatus again, despite my renewed struggles, when suddenly he changed his mind and pulled me toward the table where the dead girl had lain. "Then again, waste not, want not."

I could keep a cool head no more. I screamed.

"*Quiet*, girl. There is no one for miles around but our apothecary friend, and even if there were, what would you say to them?" He laughed a little as he shoved me back onto the table, locking one of my wrists in a cuff. "You are here unchaperoned, in the small hours, dressed in *trousers*. Nothing I will do to you will be as damaging or permanent as the hurt you could do your own honor."

I felt a hot bloom of shame at that. When my sister Lydia disgraced herself by running off with a man, I had thought no one could bring more shame on us—but at least she had not shown her legs. I was scratching and kicking, but it was no good. He soon had me strapped down to the table, barely able to move. He gave me a cheeky grin and chucked my chin. "How's it feel to be the one on the table, love? Turnabout is fair play, you know."

"I saved your *life* on my table."

"Not saved. Reinvented. Prolonged. And, as you know, I rely on your serums and secretions to maintain it. Now be a good wife and give me my medicine. I am partial to the red, you know, and yours is particularly piquant." He stepped back for a moment, regarding my struggling form. "Now, let's see..." he murmured, as coolly as a gentleman choosing how to carve a roast. "Your wedding gown will have sleeves, but there will be balls and parties, and you will open the dancing—no, an arm won't do." He stepped down to the end of the table, seized my foot, and shoved my trouser leg as high as it would go. He gave a fond chuckle when he saw the scar his teeth had left. "Not to worry, dearest, I won't leave a scar this time."

I let out a moan of shame. How could I have let it come to this? I had thought myself so careful, so attentive to everything Quindley and his ilk could teach. How was it that I had not seen how wrong I had been?

It was as though I were another woman at night. I had felt so free, out from under everyone's eyes, doing my experiments, dressing how I chose, consorting with Georgiana. Well, I was not *meant* to be free.

"Yes," he was saying, examining the bare expanse of my leg. "No inconvenient questions for the bride if I cut you there."

"You think," I gasped, "that after all this I will still marry you?"

"Hush," he murmured. "I think you will do it as gladly as I bared my bones to you. Now hold still. I've no desire to drain you dry, dearest." One of his hands gripped my leg just above the knee, holding it still. The other flashed a silver blade, and a slash of pain opened on my thigh. I fought to stay silent but only succeeded in making my whimper a sort of growl.

He patted me on the head, like a puppy. "Good girl. Not too long. Fear not." I felt him line up the funnel below the wound and heard my blood begin to trickle down into the basin.

"I hope it doesn't work," I said through gritted teeth. "I hope it makes you as stupid as a turkey that drowns drinking rain."

He looked at me in surprise. "Is that what you still think the red is for? Intelligence? Oh, Mary." He shook his head. "It is a good thing that I have taken charge of this endeavor. Your discovery of the serums was brilliant, but your own limitations have kept you from understanding their true potential."

"What do you mean?"

"You still think that each color of serum has one clear, simple effect," he said. "You would like that, would you not? If each person you knew could be literally boiled down to one trait that you could label and put on the shelf? That is nonsense, of course. The effects of each serum are far more varied and subtle than you realize. Some people even produce different colors over time. Do not feel bad—I have had access to a far larger subject pool than you have."

A much larger subject pool. All those poor girls. How blind I had been.

He patted me again. Then, as the blood from my wound slowed to a trickle, he seized my leg and squeezed it as though he were juicing a lemon. I fought back a scream.

"Now," he said, close to my ear, "I do find that your own lovely scarlet serum *is* essential to maintaining my intellectual faculties. But the principal effect is something quite different. In general, it fills me with rage."

"Rage?"

"Mmm. A delicious, hot anger that flows through my veins and warms me like mulled wine. Oh, it is wonderful—makes me feel like *me* again. Without the red I never could have shaken off the stupor that your friend's rib threw over me."

"You're lying," I gritted out. "My serum cannot possibly induce rage."

He looked surprised. "But of course it does. How could it not? You are the angriest person I have ever met." He chuckled. "Well, barring myself, perhaps. We *are* well matched, dearest."

"I am not angry."

"Your powers of denial are astonishing. But I assure you that you are. If you could see yourself—the way your jaw clenches when people talk over your piano playing; the tightness around your eyes when your father condescends to you about some matter of science that you are ten times more master of than he; the stiffness in your back when they call you plain, not even bothering to see if you're in earshot. My God, you are angry all the time."

For a moment I forgot the pain in my leg and my deadly predicament. His words rang in my ears.

You are angry all the time.

Pike was mad, and selfish, and dead into the bargain. Nothing he said about my character ought to matter at all.

So why did I feel as though he'd opened a window I'd never even realized was there?

My headaches. My shaking hands. The way my words deserted me and I had to fill the space with Quindley—not that it mattered much, for I was scarcely asked what I thought.

It does not matter that my mother never loved me. It does not matter that no one asks me to dance.

It does not matter that no one asks me anything at all.

It does not matter that the world is so vast and so interesting and so full of snails and stars and sodium and wonder *and yet when I try to speak of it, even for a minute, I am the odd one.*

All the things I told myself, every day, over and over, with the discipline of practicing scales at the piano. I did not even notice anymore. I did not see what that silent litany had been put in place to drown out. What my head ached and my hands shook to keep at bay.

I am angry all the time.

This was not the moment to consider that revelation, for Pike was examining my wound with an expert's care, and then he took out a cloth and began bandaging it. "I daresay you could give more," he said, "but I am feeling rather more cautious after Siobhan's misadventure tonight, so let us move on to the next step."

The next step?

He went to one of the large barrels against the back wall and drew off a glass of brilliant cyan liquid. I cried out. There were at least a dozen barrels, each as large as a beer keg. "Surely those are not—"

"Yes. Each a different color. They're not full yet, but they soon will be. I told you, my innovations have allowed me to far outstrip your paltry operation. And I've an abundance of the blue." He gave me a friendly wink. "Since I've no use for it myself." He poured the liquid into a little copper pan over a flame. It began to hiss and bubble almost immediately.

Before I knew what was happening, he was loosening the straps that held me to the table.

I began to struggle, of course, and even managed to make it a few steps back toward the river—but the man I made is strong and fast, and his veins are flooded with my own anger, and before I had gone ten feet he caught me again and marched my struggling form back toward his apparatus.

"You see," he said, his mouth pressed near my ear, "this is my greatest insight. It is true that the serums do not have the desired effects on living subjects—but I realized that it was merely a matter of certain tweaks to the formula and to the vehicle by which the dosage was administered." The blue liquid in the pot was boiling now, billowing pale clouds the color of shadowed snow into the air. Pike seized me by the back of the head and thrust my face into the steam.

I coughed and choked. I was far enough from the flames not to be burnt, but I'd taken in a great lungful of the blue fumes. I coughed again, which only made me breathe in more, for Pike still held my head in the cloud.

"If a living subject drinks it, he merely gets ill," Pike said, not even out of breath. "If it is inhaled, however..."

The liquid was not burning in my chest anymore. Rather, it seemed to have a cooling effect—not merely on my poor lungs, lacerated with steam and river water, but on my whole enervated self.

Why struggle like this? It was obviously futile. Wasn't that always my problem—trying too hard? Would it not be better...kinder...more restful to let someone else make the decisions for a while?

"It's better, really," Pike said. "From a business standpoint, I mean. Why will people want these serums? Not to dose *themselves*."

Oh, God.

"A bit in a wife's smelling salt bottle," he said, "and marital harmony is restored. A bit of it sprinkled over the stove in a factory, and the workers will never revolt. Oh, the applications are endless. I daresay we shall soon be the richest couple in England, dearest." He chuckled through the calm blue haze blanketing my mind. "And the most harmoniously married."

No.

I sealed my mouth shut. No more breaths.

"Ah, ah." He shook me a little. "Breathe deep, dearest. I shall need you sweet and biddable for our wedding tomorrow."

I held my breath.

"Oh, for—" He sighed. "This is pointless. You have already breathed in more than enough of the blue. It will take hold of you soon enough. Do not make yourself faint in the meantime."

That damp blue haze was, indeed, settling more heavily upon me. It felt rather nice, actually, like lying down at the end of a long day. Parts of me that had been tense and sore all my life were letting go. Surely Pike was right. Surely I ought to just do what he said? It would feel so good. And what choice did I have, really?

No.

If I was as angry as he claimed, surely decades of suppressed rage could not be simply vanished by a few lungfuls of bad air? Grimly, I held on to that one stale breath, burning in my lungs as my whole body screamed for air. I hated my anger—hated it—but surely it would at least be good for this.

A lady is sweet tempered and low voiced whenever possible, said the Quindley in my mind. I shoved him aside. Apologies, Harry, but for once in my life he was not what was needed—no, I needed what he had always tried to quench.

If Quindley could see my rage—a red, black, pulsing, spiked thing, as I pictured it—he would think me an even greater monster than Pike. One thing about monsters, though—they are hard to kill.

I knew Pike felt little, if any, pain. I could not make him recoil with a sudden slash of my nails or a well-placed kick, as I might with a normal man. However, he'd cantilevered his body into an awkward angle to maneuver my head into the blue steam, so I might, if I caught him off guard, have a chance. Just one. I waited till I felt him lean a little farther forward, then I went limp, as though I'd passed out. He leaned down as though to lower me to the ground, and, when he was as far off balance as possible, I braced my lower body, grabbed the arm around my neck, and threw myself backward.

Archimedes once said that if you gave him a long enough lever and a place to stand, he could move the earth. I do not know about that, but with a grunt from me and an *oof* from him, I managed to send Pike flying. My back and shoulder muscles screamed in protest, but I did it, and he fell over his apparatus with a crash. There was a tinkle of broken glass and a clatter of metal as his feet flailed wildly, then his head struck the ground with a *crack* that would have been fatal to a living man. I did not stay to see what had become of Pike, because I was already sprinting for the exit.

The factory was dim beyond the pool of lamplight. I prayed that my mental map was accurate as I dodged dim piles of crates.

Suddenly, a hand closed around my ankle.

I looked down. Pike, dragging himself on the ground, had caught up. All I could see in the shadows was the furious glitter in his eyes. In panic I kicked out at him, but he held on. His grip was as firm as iron, and as cold. No one would mistake him for a gentleman now. No one would think him a living man at all.

I could not break his grip. It was over. Judging from the feral snarls now issuing from him, I doubted whether his plan to carefully drug and preserve me had survived his rage.

Goodbye, Georgiana, I thought, as he jumped to his feet and his hands closed around my neck.

Whoosh.

There was a strange sensation on the back of my head. A sort of buzzing flutter. Then a scratch. Then a high, fluting scream of fury.

With a roar of irritation, Pike stumbled back. His grip loosened, and he wrenched free.

With a shriek of triumph that would have been more comfortable in the throat of a falcon than a songbird, Cariad fluttered after him, flying in his face, scratching and pecking at his eyes. Pike reared back and stumbled into a pile of crates, which tumbled over. I turned to make my escape.

Then I smelled it. Smoke.

I looked back over my shoulder. Flames licked from a pile of crates near Pike's decimated machine. When I'd thrown him into it, one of his boots must have knocked over a burner, or perhaps several. A tiny calm part of me pointed out that having so many open flames on one machine had always been foolish on his part, especially in a fabric factory—such an accident as this was only a matter of time. Even as I watched, a piece of canvas and the thread from one of the looms caught. It would all go up in no time.

I would be safe from the flames in the river. My heart screamed for Cariad, but I could not waste the chance he was giving me, and I sprinted back to the wheel room. I had one foot down the trapdoor before I remembered. Mairead. The others.

And I was almost free! Ah, well. I turned and ran back into the burning building. I raced to the other end and through the small corridor. Smoke was already stinging my lungs in the open air as I yanked at the door. It was locked.

I pounded at it with all my strength, screaming a mixture of English and the scraps of Irish I'd acquired. "Get up! Fire! Up, if you would live! Thuas! Amach, amach! Wake up!"

One pale, frightened face appeared at the window, then a second and a third. At first blinking in confusion, they quickly grew wide-eyed and awake. My poor Irish had little to do with it, I expect—by now I could see flames reflected in their eyes as they looked behind me at the factory.

"The door is locked," I babbled uselessly. Why hadn't my lessons included *door* and *lock*?

The girls were screaming now, yelling something at me that I could not understand. Why did they not unlock the dashed door? Then my eyes followed their pointing fingers. Scrabbling across the brick wall, my hand closed around a bit of string, tied around a metal hook. From the string hung a key. I was not locked out. They were locked in.

If I had not already given up all hope of redeeming Mr. Pike, I did then. He'd locked them in, the—well, I had best not record here what I called him in my head, lest it fall into the wrong hands. But even Quindley would have to admit that he richly deserved it.

I shoved the key into the lock and turned it with trembling fingers (trembling with rage! Thank you for the insight, Pike, you ██████████). A dozen girls in their nightdresses came running out, and just in time, for just then the roof of their dormitory caught.

We stood in the woods for a time, huddled together, me in my soaked, smoky boys' clothing, them in their damp nightdresses and bare feet. We could feel the heat even twenty feet off. There was a collective moan when the roof fell partially in. I kept expecting to see a dark figure stumble from the flames, but there was none. Nor did a little bird come fluttering out.

My throat burned harder. I wished I could cry. *Thank you, Cariad. God rest your little soul.*

Bang! The moans turned to screams as the fire suddenly exploded with a brilliant flash of red. *Bang!* Hands covered eyes as there was another brilliant flash of light, green this time. The barrels. That fool Pike had packed his factory with cloth, thread, wooden crates, and open flames, and now that the inevitable had happened, the barrels of serum were heating up into bombs. "Get back," I said in useless English, pulling them farther into the woods. "Do not breathe it in. Back."

They followed my urgent movements, probably more out of fear of the explosions than from anything I said. A hand gripped my arm. I turned. It was Mairead, her dark eyes hooded in the light of the flames.

"Gliondrach," I said awkwardly. "Gliondrach tu abhus." I hoped she understood my broken words as I meant them: *I'm glad you're here. I'm glad you're alive.*

She said something, too quickly for me to catch. She turned me by the shoulders toward the road to Meryton. The church bells were tolling. Others would be here soon.

Still upbraiding me incomprehensibly, she gestured to my shirt, tugged at my trousers.

Oh.

I could not be seen here. Not like this. I took a step back and then hovered uncertainly.

Surely I oughtn't to leave them this way.

Mairead seized me by the shoulder again and gave me a shove toward the road. She shouted something in which I could discern the word *go*. I started away at a slow jog, quickly growing faster as my full situation dawned upon me. If Miss Mary Bennet of Longbourn was found, in the middle of the night, dressed as a boy, at the site of her fiancé's presumed fiery death, it would make Lydia's scandalous elopement a mere footnote compared to my infamy.

I found myself at home just as the sun was beginning to bleach the horizon. A column of smoke rose from the woods. I stared at it, mesmerized, until I fell asleep against my windowpane.

No one knew quite what to make of the fire. It erased most evidence of Pike's sinister apparatus, and the barrels of serum had all burst by the time the good people of Meryton arrived.

Luckily it had been a damp autumn, so the woods did not catch, but Pike's factory burned quickly and thoroughly. When he failed to reappear, he went down into the parish record as perishing in the flames. Miss Figg, too, was lost to the disaster.

The factory girls were housed in the church for a few days. Then a collection was taken to send them home. They left with no protest.

Did Meryton know that something terrible happened out there at the old mill? More terrible than just the fire, I mean? Perhaps they suspected. However, they had no wish to know more. No one spoke the girls' language but I, and no attempt to find a decent translator was made. I tried once to speak to Mairead. Her eyes went right past me as if she did not know me. I do not know if she was angry with me or still trying to protect me.

If they knew where in the woods their sister weavers' bodies lay, they told no one. I suppose I cannot blame them for that.

Pike is spoken of now with some sorrow, as a promising young gentleman who was felled by a tragic stroke of bad luck. The lack of much *actual* sorrow makes me suspect that they knew at least a little of what went on. However, Meryton has never had the words to talk about Septimus Pike, in life, death, or anything in between. I suppose that will never change now.

No one knows quite what to make of me, either. But I suppose no one ever did.

I am a bit ashamed to admit it, but the one I grieve the most is Cariad. For days, I hoped to hear his little beak tapping at the window, but I never did. I suppose I deserve that much for my role in all this, but I could wish it was not my valiant little friend who paid the price. I find myself absently reaching up to my shoulder to stroke a feathered little head that is no longer there.

That is all, Harry, I believe. Everyone has left me—Cariad, Miss Darcy, even Pike's poisonous obsession is laid to rest at last—but that is no more than I deserve. Two monsters, me and Pike, and between us we have caused so much sorrow. Now one of us is dead, and the other is alone. I shall do my best to be grateful for that much and to live quietly for the rest of my days, doing no more damage. The scarlet rage of my nature will never erupt to the surface ever again.

A sorry tale, all in all, Harry. I daresay if you were real you would despise me. At least it is over now.

CHAPTER 34

A Letter

From the pen of Miss Georgiana Darcy, Pemberley
30 November, 18--

Dearest ~~Mar Miss Benn~~ Sir Gregory,

Forgive me for my style of address. I am sure I have lost the right to call you by your Christian name, and I cannot bear to return to the formality of Miss B——, not after all we have been to each other. So if I am to write you—and I find I must—I can only return to the name I first knew you by.

I would leave you alone if I could, really I would. If it was only that my troubles made you dislike me, I could bear that, I think. But if the Problem has made you believe that I hate you, well, that I cannot bear. You have become far too dear to me for that. You will not thank me for it, but I will tell you all.

The Problem has been upon me these nine months. A spiteful woman laid it upon me for reasons that I cannot share, for they would mean breaking another's confidence—but suffice to say, they had nothing whatever to do with me *qua* me, for I was merely the vessel for another's attempt at vengeance. My malefactor had the sort of nonsensical, tortuous path of reasoning that you and I have always despised.

I have found it best to think of the Problem simply as a disease. I did not ask for it and did nothing to deserve it; therefore it serves nothing to be ashamed of it. And yet, of course, I am ashamed of it.

The Problem will be with me all my life. How I despise myself when I think of it! I, a Darcy, one of a proud and noble line, with such parents and such a brother to live up to. I can never be the girl they wanted me to be, and sometimes I am so wretched over it I do not know if I can go on.

I used to transform every night. What a trial that was. A bit of experimentation has reduced that—now I must merely spend a week a month "indisposed." But the tonics are unreliable. One works for a while and then loses its effectiveness. This is why I pilfered your serums. I hope you can understand. I suspect I shall always be forced to continually change the formula. All my life, I shall be chasing whatever scraps of normality I can get, that other people take for granted. I shall never marry. Never have children.

That is the bad side of it. Some days it seems very bad indeed. But there are other things, too.

There is the feeling of winter wind ruffling my wing feathers. The way the blood sings in my ears when I spot my prey far below.

And there is my mind, which I still have. There was—once—the prospect of a complete cure of the Problem, but it would have hobbled my mind forever and left me a shell of the scientist you know. I chose to remain myself and remain a problem.

When one accepts that one will never be all right, will never be just as a young girl ought—well, there are pleasures in being formed wrong.

This life can be lonely. But it is who I am. Which brings us to you.

I am so, so sorry about the garish way I revealed myself to you. I have not much control when I am deep in the Problem. Still, I regret it more than anything I have ever done in any form. I would not hurt you for the world, my dearest, dearest one.

My Sir Gregory, knight of my heart, lord of my laboratory—your life would in every way be easier without me in it. I do not fit. I violate the rules that govern your existence. Explaining things is your passion—and mine!—and we will never be able to explain the Problem.

Does it undermine you too much? Is it too repugnant to you? Perhaps so. Perhaps it would be better for us both if I withdrew. I know it felt miraculous to us both to find a friend in each other—but considered from a logical standpoint, it may actually be sampling error. If you and I, quite by chance, wrote to each other under male pseudonyms—well, does that not suggest that there may be hundreds of other girls all over Europe doing the same? Perhaps half the letters in the journals are from lonely girls like us, laboring in isolation, unaware that there are so many others in our sisterhood. I am sure you could find one to aid your research who does not come with the Problem.

I do not want you to. I want it to be me.

Oh, it is vexing. I am a natural philosopher, and it is against nature. Consider the problem of mass—I am a well-grown girl, of a mass proportional to my height and width, and yet in the grip of the Problem I am sure I cannot weigh more than thirty pounds. Where does the rest of me go? It violates the law of thermodynamics! If Newton's *Principia* was a book of etiquette, the universe would cut me dead when it saw me in the street.

So, yes, your life would be easier if you, too, cut me dead. I like you enough, and care so very much for your happiness, that I almost advise it. I complicate your story in truly unconscionable ways. But I am too selfish for that. I want to be in your story. I want that so very badly. I want to do midnight experiments with you and turn the pages for you at balls. I want to wake in the morning knowing that you are under the same roof, and that our days will be passed together.

It will not be easy, cleaving to each other in that way. It will severely limit our options.

Many will not like it. I have a large income, but we may find it reduced.

So I do not demand, or beg—I merely ask. Let me be a part of your story. It would make me so happy, and I would do my very, very, very best to make you happy, too.

Yours, yours, yours,
HOLZMANN.

⁓

7 December, 18--

After reading Miss Darcy's last letter, I stuck it in the back of a drawer, under a pile of journals I never open anymore. Then I climbed into bed, pulled the covers over my head, and stayed there the rest of the day. When Mamma saw how I shook, she thought I had had an attack of grief. I suppose perhaps I have.

What am I to do? It is absurd. She believes she is a *bird*. And I...I love her so much that somehow she made me believe it, too.

I will not accept it. I will not reply. If she is to recover from such delusions, it will be with the help of good, sound people. Not a monster like me. Henceforth we shall be strangers to each other.

A life of dependence is all that awaits me now. I fought it for years, but I shall fight no longer. The farthest seat from the fire, Pike called it once. I shall strive to be grateful for it.

I shall get up in a moment. Stop shaking. Move on. Decide what I'd best do.

In a moment.

CHAPTER 35

Longbourn

13 December, 18--

I thought things could get no worse since last I wrote. I was wrong.

For three days I lay abed. Stupid! Lazy! I was feeling self-pity when I ought to have *forced* myself to my feet. Quindley would box my ears until I went deaf, and I should deserve every ringing blow.

On the third night, I awoke to the now-familiar scent of fire. I opened my eyes. Longbourn, our Longbourn, was engulfed in flames.

"Mary!" my mother was shrieking. *"Mary!"*

Coughing and choking in the smoky air, I made my way to the door, and then screamed. The doorknob was hot. I turned and climbed out onto the windowsill instead.

As I sat on the threshold, I saw, at the edge of our little park, a tall, dark figure. He waved at me, patted a nearby elm tree, then vanished into the shadows.

It was too far to jump to the ground, but the wall was covered in ivy, which, thank God, my father had been too lazy to have cut back. Scrambling for purchase, I managed to climb down far enough that I could jump onto our stable roof, and then into a groom's arms. He tried to carry me, but I shoved my way onto my own two feet. Icy grass lashing my bare feet, I joined the little knot of Longbourners standing numbly in the garden. My mother was wailing. When she saw me she shrieked and put an arm around me, more for her own support than out of any evident affection.

The fire was fierce, but, thank God, quickly contained. When it was out we walked through the smoldering, blackened ground floor. The fire had destroyed the kitchen and dining room, and greatly damaged the parlor and stairs. The bedrooms were mostly all right.

We found my father in his bed. His body was untouched—it was the smoke that got him. I shall never forget the noise my mother made. Not the dramatic wail you'd expect from her—just a ragged gasp that sounded like she was breaking in two. I turned and found she'd stuffed her fist to her mouth.

"Is he—" she asked.

"He's gone."

She came to him, slowly. Took his right hand in hers, as though they were being introduced.

"Bring him back," she said.

My jaw dropped. "What?"

She turned to me. "Bring him back. Fix him. I know you can. Do you think I am so ignorant of what you and Miss Darcy got up to under my own roof?"

I was still gaping at her. "I-I already did him once. I don't know—"

"Do it."

"You don't know what you're asking...He won't be—"

"I do not care." She seized me by the shoulders. "If you do not do this, we will have nothing. We will *be* nothing. Is that what you want, Mary? For your mother? For yourself?" She gave a bitter laugh. "I know it is not. None of my daughters has ever wanted so badly to *matter* as you do."

"Mamma—"

"Do not 'Mamma' me."

That man out there. I know who he was. This fire—this too is my fault.

"Take his arm," I said. "Help me get him up the stairs."

I thought I might not be able to do it with Mamma watching me. However, I have enough experience now that my hands almost prepared the apparatus on their own. I have improved its structure to provide more galvanic energy; even without a lightning strike the power was sufficient to make Papa's body arch off the table.

Once. Twice. Three times. Then he gasped and opened his eyes.

Mamma gave a low moan when she saw his black eyes. "It's all right, it's all right," I babbled. "He just needs medicine." And as quickly as I could, I poured him a draft of chroma serum.

It took nearly every drop I had to bring him back to himself. Perhaps because it was his second trip through the apparatus, perhaps simply because he has such a contrary personality, but Papa required much more serum than any previous patient.

"What happened?" he said at last. "Where am I?"

"The attic," I said. "There has been a fire, Papa. Longbourn is badly damaged."

"Then why the devil have you got me up here?" He tried to stand and staggered.

"*You* have been badly damaged."

"Stuff and nonsense. Out of my way."

"Mr. Bennet," said my mother in a quavering voice. "You died."

"Oh, Lord, woman. Might you delay your hysterics a day or two?"

"It's true, Papa."

He stopped and touched his own hand. He flinched at how cold it was. "Oh God," he moaned.

"I will provide you with medicine," I said. "No one need know."

He turned flat eyes to mine. "*You?*"

"I."

He gave me a long look. I am not sure he had looked at me so closely in all the years since my expulsion from his library. "Well, then," he said, "you had better get to work making more."

My throat was so tight I could barely speak. "Yes sir."

For the next three days, as Papa and Mamma took stock of the damage, that is what I did.

My laboratory was, thankfully, untouched. I made every drop of serum I could manage. Everyone thought me a very unnatural daughter, I believe, disappearing to my room at such a terrible time when my father needed all the help he could get and Mamma kept falling into hysterics—but it soon became clear that my father's need for a large volume of serum was not a one-time issue. I shall have to spend most of my time henceforth producing more. I offered to treat and reinsert his ribs, but he flat out refused. Luckily, he does not seem to mind the shade of the serum as much as Pike did.

The morning after the fire I found a few moments to sneak away to the old elm tree. There was a note stuck in the crook of its branches.

M—
  A fire for a fire.
P

Today the servants are packing up such belongings as can be salvaged. Tomorrow, we Bennets leave Longbourn.

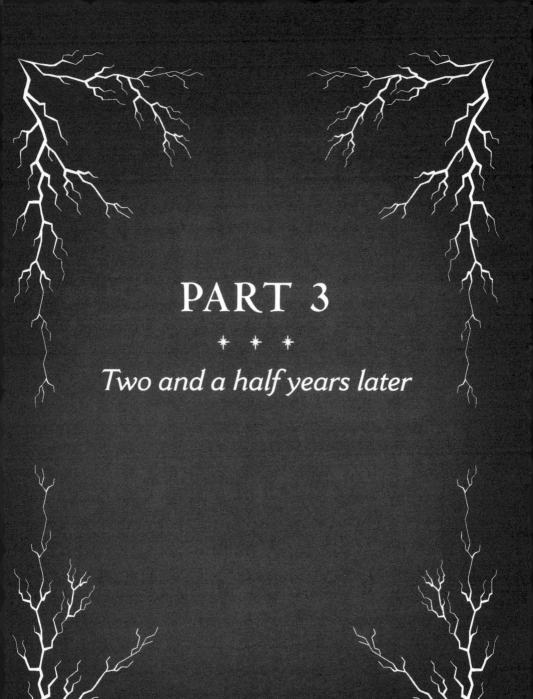

CHAPTER 36

Visitors

23 April, 18--

"Well," said Mamma, settling into the carriage with a sigh, "at least we are away from *them*."

I did little more than nod. So much carriage travel in the last two years may have allowed me to see a bit of the world at last, but it has also educated me thoroughly upon how much I dislike carriage travel. Our poor carriage is getting worn out, too, and Papa says we've not the money to replace it, so every ride is more jarring than the one before. I have learned to carry a small discreet bag with me, in case I am sick on the king's highway.

It helped a little to look out the window, but I did not much like that, either. Sometimes when I was tired I saw things.

"They were very kind to have us to visit," I said automatically.

"Hah! Kind!" Mamma sniffed. "I believe that Mr. Collins only agreed to take us at all so he could show off those nasty creatures."

"You mean his sons?"

"I shall not dignify them with the name until they can manage to go three minutes without whacking someone with a toy sword, and someone wipes their noses. Eugh!" She shuddered. "I am monstrous glad that *I* never had any sons myself. I'd have hated it."

"Yes, Mamma." Every problem my mother had ever concerned herself with would have been solved by birthing a son, as well she knew. But in this case I was too tired to resist her efforts to rewrite history. Besides, I shared her dislike. Three weeks with the Collinses had made me, too, wish that I could rewrite history, so that it contained fewer Collinses.

Hello again, Harry. I suppose you wonder why I take up my pen again after all this time—and, perhaps, why I voluntarily spent more than a fortnight in the home of Mr. Collins. Read on.

After the fire, my father had taken lodgings for himself, me, and my mother in Bath. Of course my elder sisters offered to have us, but my father refused, having a horror of accepting favors out of the dark suspicion that he would one day be expected to offer one in return.

Mamma was happy enough to go to Bath, but our lodgings were unfashionable, which vexed her, and too small, which vexed us all. Such peace as we had enjoyed at Longbourn, it became clear, had been a result of all of us being able to retreat to different sides of the house and close the doors. Besides, I had a job to complete.

I now divided my time between our Bath apartments, making medicine for my father, and visiting friends and relations. Most of these were very surprised to hear from me, as I had never been an enthusiastic visitor before, but now that I was sister-in-law to two of England's richest men, I had only to drop the slightest hint and an invitation to visit would promptly be issued. Mamma, who loved Bath but hated our lodgings, usually accompanied me.

And how did I choose which invitations to solicit? Anywhere there were rumors. A new factory in town. Disappearances. Gossip of an eligible bachelor with dark hair and an attractive Byronic manner. Uneasy mutterings about blood.

I was hunting Pike.

It had expanded my skill set in surprising ways. I found that, though I still went awkward and still at parties, I could chatter away charmingly if it was necessary to draw someone out who might have a nugget of useful news. I could dance all the dances, though my head and jaw ached with the effort of not counting, and I could dance them flawlessly while smiling. I could play every card game that a hostess could conceivably want a fourth for, and had learnt to keep sweets about my person to bribe any children of the house who might be inclined to resent an intruder.

In other words, I was now essentially the poor relation I had always feared becoming. I was better at it than I expected, but I hated it even more than I expected, too.

Once or twice I nearly caught up to him. Each time he managed to escape me.

His need to make his own medicines made him easier to track, but he was still stronger and faster than I, and he had all the advantages of being wealthy and male. He had no need to wait on invitations. He could just go.

I was not poor, exactly, and the reflected glory of the Darcy connection certainly helped, but most of Papa's money went into repairs at Longbourn, and the allowance he gave us barely stretched to cover travel. Our life on the road was uncomfortable, all fixed smiles and pretending not to be cold or tired or lonely or about to be genteelly sick in a bag.

The Collins visit had been the worst of them all. Mr. Collins had never recovered from Lizzy's slight, and he did indeed thrust his two odious sons upon our notice at every opportunity. Sons were the only area where he had excelled and we had not, and so Thaddeus and Arthur were continually paraded before us.

"He is just proud of his family," I said weakly.

"Ha! And Charlotte!" Mamma shook her head. "I bounced that girl on my knee. And now she has the nerve to scold me!"

"She was just being sympathetic, Mamma. Everyone agrees the fire was terrible."

"She was not being sympathetic; she was scolding. She asked me where I kept my curling iron!"

Charlotte Collins had not exactly *scolded* my mother. However, it was true that her repeated expressions of horror contained, from time to time, a hint of proprietary reproof. That such damage should be allowed to come to the future home of the Collinses was, she implied, something we ought to apologize to *them* for.

All in all, it was almost a relief to be getting queasy in the carriage again. At least when I was here I did not have to plaster on a smile. I could, for a little while, speak freely.

Which reminded me…

With an effort, I focused on my mother. "Mamma, I have been meaning to ask you—is that a new bonnet?"

She looked guilty. One hand flew to her head, as if to hide the offending garment, which was far too large and garish to be so hidden. "Er…is it? I forget."

I sighed. "You know it is."

"Well, and why not? We are going to Pemberley. We shall have no expenses there."

"You know very well that we shall have to tip the Pemberley servants who wait upon us."

Mamma waved this off. "Ridiculous. I am quite sure Mr. and Mrs. Darcy are more than able to pay their own servants. Why should they expect us to do so?"

I bit back a sharp retort. I had a little money held back. I had hoped to put it toward our luncheon on the road. Ah, well, I could go hungry. Mamma knew perfectly well that one must tip the servants in great houses, but she was tired, and if she ever put her foot down and refused to travel with me anymore then my pursuit of Pike would be at an end. That must not be. I am the reason he is still at large.

In truth, I was now used to giving up such small comforts as regular meals to keep Mamma happy. It was our destination that was making me snappish. Pemberley.

This was not a visit in pursuit of Pike. He had not been seen in Derbyshire. No, this was a true social visit. The idea of having to do my gushing-visitor act for my own sister made me want to hit something. And, of course, at Pemberley I would find *her*. When our carriage wheels whispered up Pemberley's wide white drive, I promised myself that I would find an excuse for leaving as soon as possible. As Pemberley itself swung artfully into view, framed by the surrounding hills and trees to make one's approach equally picturesque and terrifying, I screwed up my sweaty palms in my skirt.

The grip around my heart eased a little when I saw that there was only one figure waiting on the steps for us, and it was Lizzy. She had changed little in the years since I had seen her, just grown a little rounder, which made her prettier than ever. When we alighted she gave a glad cry and, to my surprise, hugged us both with what seemed to be genuine delight.

"Come in, come in," she said. "I am sure you are dying to refresh yourselves, but do have a drop of tea as soon as you have changed. Georgiana sends her apologies. She has got the headache. Oh, it is so long since I have seen you both!"

As she led us down a hall that would have admitted a coach and four without difficulty, she continued chatting away happily at a speed that would have put Lydia to shame. When she married Darcy, Lizzy quitted Longbourn with barely disguised relief, and life at Pemberley appeared to suit her. Her dress was a simple one in the Grecian style, but very finely made. Her hair, too, was simple, but Mamma's maid never could have dressed it so neatly and elegantly. She was undoubtedly a fine lady now. Yet I suppose even fine ladies find they miss their mothers.

I began to discern the reason for this unexpected warmth. "I've had no callers these five days," she said. "My husband has been away tending to business in town, Georgiana is always resting or reading, and I am stuck here in Pemberley awaiting my next confinement." She brushed a hand fondly over her belly. "Of course, playing with little Charlotte is a joy, but a child of two is hardly company, and because I am Mrs. Darcy, no one hereabouts will have a comfortable chat with me." She sighed. "I had high hopes for Mrs. Andrews, our vicar's new wife, for I had heard she was an educated woman, but she is so afraid of me that her teacup rattles in its saucer because she is trembling so hard."

"No fear of *that*," said Mamma. "*I* shall never be afraid of you, Miss Lizzy. And I call it very ill-bred of this Mrs. Andrews to behave in such a ridiculous manner before Mrs. Darcy of Pemberley."

"For heaven's sake, Mamma," Lizzy said, and they fell to bickering as of old. They both appeared to thoroughly enjoy it. After that Lizzy had a thousand questions about our old neighbors, and about the fire, and about Bath. I began to think that Lizzy's loneliness might save *me* from the things I did not wish to discuss.

Of course Lizzy had many kind inquiries for me, too. In the old days she seemed always to be cross with me or ashamed on my behalf; she seemed now to remember us as the best of friends.

"And of course you must play our piano while you are here," she said to me. "It is a very fine instrument, and I do not take advantage as I ought, I am so busy with the house. I know *you* have not been so lax, Mary."

I winced a little. In truth, all my travel had made it difficult to practice, and my dear Longbourn instrument was lost in the fire. Even with all that, I might have kept it up, but I had another reason for my slackness. My right hand drifted to my left forearm.

My mother jumped in and said, "Mary has not been strong, you know, and so cannot play so often. Jones said she must preserve her strength."

"Oh, Mamma, you are not still listening to that charlatan Jones?" She turned to me. "Come, Mary, I entreat you to play something for us. Surely you will? I have not forgotten how you enjoyed an opportunity to exhibit your skills."

I thought of that night that Pike had jilted me. The way the dark music seemed to flow from my fingertips. The way Lizzy had dispatched Papa to practically drag me from the keys, in front of all we knew. I tried not to react, but a flinch ran over my body, involuntary as the twitch of a horse's flank. "No, thank you."

Lizzy, to my surprise, looked stricken. "There, you see," she said. "If I had said anything so thoughtlessly nasty to one of the ladies hereabouts, she would force a laugh and pretend to think it a great joke. I did not mean anything by it, truly—only that I really wish to hear you play. You have come just in time to save me from growing too sharp-tongued to be borne, Mary."

"But surely you have company in the house," Mamma pointed out. "Surely you have Miss Darcy."

"Yes, but she is too shy and obliging. She will never check me." Shy? Obliging? My Georgiana?

No. Not *my* Georgiana. We had not laid eyes upon each other in years.

"And how is Miss Darcy?" said Mamma. "We miss her. I hoped she would be here to greet us."

Lizzy, in the course of pouring more tea, froze for an instant. "She is well," she said.

"Does her illness trouble her still?"

"Sadly, yes. But she manages very well."

"Well, I hope we may see something of her. She and Mary are such friends, you know." My mother laughed. "I once found them sleeping with their arms round each other, as innocent as two babes."

I made sure, this time, not to flinch. What she had seen us doing that day was not what I would call *innocent*. I have never been able to look at blackcurrant jam the same way.

Lizzy smiled. "I am sure she will be glad to see you if her health allows." Whatever Mrs. Darcy knew about Miss Darcy would not give itself away with the rattle of a teacup.

Presently Mamma went upstairs to unpack her things. Lizzy drew her chair a little closer to mine. "I got your letter of last week."

My heart leapt into my throat. "Oh yes? I have been on the road, so if you replied—"

"I have not."

"Ah."

"I knew you were coming, and"—she drew a deep breath—"I thought I had better tell you this in person. Mary, I cannot send you any more money."

I deliberately smoothed out my brow. Be agreeable. Be charming. *No is not always no.* "I am sorry to hear that," I said. "Of course I would never want to strain the Darcy finances." I dabbed at my lips, then let my eyes steal to the gold candlesticks above the fireplace.

She sighed. "You are not straining the Darcy finances, naturally. However, my own funds are not infinite, and a great deal goes already to keep Lydia and Wickham out of the gutter."

I had often wondered if my wayward sister and her husband would do better if they had to fully fend for themselves. They both struck me as possessed of more cunning than they were generally given credit for. However, it was hardly my place to demand harsh measures be taken. "I see. I will manage." Though I had no idea how.

"Manage *what?*"

"My travels."

"Why must you travel?"

"Quindley says that appropriate travel, such as to visit sites of historical or religious importance, is salutary for a young lady's moral development."

Lizzy passed a hand over her brow. She looked as though she was beginning to remember why she had found me so irritating. "I cannot *believe* you are still so attached to Quindley, that—" She took a deep breath. "It is to your credit, Mary, to wish to improve yourself. However, I am not sure all this travel is really good for you."

I frowned at the floor. Seeing a sister I had not met for some years made me feel about twelve again. None of my own words would come to mind. "Quindley says—"

"*Bother* Quindley." Lizzy leaned forward. "I mean it, Mary. I have had letters from Charlotte, from the Gardiners—everyone says how pale and thin you have grown, and now I see it is even worse than they said. I know how you have suffered. If I lost Darcy—" The sympathy in her eyes made me squirm. "But you must not wear yourself away like this."

I glanced down at myself. I had indeed grown thinner. It was hard to keep my figure up, skipping meals to fund Mamma, and, of course—my left arm gave a throb—I had Papa to care for as well.

"Stay here," she continued. "Stay at Pemberley. Just for a little while."

I stood up so fast that my delicate little cake plate tumbled off my knees to the ground.

Luckily for the strained Darcy coffers, it was cushioned by the thick rug. "I cannot. Thank you, I—No."

"Then your only other choice is to go back to Longbourn." A cold sensation crept down my back.

"To Longbourn?"

"Yes. I have had a letter from Papa. He says the repairs are nearly finished. You and Mamma are to go home straightaway."

I sank back to the chair. "Oh."

"That is the only journey I will fund, I am afraid," she said gently. "Jane feels the same. It is no use applying to her."

If Jane, usually a soft touch, had employed Lizzy to cut me off, they must have discussed me extensively. My cheeks burned with embarrassment even as my mind was working furiously. I could not stop now. Pike was still out there.

Lizzy sighed again. "I can see you are by no means resigned. You always did have to take the most difficult path. Go and rest before dinner. Perhaps with a little time to think you will feel differently."

I rose and gave her a deep curtsy. "I thank you for all your generosity to a poor girl, Mrs. Darcy." I felt rather than saw her flinch. Lizzy might have mountains of money, but at least I could still make her feel like rubbish. Cold comfort as I swept from the room.

"Mary?" her voice called as I exited. "What passed between you and Georgiana?"

I pretended not to hear as the door swung shut behind me.

I did need a little time alone, in any case. Not to rest, though. As soon as I was alone in my borrowed room, I set out my travel kit, took out my razor, and ran it down the inside of my left forearm. No fashionable ballgowns for me anymore—both arms were streaked with scars. Every dress I owned covered me to the wrists.

I stared at the ceiling as my blood plopped into the little basin. *Bother Lizzy.* I had so counted on wheedling a little more money out of her. Without it we could go no further.

Well. I had thought this might happen. It would be a difficult conversation, but I had to speak to Miss Darcy anyway. May as well add this to my list of demands.

Once my blood had filled the little basin up to the mark I'd scratched in the glass, I quickly bent and bandaged my arm. This had been awkward at first, but I had done it so many times now that I could quite easily manage one-handed, even though I felt a bit lightheaded as well. The bloodletting always seemed to hit me harder if I had not eaten. Perhaps Sir Gregory could write a monograph on it, if I lived out the year.

Mamma came in from the adjoining room. "Still at it? We will be called for dinner."

"I am sorry I could not bleed faster."

She clucked. "You ought to let me."

I was lighting the small burners on my travel kit, a folding metal apparatus of phials and burners that was cunningly made to fold into a small suitcase. Cunningly, and expensively. This, at least, my father had been willing to fund. "You know he prefers mine."

"He will take what you send him," she said. "Me next time. I insist."

She often insisted, but when it came time to cut her she always spent thirty minutes screaming and fluttering and considering falling into a faint, and most of the time could not actually bring herself to lose a drop of blood. I found it far easier to use my own. Besides, Papa did not like her bright pink serum, which he claimed made him nervous. He preferred my own red. "It's all right, Mamma."

"It is *not* all right. You are a single girl, Mary. You will never get a husband if you scratch yourself to ribbons."

"Mamma, you know perfectly well I will never get any husband at all."

"Nonsense." But her answer was halfhearted, and she sank onto the bed and watched me prepare Papa's next phial.

I joined her on the bed while the mixture steeped and leaned on her shoulder. Mamma has many faults, but her shoulders are very soft. When the bell rang I sprang to my feet, only to find the world going gray.

I was in the carriage again. The rattling journey would never end. Out of the corner of my eye I saw a tawny owl sweep past. When I looked right at her she was gone.

I awoke once more on the bed. Mamma was just stoppering a little red bottle. I groaned. "What happened?"

"You fainted, my girl."

I tried to sit up. "The serum—"

She brandished the bottle at me. "Finished."

Mamma was no great hand at making my serums, but she had watched me often enough, and it was too late now, anyway. Then when the dinner bell rang, she rebound my arm, which had begun to bleed again, and helped me into my evening gown. It was a grayish-brown color that even I knew was hideous and far too old for me, and the long sleeves made me look either eccentric or hopelessly out of fashion, but it covered my arms and the fabric had been cheap. For a moment, she stood behind me in the mirror, looking at us both, her hands at my shoulders. I had a sudden flash of memory of being very small, leaning against her leg and practically disappearing into her skirts. Now, of course, I was taller than she was.

"Nothing to be done, Mamma."

"But it's so ugly," she said. "I have nightmares, sometimes, about those arms of yours. It is not right for a gentleman's daughter."

"It is because I am a gentleman's daughter that I must do it. For Papa. For Longbourn."

Her lips thinned, but she said nothing, patted my good shoulder, and led the way downstairs.

However, Mamma was correct that I had taken too much blood. As soon as I turned the corner outside the dining room, my vision began disappearing in a veil of gray mist again. For there, standing at the door on the arm of an unknown young man, was Miss Darcy.

This is the true reason I am writing you again, Harry. I am under the same roof as my former ~~coll to~~ friend, and I find I cannot face her without you. There is much to tell, but even this much has taxed me. More anon.

CHAPTER 37

Georgiana

27 April, 18--

It has been four days. In truth, I feel no better, but perhaps writing you will help me tame my flying thoughts. Let us resume where I broke off, in the dining room that first night.

Through sheer force of will I pushed the fog back and kept my feet. Miss Darcy's eyes stayed locked on mine. Gone were the extravagant colors and wild patterns of her attire in former days. Miss Darcy now wore a very simple white gown trimmed with the palest pale blue satin. She could out-virgin the Virgin Mary in it, I thought woozily. She looked extremely pretty in it, and rather younger than she had two years ago.

"Mrs. Bennet," she said, "Miss Bennet, how do you do. May I present Mr. Arthur Bascombe, my fiancé?"

Fiancé?

Two years as a poor relation had prepared me to come through more trying social occasions than this. With a smile that felt like it was stretched over a tanner's frame, I gave a curtsy. "Miss Darcy. Mr. Bascombe. I wish you both joy."

I wish you both in a deep, dark hole.

My thoughts become somewhat overfree after blood loss.

"Ah! Bennets! Capital!" He hurried forward to pump our hands. I stifled a wince. "Always Bennets and former Bennets about the place. I've developed quite a taste for 'em." He guffawed to himself. "Always a welcome addition to our little party, of course. Heard about you, naturally, from my beloved here. Play cards? Yes, yes, capital, we must have a game. Oop, second bell." And with that, he bowed to my mother and to me, offered Miss Darcy his arm, and swept her in.

I watched in wonder as he dined with us. This bit of posh fluff! Marry ~~my Geo~~ Miss Darcy? Why, she would be bored stiff. I had spent only an hour in his company, and already I was sure that if he told me once more which of his hunting bitches he planned to cross with which hound to produce precisely what length of ear, I would seize the silver vase from the centerpiece and dash his brains in. Surely Miss Darcy could not contemplate a lifetime of this sort of thing?

But it seemed she could. Even her brother, Mr. Darcy, seemed pained by Bascombe's company, and Elizabeth looked like she might beat me to the vase, but they paid him all the courtesy a soon-to-be member of the family was owed. As for Georgiana, she merely offered him quiet replies to his queries and smiled at his loud guffaws.

Once, while he was saying something particularly stupid, my eyes caught Georgiana's. She flushed a light pink, which made me ache to press my hand to hers, and quickly looked away.

Those few words outside the door remain the only ones we have exchanged since my arrival at Pemberley. Since then she is like the moon—usually visible, but utterly remote. If there are cards, she is at another table. If there are walks, she is on someone else's arm. And if I go to her sitting room directly, to beg a quiet word, she is not feeling well, thank you, miss, you'd best try another time.

I shall have to change my tactics. I must speak to her. It will be tomorrow night. I've a plan.

---

28 April, 18--

There was a ball tonight, a sort of unofficial engagement ball for Miss Darcy and *him*. How I loathe him! Gossip at the ball told me that he has ten thousand a year, that he comes of a family even older than the Darcys, and that he is popular belowstairs, too, for he tips liberally and cuts a fine figure as a hunter. I'd like to cut him a fine figure, all right. I wonder how he would feel about being dissected and then dissolved down to his bones in a vat of acid?

Ugh. Listen to me. Rest assured, Harry, I know what a monster I sound, and I never let such bile spill forth to anyone but you. He is not a bad sort, really. Quite kind, in his bluff, stupid way. I want to drop him off a cliff.

There I go again. I assure you, Mr. Bascombe is quite safe from my machinations.

Well, as safe as anyone can be when I am about. Death does tend to dog my steps.

He and Miss Darcy opened the dance, of course, and it happened to be the country dance I once danced with her in the sitting room at Longbourn, and for a moment I was miserably certain she'd chosen it to torment me. Nonsense, of course. My monstrous conceit making itself known again. How loathsome I can be. I am sure it was pure coincidence.

I made no little sensation myself when I entered the hall. Over Mamma's strenuous objections, I had borrowed a pair of shears this afternoon and restored my hair to its *à la guillotine* style. I doubt very much if anyone else would have done such a thing, for it is now long out of style, but I am so far past the possibility of pleasing that I may as well try to shock.

It worked, I saw grimly. When Miss Darcy caught sight of me she stumbled in the middle of a step, and she would have fallen had her partner not hauled her along bodily like a sack of potatoes.

I could not even have a moment to fancy that she'd been struck by my beauty, for in turning away, I caught sight of myself in one of the french windows. Shorn, pale, and gaunt, in an unfashionably scarlet dress with gauchely long sleeves—I looked more like a vengeful spirit than a girl. Perhaps I am more revenge than woman now.

Still, she managed to avoid me. I felt her eyes upon me all evening, as we circled opposite ends of the room, repelling like two magnets. Once or twice I danced—it could not be avoided—and saw her face in the whirl. One-two-three-*her*, one-two-three-*there*.

She was not the only one who stared, either. My mother's pained gaze met mine more than once. I turned away. What did it matter? She had married all her other daughters off, and obviously no one would marry me, so why keep trying to pass off dirt as diamonds?

I expected Lizzy would be livid. She just looked puzzled and sad.

At last, though, I cornered my quarry. Somehow, despite the perfection of a Darcy party, a series of twisted ankles left us light on gentlemen. That was my chance, and I seized it.

"Excuse me, may I have this dance?"

Miss Darcy turned to me in astonishment. The girl she was conversing with, some distant Darcy cousin, tittered behind her fan. My cheeks burned, but I did not drop my gaze.

"You…want to dance with *me*, Miss Bennet?" Miss Darcy asked.

"If you would be so kind. I know we are too old to stand up together, but we are all friends here, and I should hate for you to miss this dance due to the scarcity of gentlemen. I know how well you dance it."

She colored at that. It was the same dance she had opened with. So she did remember it, after all.

Her friend's mouth was hanging open at my daring. However, the good thing about such a bold and eccentric request was there was no graceful way to say no. Young ladies are taught to meet gentle ripostes with parries. There is no provision for a cannon blast.

I held out my arm, as a gentleman would. I am a cannon.

"What are you *doing*?" she hissed under her breath, her hand resting lightly in mine. She looked every inch the lady, but her gloved fingers trembled a little.

"I had to talk to you," I returned calmly. I led her over to the side of the floor, where several other young girls had also paired off with each other. I almost wished they had not. In my strange humor, I wanted full credit for my eccentricity.

"I have made it quite clear," she said, as the movements began, "I have no wish to talk to *you*. Really, Mary, your behavior is shocking. How dare you be so rude under my brother's roof."

The dance drew us apart for various twirls and dips. Under the strange calm that had overtaken me, I had the feeling that I had never danced so well. Apparently all it took was a willingness to destroy all the goodwill in the room.

When we were together again, I slid my arm a little farther around her waist than the steps demanded. "How dare I?" I whispered. "How dare *you* act so prissy? Have you forgotten the things I have seen you do? The things we've done together?"

A flash of hurt crossed her face. I had been referring to things like electrocuting the skull of her ancestor, but it was clear from her face that that was not what she was remembering when I said *things we've done together*. "Georgiana—"

She nearly threw my hand from hers as she turned to curtsy to the others. I bowed, as I was dancing the gentleman's part. "Speak, then," she said, "if you are so determined to ignore my feelings. Speak and get it over with."

I had limited time and a great deal to get through. I knew I ought to divulge the plan immediately. Instead I found myself asking, "Why are you marrying him?"

"Because I love him."

"*Ha!*" My scornful laughter was so loud that the musicians missed a beat. Miss Darcy, through a frozen smile, gave a genteel trill of laughter as though we were sharing a joke.

"All right," she whispered. "Because he is kind, and rich, and will never embarrass me." Her eyes were daggers on mine. "Such friends are to be treasured. One meets so many who are the opposite."

"Oh, please. That's not it, either."

"All *right*," she hissed. "His father has a similar…affliction to mine. His family will understand. Apparently this kind of thing is not unheard of in old families. He and I can…shelter each other." She looked so tired suddenly that I almost let her go. "Is that why you accosted me? Everyone in this ballroom is frightened of you, you know. You look like a fallen angel or something."

"No," I said. "I need your help."

Something I couldn't parse flickered in her gaze. "Help with research?"

"I would not ask you for that. I am sure you are busy preparing for your nuptials. I need money."

Her eyes had gone flat and tired again. "Ah. Of course."

"To capture Pike," I pressed on. "To end him. I'm close, Georgiana." The other female couples, growing bored, had drifted away to the refreshment table. Now we were alone, dancing in a pool of darkness between tables of candles, right in the middle of the ball, and yet, I fancied, almost unseen.

Her eyes glittered. "Miss Darcy."

I swallowed. "Miss Darcy." She spun under my arm. As she whirled past me I swear I felt her eyelashes brush my cheekbone.

"I needed something from you once, Miss Bennet. You never even deigned to answer."

"I'm sorry," I said. "It was only, I thought—"

"No." The dance had come to an end. She wrenched her hands from mine. "Whatever hopes you cherished, pray smother them. We are nothing to each other." She lowered her eyes and offered a slow curtsy. "Thank you for the dance."

I left with Mamma shortly after that. Her iron grip on my arm left me little choice. I had disgraced the name of Bennet enough for one evening, it was clear.

Now here I am in my nightshirt, curled in a window seat that is far too large, overlooking an unfamiliar park.

If she thinks I will give up that easily, she does not know me at all.

29 April, 18--

Last night as I sat writing there was a rustle. A tap at the window of my third-floor room. The curtains moved. The next thing I knew, Georgiana Darcy stood before me in the moonlight.

I stared at her for a long moment. Then I stepped past her, parted the curtains, and peered out.

"There is a balcony," I said. "Connecting our two rooms. You walked across."

She smiled faintly. "I never said otherwise."

Her hair was down, her white sleep shift blowing in the breeze. I turned away. "To what do I owe the pleasure?"

"I thought we ought to finish our conversation."

"I thought you had finished. Oughtn't you to get your sleep? To look pretty for your fiancé?" I could not keep the jeer from my voice on the last word.

"You don't like him much."

"Nor do you," I accused.

"He's all right. His father, too, is tied to the full moon, though he does not become an owl."

"Stop. It has been years. Must you still mock me in this way?"

"Mock you?"

My head was beginning to hurt. "I know I offended you. I know it must have been a blow when I would not do as you ordered. After all, I am a mere country spinster, and you are Miss Darcy. But I know perfectly well that girls cannot turn into owls."

She took a shuddering breath. Anger drew her half a step closer to me. "You know so much less than you think. There are worlds other than the one you see. Every one of us has a different world between our ears, so why should we ever expect to understand them all?"

"Nonsense! Some scientist you are, if you throw up your hands at the mysteries of the universe!"

"I *am* a scientist, and I *do* turn into an owl several nights a month! What is there to do but throw up my hands?"

"Oh, please."

"It is true. I swear it."

"Then prove it. Change now."

"I can't do it on command. I am not a dancing bear."

"Tell me everything then. How did it happen?"

She swallowed. "I cannot. It is not my secret to tell."

I laughed. "Of course." I hated the bitterness in my own voice—but how stupid did she think I was? "Please go back to your room."

She drew herself up. "I cannot fund your travels. Most of my money is held either by Fitz or by the lawyers, preparing to transfer it to my husband."

"Your husband," I said. "You will be Mrs. Bascombe."

"I will give you what I can," she pressed on. "As well as the modest laboratory equipment I possess. You will have to make it be enough. I cannot do more. I am trying to be the sister Fitz deserves. I must prepare for my wedding."

"If I cannot catch Pike—"

"You never *will* catch him!" she said. "To be honest, you are acting foolishly, Miss Bennet, to chase him all over England like this. He is a young man with wealth and resources. You are an unmarried lady of modest means. He will *always* be able to move faster than you."

"Then what do you suggest?"

"I don't know," she admitted. "You can find another way. I know you. But better yet—don't."

"Don't?"

"Forget about Pike. You've done all you can. Take what I can give you and use it to make a life somehow."

I closed my eyes. My headache was pounding ever more fiercely, and I had the horrible feeling that she was right about the futility of my pursuit. Had I really been wasting my time these last years? I scrubbed my hand over my face, willed words to come.

She gave a cry. The next thing I knew she was beside me, two hands pulling my forearm into the moonlight. "Mary! What in heaven?"

I tried to pull away, but her grip was strong. Of course. My night shift's sleeves had grown loose with my weight loss. I had not bothered to take them in, and one had ridden up. My network of scars and scabs showed up plainly on the bare skin of my arm. Georgiana gave a *tch* of outrage, turning my arm this way and that. "Who is this for?"

I thought about telling her. I was so tired, and so cold, and my arms throbbed so badly. I wanted to sink into bed with her, let the warmth close over us, and whisper the whole sorry story into her ear.

I wrenched my arm away. "If you will not tell the whole truth, why should I?" There was a dampness seeping over my skin. One of my cuts had reopened. It still hurt less than her touch.

She backed away. "You must stop this," she said. "It's killing you. It's shaming your family. Today we cut you off, but if you persist, you will find yourself in a madhouse."

I laughed. "If my father tries—"

"If your father tries, I will back him, for your own good. So will we all. So *stop*."

Gravity seemed to be malfunctioning. It could not be Georgiana, my Georgiana, saying such things.

But then, I had made quite sure she was not *my* Georgiana at all. She could no more abide me than the rest of them.

I waited till she had left, till I heard her window shut. Then I whispered, "Good night, Georgiana."

I lay awake for some time, waiting for the pain in my arms to die down. I drifted off before it did, and the pain chased me through my dreams. I awoke as the sky began to shade from black to gray. Heedless of the cold, I leaned my head out the window, looking over Pemberley Park. It really was extraordinarily beautiful. The hills, the ancient trees, the winding garden, the lake.

My father would never put me in a madhouse. That would be mad indeed, since he was the recipient of my serums. But...if my sisters pressed him, he might put me under lock and key. Longbourn was back on the map. It would be the easiest thing in the world to imprison me there. I had, in some sense, been a prisoner there most of my life.

I still had the strange feeling that gravity was not quite itself. The floor would not settle under my feet. I found myself gripping the windowsill.

I see, now, Harry, that Georgiana was right. I must stop chasing Pike. The only sensible course of action is to bring him to me.

[The following appeared in all the London and Manchester papers for three days.]

To S.P.—
I give in. Find me in Derbyshire. I've nowhere else to turn.
—M.

CHAPTER 38

Pike

15 May, 18--

The delightful thing about going up against an obsessive personality is that they are so predictable. Pike must have known I was attempting to lure him into a trap; and yet, I had no doubt he would come. He had to. Any whiff of surrender from me, of unrestricted access to my brains and my blood, would be enough to draw him.

It was a cold night. The air blowing off Pemberley's small ornamental lake made it still colder. I pulled my cloak closer about me and leaned against the low fence next to the lake. Young Charlotte Darcy seemed determined to teach herself to swim, so her desperate parents had erected this barrier, though it marred the view. I had wanted to dress as a boy again, but I suspected that Pike would be more receptive to what I had to say if I wore women's clothes. It was less safe—I could move better in boy's attire—but then, nothing about this was safe. There was every chance I would not survive this night. It made no difference. Pike was not the only obsessive one.

"Hello, Mary."

I started. Despite my constant vigil, he had managed to approach unheard. With the way the wind was moaning through the trees, it was no surprise. All this land was part of Pemberley's grounds, but in the deep of the night, it felt like the wildest, loneliest woods.

I turned. Pike was standing a few feet behind me. He looked just as he had the last time I saw him. No older, no less handsome. His face and eyes looked perfectly human. Clearly he had had no trouble finding other sources of chroma serum than mine.

"Mr. Pike. You look well," I said. "You must be killing some lovely people these days."

He inclined his head slightly. "Thank you. Actually I have taken the lessons of my Meryton factory to heart. No need to cause such a stir to get what I need."

"Isn't there?"

"No." He was walking slowly around the clearing, pacing a large circle around me. "Do you know that once in a London slum a woman sold her baby for a ration of gin? I've no need to kill that sort to get a little blood out of them. There are plenty desperate enough to sell it directly, and despicable enough that I need feel no scruples."

"Sounds as though you have an excellent situation."

"Indeed."

"And yet, Miss Carrie Baker in Manchester, Mrs. Josephine Smith in Derbyshire, that Lascar in London—"

"Yes, well. One tires of the blood of gutter rats." His eyes raked over me. "Speaking of fine fare. Why am I here, Miss Mary?"

"Is that what I am? Fine fare?"

"You know you are."

"And yet you come no closer."

He laughed darkly. "If I did, I suppose I'd fall through a trapdoor or something. I know you."

So he was at least a little afraid of me. Good. "If I am so dangerous, why come at all?"

He laughed. "It is rude to ignore an invitation from a lady."

"And I am fine fare."

"The finest."

So he was still afraid of me, but he still wanted me, too. Good.

"Come, tell me why you brought me here. I believe the words *I give in* were mentioned?"

I drew in a deep breath. "You were right," I said. "The last time I saw you."

"About?"

"I'm a monster," I said. "Like you."

His prowling half circle drew a little tighter about me. "Oh?"

"I've tried for two years now to repair my mistakes with you," I said. "I've got nowhere." I laughed a little. "Worse than nowhere. I'm...a burden. An embarrassment. They all despise me." I shook my head. "Then suddenly I realized that I've been going about it all wrong. I cannot stop you by force, but you and I cannot stay away from each other. You understood that long before I did."

His circle drew tighter still. He was almost close enough to touch me now. Instinctively, I took a step back.

"I would never despise you," he said softly. "Never overlook you."

"I-I suppose." In spite of it all, my chest ached like an old scar at his words. Why did it have to be he who spoke that way? And why did part of me still respond to it?

"I have not always been kind, I know, but you never wanted kind, Mary, not really. 'Thou and I are too wise to woo peaceably.'"

I shivered. Apparently he had found time in his wanderings to take in some Shakespeare. "You have fascinated me always, you know," he said. "Since the day you marched into your uncle's office with a bag of gunpowder. You were never a creature of ballrooms and soft politeness." He waved his hands. "This is you. Midnight, in a deserted patch, with a man you have twice tried to kill." He smiled a little. "Once successfully. You could never love any but such a man. For you, any lover would have to be your fiercest enemy, too."

His voice was oddly soothing. I was so tired these days. He was coming closer. My hand slipped into my pocket. *Just stick with the plan, Mary.*

One more step...

I whipped my hand out. The knife flashed in the moonlight, almost too fast to see. Bound straight for his heart.

Just before it sank into his chest, he grabbed my wrist. I struggled to complete the blow, but it was no good. His grip was like iron.

"There, you see?" He wasn't even out of breath. "You cannot seriously have thought that would succeed, dearest. This is mere flirtation. Admit it. You thought the words of your message were a subterfuge, but you inadvertently told the truth. You are ready to give in."

My wounds were seeping again. Was the gray mist creeping over my vision once more? It was hard to tell in the dark. My brain felt fuzzy.

Pike waved a hand at the sky. "No lightning tonight," he said. "Skies are clear. Your arsenal is bare, dearest."

I wondered if he was right. Would everything be easier if I just went with him? We were two of a kind. Perhaps the obsessive loathing I felt for him was as close to love as someone like me could come.

"I know you," he breathed. "I know you. Come with me now. I won't take too much." He reached out a hand toward my face.

Oop! Jam.

Georgiana dancing. Georgiana in the world's busiest hat. Georgiana touching a Leyden jar, laughing as her hair stood on end. Georgiana crying, screaming, turning away. Georgiana waking up, finding me beside her, and smiling.

"Come," he said, as he moved his hand toward mine. "Take my hand."

I did.

"You know," I said, "you have bested me many times now. There are parts of me that no one but you seems to see—even me."

"I know." His fingers tightened around mine. Like a dance hold, except we were gloveless.

"But," I said, "you don't know me." And with my free hand, I seized the metal fence.

I have, of course, been electrocuted before. If being struck by lightning was, on a scale of 1 to 100, a 92 for intensity and a 95 for pain, this was perhaps a 99 for both. It also seemed to go on for longer. The voltaic piles I had wired to the fence were perhaps less powerful than lightning, which resulted in continued consciousness and, hence, continued pain. If Mr. Franklin of Philadelphia is still among the living, perhaps I shall write and solicit his opinion.

Pike and I were flung in opposite directions. As I flew through the air, there was room beneath the pain and fear for a drop of satisfaction: It had all gone off just as I had designed. The voltaic piles, which I'd constructed of copper and zinc discs collected over the course of my wanderings, were occasionally used in my serum production, but only one or two stacks. Now every one I had was wired to Darcy's fence. When he had stepped on the plate attached to the piles, which I had barely concealed under some sod, he inadvertently became a part of a circuit, which I closed when I grabbed the fence. All I had needed was for him to draw close enough to me that I could serve as a connection between the fence, charged by the piles, and Pike. Two poles repelling, to spectacular effect. There was a shower of sparks and a tinkle of broken glass as I flew across the clearing.

"If you're interested..." I panted. "That was my plan."

No response. I hauled myself up on my elbows. My hair and dress seemed to be smoking a little, but I was absolutely alive.

"Pike?"

He lay quite still. Flames licked at his cravat. "Pike?"

No movement. No hint of breath. I found the knife, crawled toward him...His eyes opened. A hand seized my throat.

I was slammed to the ground. My ears were ringing—he'd hit my head on the fence. His eyes were open, but fully black now. The black traceries were taking over his face. He barely looked human anymore. There was nothing behind his eyes as he calmly squeezed.

The world began to go dark. *Sorry*, I thought. *I tried.*

I was falling backward. My eyes rolled up to the sky. A lovely clear night. A dark shape against the moon.

"Help," I whispered. Over the pounding of my heart I could not tell if I even made a sound.

It takes longer than you may think, getting strangled. I kept my eyes on the moon's glow for as long as I could as it faded.

Fumf.

Suddenly, I was free. I could breathe. I gave a ragged breath, then another, clutching at my throat, scrambling away.

Pike was struggling with a large pale shape. A ghost. No—an owl.

It—she—beat her wings against his face. He struggled to get free of it. For a moment she had the upper hand, but owls are not well equipped for close combat, and Pike managed to get her by the throat. He slammed her to the ground, raising a knife with his other hand.

No.

I was running before I knew what I was doing. I had lost too much to him already.

There was something in my hand. I smelled woodsmoke. My little trap had set one of the fine old trees of Pemberley aflame, and I was clutching a burning branch like a club.

Pike was so strong, and it was terribly difficult to hit him without striking the owl. Perhaps, I thought miserably as I flailed with it about his head and shoulders, it was no good. Perhaps I had pulled him away from death too many times. Perhaps this evil I had put into the world was here for good. All I could hope to do was distract him long enough for the bird to escape.

Then I realized that there were flames licking at his form.

It took him a moment to realize it himself. There are downsides, I suppose, to feeling no pain. When he did, he let go of the owl, who fluttered upward, and he began trying to beat out the flames.

Yet, that black, powdery dryness that made up his insides, whatever it was, it had no fire-retardant properties. Indeed, it would have made excellent kindling.

I backed away and sat in the damp grass, hands around my bent knees, watching as Septimus Pike burned to a fine ash.

Then I passed out again. When I awoke, the owl was perched on a low branch, staring at me.

"Georgiana?" I wheezed.

She cocked her head.

"Thank you," I said.

The great bird spread its wings and took off noiselessly into the sky.

I am tired. I will continue the tale tomorrow.

Chapter 39

Back to Longbourn

16 May, 18--

I fainted again for a time. When I woke again, I found I was being half-carried, half-dragged across the lawn. My left arm was flung across someone's shoulders, my waist clutched tightly by an unknown hand.

No. Not unknown. Even under the smell of dirt and blood, I knew my benefactress. I mumbled her name.

She paused. "Can you stand?"

I tried, and immediately crumpled back against her.

"Right. Just hang on to me. Courage, Sir Gregory, we're almost there."

Indeed, I could see that Pemberley loomed in front of us, a dim outline against the rising sun.

"You saved me."

"I don't know what you're talking about."

I felt a little drunk. My head lolled against her shoulder, my feet stumbling in the morning dew.

"You are hurt," she said. "Your mind is in disorder. No need to talk."

We had made it to a door. A tradesman's entrance, I believe, tucked in a stone alcove. She propped me against its wall so she could deal with the door. I promptly slid to the ground.

She tried the door, then sighed when she found it locked. "Dash it. Listen to me, Miss Bennet. We went for an early morning walk to catalogue mushrooms, and you slipped and fell. They will believe that. I've done it before. Can you remember that?"

I nodded, then winced. My neck felt like it was broken in eight places. "Mushrooms."

"Mushrooms." She would not look me in the eye. She raised her fist to knock.

"What mushrooms?"

"Oh, for—*Agaricus arvensis*, all right?"

I nodded again and then winced. With an effort, I looked up at her. Again, she was about to hammer on the door.

"Wait!"

"What now?"

I held up a hand. In it I clutched a soft white feather. "You'll need this," I said. "Next time."

She bit her lip. For a moment I thought she might cry. Then, ignoring my proffered feather, she hammered on the door.

"Open up!" she yelled. "It's Georgiana Darcy! Open up, Jenkins! There's been an accident!"

There was a commotion within. The commotion grew louder, then the door opened, and the commotion enveloped me. There seemed to be dozens of sleepy maids and flour-covered kitchen girls around me. As they lifted me everything went fuzzy again.

The next thing I knew, I was waking up in bed. Mamma was seated next to me, reading something.

"Georgiana?"

Mamma jumped. "Oh. Mary. Thank the Lord."

"Georgiana…"

She tucked away her letter and took my hand. "Shh. Rest, little one."

Against my will, I did.

The next few days passed in a haze of sleeping draughts, physicians, and Mamma and Lizzy arguing in hissed whispers about which physicians should be admitted. I do not know what they made of the black and blue marks round my neck or of the scars down my arms, but I suppose a physician sees all kinds of things. After a few days Papa turned up as well, though his visits to the sick room were brief—leeches make him ill. As I regained my strength, I began pushing away the sleeping draughts. Again and again, I asked for Georgiana, until finally my mother said, "She's gone, child."

"Gone?"

Mamma was fidgeting with her apron, folding it into little pleats. "She is visiting her future mother-in-law. The visit was long planned." She hesitated. "She left this for you." She placed a folded letter on the coverlet.

I picked it up. My name, written in Georgiana's hand. The seal was broken. "Open?"

"It was like that already," she said quickly.

I opened it. Here it is.

Dear Miss Bennet,

It was terribly unfair of me, that last letter. Of course you did not believe me. No one with as fierce and fine an intellect as yours could believe such a fantastic tale. Forgive me.

I think it is best if you go on not believing me. I am sorry for not saying goodbye in person, but I find the thought too difficult.

When first we met, I could hardly believe my luck. We seemed so utterly alike, so utterly complementary in every way. But of course the opposite is true.

We were not really good for each other, were we? It felt as though we had created a world just for us—but that was an illusion. That kind of folie à deux ought to be avoided. However intoxicating it may be, the world will always shatter it in the end.

I believe the done thing at this juncture would be to return your letters. Forgive my failure to do so. I must have something.

Goodbye, Mary. Be well. I will picture you, always, happy among your phials and Leyden jars. May the world bring you a clear answer to your every question.

Your servant,

Miss GEORGIANA DARCY.

What am I to make of this? Is she saying that it was all a lie? But that night I saw—

I was concussed.

I suppose she is right. We are not good for one another.

We are to leave Pemberley soon. I am glad.

30 June, 18--

We left Pemberley as soon as I was able. Before I was able, really, and Lizzy scolded Mamma and Papa roundly for it, but there was no more time to lose. Papa was low on serum again, and he was wearing smoked glasses to keep anyone from seeing how black his eyes were becoming. (Luckily his sideburns hid the worst of the black veinage.) Even when low on his medicine, he seemed to lack Pike's propensity for arson—but his elderly body was unable to bear the strain. His breathing would become labored, his speech garbled. He would refuse food and drink and would not, or could not, walk. It was only the serums that kept him alive.

We made our way back to Longbourn slowly, in care for my health. A journey that would normally take two or three days now took a full week. We were just in time. Had we not arrived in the dark, anyone could have seen what a sorry state Papa was in.

The next day I got up and made him another batch of serum. Mamma made a little noise when she saw me open a vein in my arm—but then she pressed her lips together and said nothing. What was there to say?

The days passed. I got up, I made serum, I rested. Papa drank it. I made more. It wasn't enough.

Papa's needs were still increasing. He became feverish. I made more.

Mamma, after an afternoon of gathering her courage, opened a cut on her arm. A good bleeder, and enough for several phials of serum for Papa.

He would not take it.

It was no mere freak of temper, either. When we made him choke some down, he was sick. The razor came back to me.

More, and more, and more. Cuts on my arms, on my legs, on my stomach and back. Papa allowed me to extract his rib; it did not respond to the procedure, and he could not tolerate one of Harry's, tearing the stitches open with his own hands. More of my own blood, then. In between, I wandered Longbourn's halls. Ours. Still ours. Empty now of sisters, but I remained.

Sometimes my wanderings turned out to be dreams, and I would awake in bed, or with my head in my arms at my laboratory table.

One day, Mamma found me in such a daze. She was now an accustomed guest in my laboratory, so I was not surprised to find her shaking me awake. "Mary. Wake up, child."

"Mmm." I sat up, my head pounding. Even in my sleep, I had managed not to dislodge the basin my arm was bleeding into.

Except…Mamma was covering the wound in cotton. She was binding it shut. "Stop it," I grumbled. "Can't you see it's not enough?"

"It is enough," she said.

There was a strange tickle. She was stroking my hair.

"Such an odd girl you were, Mary," she said. "I never knew what to do with you. So different from your sisters."

I tried to shove her off. "Enough. I've got to make more serum."

"No."

"What? Yes I do." I reached for the bandage.

She stilled my hand. "I said no."

"I've got to," I said. "Papa…Longbourn…"

"Would have both been lost years ago, without you." She sighed. "We were only ever keeping it warm for the Collinses, anyhow."

I finally focused on her. Was she saying what I thought? Everything Mamma had done since Jane was sixteen had been aimed at keeping this house. "You shan't mind being a poor relation?"

"Poor relations! Us? The very thought!" She sniffed. "We are no such thing. Lizzy will set us up beautifully. I shall make her. Why, she never would have caught a Darcy had I not sent Jane to Netherfield on horseback in a thunderstorm."

"Yes, Mamma."

Papa died five days later. It was very peaceful, actually. The physician said it was blood poisoning, which I suppose was true in a way. He slipped into a coma, and then three days later he went. And so ends the tenure of the Bennets at Longbourn.

CHAPTER 40

Flora Britannica

22 July, 18--

Oh, Harry. All these years I've been writing you—you must have been so vexed.

Papa's death was three weeks ago. Mamma and I have spent the last few weeks overseeing the removal of our belongings. It was a tiresome business. Mr. Collins sent multiple letters each day, which both poured forth sympathy for our loss and also managed to imply that he suspected we would make off with things that belonged to him. He begged us to take all the time we needed, to be in no hurry to quit our abode, while at the same time informing us that his family would take possession at the end of the month.

It is tiresome work, but it grows a little easier each day. For the first time in years, I can call my blood my own. Little by little, my strength has returned. My figure, too, has begun to fill out the dresses that had sagged around my wasted frame. Mamma seems grimly determined to eat everything on the farm that we can, and she presses all the best cuts and the richest cream upon me.

The Shocking Experiments of MISS MARY BENNET

This morning, my mother called me into the place I had so rarely been allowed: my father's study.

"Mary! Mary, come here, child, I want you!"

At the strident sound of my mother's voice, I reluctantly put aside the book I was reading whilst curled up on the windowsill. No doubt my mother wanted company for a morning visit, or someone to do the fine needlework on a napkin she was sewing, or something else like that. But Quindley says, "a young lady is not to become obstinate or stubborn, but she must obey her parents in all things, as she will later obey her husband," and I had not been strictly adhering to Quindley's strictures lately, so I resolved to do as she asked with no complaint. Poor relations must behave themselves.

Golden morning sunlight poured over Papa's volumes, making the dust motes dance as I slipped over the forbidden threshold. I looked around silently, looking for my favorite volumes like I was greeting old friends. Hello, Newton. Hello, Homer. Hello, publication of the Royal Astronomical Society, containing comets and nebulae discovered by Caroline Herschel. If only I had an astronomer brother I could keep house for.

Mamma, a streak of dust smudged across the frill of her cap, popped up from behind my father's desk. "There you are. I've a task for you, Miss Mary."

"Yes, ma'am? I can dust in here, if you wish."

"Dust! I'll thank you not to talk such nonsense." She shook her head, puffing as she got to her feet. "No, your task is all these books. We must know what we have before they're got rid of."

I felt cold. "Got rid of?"

"Well, yes. Some will stay with the house, when we—" She swallowed, then continued. "In any case, we need to know which ones are to be Collins's and which can be sold."

Sold. Of course. Most of these books would come to Mr. Collins as part of the estate. I would never see them again. The rest would go, since we no longer had an income or a house to keep them in.

Well. At least I could say goodbye.

"I should be glad to make a catalogue for you, ma'am," I said. "I know the provenance and ownership quite well."

"Good, yes, I thought you might." She patted something behind the desk. "You'd best start with these."

I came around the desk to find a small wooden chest I did not recognize. Mamma lifted the lid. Within were a half-dozen books I had never seen before.

My fingers itched with the old book lust even as I felt a pang of irritation. There were books in our house that I did not know? Outrageous.

"These must be the valuable ones," my mother said hopefully. "They were locked in a chest, hidden beneath his desk. See what you can find, please, dear."

"Yes, ma'am," I said absently, already drawing forth the first volume.

All afternoon I sat in that puddle of sunlight, just as I had when I was a child, soaking luxuriantly in book after book after book. My mother was not entirely correct—some of the books, I realized, my father had put away not because they were valuable but because they violated some kind of decency act. My face flamed at the illustrations in a certain French volume with a long title. So graphically did it illustrate the act of copulation—not to mention a number of acts so exotic I am not sure what to call them—that I quickly put it aside and covered it with a pillow. Curiosity soon made me take it up again, and then I thought of *my own father* looking at these pictures and stuffed it under three pillows. And I thought *Fanny Hill* was bad.

We shall have to see what to do with those, Harry. Indecent they may be, but I suspect they are not without value. I wonder what Tim Lucas would give me for them.

Some of the books, however, were just what my mother surmised—rare volumes, first editions, everything my father thought the greatest and dearest of his collection. There was a large folio edition of Smith's geology monograph, with colored plates so lovely they took my breath away, and an astronomical map that said it was made by the Herschels themselves—how did he get a hold of such a thing?

Then, at the bottom, I found one more book.

It did not appear as fine as some of the others. It was just two little green volumes, volumes 1 and 2. I picked one up.

"Smith's *Flora Britannica*," I whispered. "Linnean Society. Volume one." I flipped open the pages. Oh!

I would not have credited, Harry, that such a shabby-looking little volume, with smudges of dirt and tea stains on the cover, could be so beautiful inside. The book is an encyclopedia of the plants of Britain, a dense and thorough reference almost entirely in Latin. It would be a marvelous gift on the strength of that alone. The margins, though—in the margins, there are flowers.

Someone with great patience, a steady hand, and an assortment of colored inks had annotated Smith's dry volume with illustrations. The hairs on my arms stood up as I carefully paged through. There were cross sections of leaves and stems, berries and seeds, in some places diagrammed carefully and in others painted almost as though the artist had forgotten that he was making a reference book and simply painted flowers for their sheer beauty. Here on page 23 was *Veronica floribus folitariis*, English name: germander chickweed, the spiky leaves climbing from the right margin between the words. Page 244, *Viola*, the common pansy, the purple and yellow petals so vivid I could almost reach into the page and pluck them.

More than a third of the pages had been so annotated. No wonder, I thought, that my father had locked it away carefully, for it must be the only one of its kind in existence.

I had meant only to take a cursory glance, but the beauty of the thing so beguiled me that I could not stop reading it. I flipped through page after page, back and forth at random, forsaking my normal systematic approach for a more self-indulgent randomness, mouthing Latin names unfamiliar to me, finding with a shock of happy recognition familiar friends like lily of the valley and dandelion, as well as more exotic blooms.

When I reached page 238—*Campanula trachelium*, the nettle-leaved bellflower—a slip of paper fell out into my lap. I unfolded it. Instantly, my hands began to shake. Not with anger, however. I knew this handwriting.

The note was in Latin, befitting a scientific tome. Here it is translated into the common tongue.

Dear niece,

Well, dear child, the time has come. The apothecary shakes his head over me. Every day, I lose a little more strength. The fight will soon be over.

One of my only regrets in leaving this life is leaving you. I never expected that one of my dearest friends would be an eight-year-old girl, but so it is. You and I, my dear, are two of a kind, and the moments I have spent with you have been some of the happiest of my life. I only wish I could see you grow up.

As I write this, sitting in the window of the rectory, I can see you in the back garden.

Your mother sent you to me for the afternoon, because she could not bear your incessant questions. She hoped I might be able to answer them, but of course in many things you have already outstripped me. I do not know why the sky is blue, or how many planets there are yet to be discovered, or what is on the dark side of the moon, or what happens when we die. When you realized I was answerless, you huffed and took yourself outside, where you presently lie in the grass, observing an anthill, frowning with a concentration that would put any gray-haired member of the Linnean Society to shame.

The Shocking Experiments of MISS MARY BENNET

To make up for this shocking lack of knowledge, I mean to leave you a legacy. I haven't any money to speak of, but this little book will be yours. I have filled it with my own poor attempts at illustrations. I hope they are of use to you in future, if you continue your research. If not, I hope they will at least hold happy memories.

I shall place this note between pages 238 and 239, atop the entry for Campanula trachelium, *the nettle-leaved bellflower. Some of these illustrations are copied from plates, but this one I drew from life, on one of my tramps through the countryside. Is it not pretty? The leaves are edged with stinging nettles, but the flowers tucked among them, if one cares to look, are such a gorgeous dusky purple-blue. It reminds me of you.*

Dear little cousin, I am so sorry to leave you all alone. The world is not always kind to people like you and me. I wish I could continue to be your teacher. Pray do not be too lonely. Pray do not try too hard to be other than you are. Pray continue to learn and continue to ask why, no matter whom you irritate thereby. Pray look for other nettle-leaved bellflower people, and cling to them when you meet them, never minding the thorns.

Goodbye.

Your loving cousin,

HENRY BENNET.

PS. I hope your father is not too offended by the legacy I left for him. He always complains of my "tiresome churchy nonsense" whenever I try to engage him on a point of theology. Therefore I have left him the most tiresome book of sermons in my collection. Even I have never managed to read all the way through Reverend Quindley's Admonishments for Godly Young Ladies. *Just my final little joke.*

A strange sound broke the air. It was a sob. My own.

Swiftly I pushed back from the table. If my tears smudged one of your beautiful illustrations, I would never forgive myself. Just in time, too, for the tears were already spilling down over my cheeks.

I tried to breathe deeply, but another sob broke my breath, and then another. When one has not cried in more than seven years, one finds it a bit hard to stop. At least, I did. It had been so long I could scarcely recognize the sensations, and part of me observed the shattered breathing, the hot liquid trails, the seizing feeling in the middle of my chest, to be catalogued later.

For now, though, I could only give in to it. I cried for everything in the last few years. For Pike, and everything with him. For my mother. Even, with surprising vehemence, because my aunt had not invited my twelve-year-old self to London, and why that was something I had held on to all this time, I've no idea.

Why did my father not give me my legacy? I suppose he simply never found the note, or, if he did, never bothered to translate it. His Latin, as I have mentioned, is execrable. I am attempting not to hate him for it. Two legacies, one a book for young ladies, one a scholarly volume for learned men—his mistake was natural enough.

But now I knew. Harry, you never intended me to take *Quindley's* as my guide. You never intended me to read it at all. At the thought a sob tore from me so violent that I almost bent double. Suddenly I saw what *Quindley's* really was: a stuffy, hateful tome written by someone who knew as much about young ladies as I know about kangaroos. I had always known, I realized. For years, I had fought that knowledge, for your sake. How could I ever think that necessary? How could I ever fail to remember you as you were—someone who liked me?

Oh, Harry, thank you. The thought of all those wasted years, making that hateful book my bible, trying to be what I thought you wanted for me—I am crying again as I think of them. But the mistake is now corrected, and I really believe it happened at the right time. I shall never read the horrid thing again.

Mamma heard my noise and came in, alarmed. "Mary! What on earth is the matter! Are you ill?"

I was sobbing so hard I could barely speak, like a child. It was mortifying. "I-I-I didn't g-go to London!"

"When?"

"When I wa-was twelve!"

"Oh," she said, still looking mystified.

"And I-I-I hate *Quindley's*!"

She patted me nervously. "Believe me, so do we all."

"And Papa is gone—and Longbourn is lost—and I-I-I don't mind." And I cried so hard I could no longer speak at all.

She put her arms around me. "There, there, love. It will be all right. I knew all those books would fracture your wits one day. Come."

So unused to seeing me in tears was she that she bade me lie down as though I had a fever. Now I am writing this in my bed, like a lady of leisure.

I do not know what is to become of me now. But I will go to my fate with good grace.

Nettles can grow anywhere, can't they?

And, dear Harry, there is another *Campanula trachelium* I must take your advice about. I do not know if she will listen. I do not know if I deserve to be listened to.

Wish me luck, anyhow, whether I deserve it or not.

Epilogue

Pemberley Cottage
Some time later

Hello, Harry. I suppose I shall call you that, for old times' sake.

It is a long time now since I wrote you. A long time since I needed to. My life now is more settled and comfortable than I would have thought possible.

Settled? Comfortable? I believe the word I am looking for is *happy*.

I write this in the drawing room of Pemberley Cottage. It is a snug little house on the grounds of Pemberley, near the lake. I have a little desk in the corner, and there is one for Georgiana in the opposite corner. We make our notes here, or sometimes she experiments with proofs. She claims she once proved Goldbach's conjecture, then forgot it. Not sure if that is an invention of the Darcy pride or the true result of Georgiana's absentmindedness. What a darling.

There is yellow-green sunshine pouring in through the window, filtered through the leaves of the trees in the garden. It is so beautiful it makes me ache. I do not believe I would have noticed that a few years ago. Taking the time to notice something beautiful—I would have considered it a shameful waste of time. I was ashamed of so much in those days.

There are those, I believe, who feel sorry for me. *Warehousing their old maids together—the Darcys will live to regret it! Such a difference in their situations and dispositions. Those cats will soon begin to scratch...*

If they only knew.

To be fair to the naysayers, it did not begin auspiciously. I shall never forget how pinched and frozen Georgiana looked when I first returned to Pemberley. I sat there in the parlor with Mamma and Lizzy and Darcy and watched her pleat her skirt with anxious fingers. I tried to tell her with my eyes how sorry I was, but she would not meet my gaze.

"Did you hear that, Georgiana? Mary has become interested in fossils," Darcy said presently. "Did you not recently attend an interesting lecture on the subject?"

Georgiana's eyes caught mine at last. "Fossils," she said.

"I adore them," I said. "A lecture, you say? Won't you tell me of it? Please?"

She leapt to her feet and ran from the room.

"Why, Georgiana!" Darcy cried, and half rose, but Lizzy put a hand to his arm.

"Mary," she said calmly. "Would you please go and see if Miss Darcy feels quite well?"

I wanted to say no. I knew I was the last person she would want to see. But the tears that were now never far threatened to spill over if I spoke, and I could do nothing but nod and exit.

I found Georgiana by the lake. She was tucked on a stone bench under a willow tree, hidden beneath its boughs until one was a few steps away. I brushed aside a curtain of switches and stepped closer.

"I am so very sorry," I said. "I was wrong."

"About what?" came the whispered reply.

My heart was pounding madly in my chest. I fought the urge to run. I fought the urge to throw my arms about her. "About girls turning into birds, for one thing," I said. "I have seen it now. Twice. I ought to have believed you."

No answer.

"And...and everything else. Pike. Everything."

"Everything?"

"No. Not everything. Hardly any of it really. Just the bits where I made you cry."

My voice broke and it made her look up at last. Her eyes widened. "Mary, *you're* crying."

I sniffed. "Yes. I do that now. Oh, dearest, *please*." I sank to my knees at her feet and seized her hand in mine.

She started. "Miss Bennet—"

"Georgiana, I beg you listen. I did not trust...my feelings. I thought I could only drag you down—that my love was as twisted and excessive as the rest of me. But darling, darling—I've been so wrong...and I know...I know I am too late. I know you no longer desire my company. But I had to tell you, just once...how sorry I am...how foolish I was...how entirely I am yours."

I drew a deep breath. My agitations had ridden up my sleeves. My scars were plainly visible. The sight brought me back to earth. I pulled back and tugged them down my wrists. "Sorry. I know I am just an eccentric, scarred old maid now. But I thought you deserved to know."

"Stop it, Mary, stop it." She seized one of my wrists before I could cover it completely. Before I could resist, she'd brought it to her lips and kissed my scars, one after another. Each touch of her lips on my skin was like a jolt of warmth so intense that I had the mad idea that when I looked again my scars would be gone. But I did not look, because Georgiana was crashing to her knees beside me, and threading her fingers through my hair, and then her lips were on mine again, our arms locked tight about each other as though we could become one creature, and I wanted to die with relief that the thing that burned between us lived on. We broke the kiss only to seize each other in an even fiercer embrace. I buried my face in the crook of her neck. She still used pear-scented soap. It was like coming back to life.

She dissolved her engagement. Mamma and I moved up to Pemberley Cottage. She joined us shortly thereafter.

Indeed, my situation appears to be exactly what I feared as a young lady. No home, no fortune, no husband, no permanent place. Dependent. Ignored. *Pitied*. I took great lengths, once, to avoid this.

Life takes strange turns.

For one thing, I am not *quite* so dependent on the Darcys and Georgiana as I appear. True, Georgiana is an heiress, and I have a scant thousand pounds to my name. True, I live in Darcy's cottage rent-free. However, while Mary Bennet is quite poor, Mr. Gregory Pike—brother to the late Septimus and, thanks to a brilliant idea from Georgiana and some sternly worded letters, his heir—has rather deep pockets. Mr. Gregory Pike elected not to continue his brother's business, but the sale of his assets proved of considerable value. Especially the sale—in an improved, bloodless form—of the formulae for his dyes.

Of course I cannot touch the substance of this money. Most inconvenient questions would be asked. Still, I can nibble at the interest, and it is a comfort not to have to scrimp and save for new laboratory equipment.

Other than that, I live as I appear: a young spinster of more breeding than fortune. I have adapted quite well to the modesty of my circumstances. Even if the snugness of the cottage means that Georgiana and I must share a bed.

We talk occasionally of setting up house farther afield. In the North, maybe, or perhaps even abroad. If we ever find that we embarrass the Darcys, we will. However, we have been surprised to find how much we like it here. They have been surprised, I think, to find how much they like us—like *me*. The older Lizzy and I get, the less irritated we are by one another's faults. Mamma has come into her own as a grandmother to Lizzy's children. She and Lizzy irritate each other as much as ever, but they have found common ground in doting on the small creatures tumbling about the nursery. Mamma *will* exceed our income, but since our income is actually several times bigger than what she believes, this causes us little trouble.

Almost every day, we make the ten-minute walk to Pemberley and call upon our family there. I never liked children, but I am surprised at how fond I am of the little Darcys. Charlotte is opinionated, talkative, and clever, just like her mother. She rules the nursery with an iron fist.

Next is Small William, as we all call Mr. Darcy's namesake. He is a comically pompous child, convinced that if anything is amiss at Pemberley it is due to some neglect of his own. I once saw him come to visit the cottage and, instead of coming straight in, he walked around it, hands clasped behind his little back, examining the roof and tutting to himself. He was six. We will have our hands full with that one, seeing to it that he not grow up into *too* much of a Darcy. To be fair, he was right about the roof, and the house is much warmer and drier now after the repairs he insisted upon.

Then there is little George. He is ours.

George was born after a terrible lying-in that frightened us all very much. Lizzy pulled through, thank heaven, and so did her son, but he is not quite like other children. He is undersized and sickly, and there is a palsy in his left side that is not fading as we hoped. He cannot ride, or shoot, or dance, and sending him away to school will likely be impossible.

His parents are very fond of him, but they are not sure what to make of him. More and more, he spends his afternoons with us. He glories in our library (smaller but more serious than Pemberley's) and far outstrips his older siblings in mathematics and natural history. He is in our back garden now, flat on his stomach, examining an anthill.

Apologies. I was startled and knocked over the inkwell. As I write this, Georgiana has come up behind me and put her arms around my neck, her cheek pressed to mine. I almost shoved this manuscript into the coal bin, as I do when I hear the creak of the front step signifying callers.

But no, read on, my love, if you like. I have no secrets from you.

All that I am is yours. From the bedroom we share in the attic, with the little skylight through which I watch you depart on your monthly flights, to the cellar laboratory, where only we two are admitted.

You may read this whole manuscript, if you like, Georgiana. You will find it amusing, perhaps, to laugh over what fools we were when we were younger. I think, though, that what I really ask is that you keep it safe for someone else.

I do not think George has an easy road ahead. If I go first, pray give him this manuscript when he is old enough. I once got a similar gift, but it went astray, and its lack cost me dear.

Darling boy, if you are reading this: Take note of how your young Aunt Mary approached life with the grim avidity of a boxer or a gambler. Everything, it seemed to me, from money, to beauty, to accomplishments, to making a good match, was just a way of keeping score. Earn enough points, and one earned the right to like oneself. It must be so, I thought, for all the things I was supposed to want seemed so totally incapable of bringing happiness themselves.

Do not repeat my mistakes, child. There is no scorekeeper. No wrong way to be happy.

Gentility may seem like a cage, but the gaps between the bars are so much larger than you think. Observe how Aunt Georgiana and I step in and out at will without anyone noticing. As a very dear relation once said to me, "Pray look for other nettle-leaved bellflower people, and cling to them when you meet them, never minding the thorns." You are not alone.

The shadows are growing longer, and I can see you begin to shiver in the grass. Time for me to drag you inside for tea.

Much love,
Aunt Mary.

THE END.

ACKNOWLEDGMENTS

Too many to name. I'd just like to shout out my sister Hannah, who, for a computer programmer, has a startlingly deep knowledge of alchemy; my sister Amanda, for all her support and patience with my G Chat meltdowns; Sophie Gee, for pointing me toward *Fanny Hill*; Jenn Joel, Jacqui Young, Anne Perry, and the rest of the team at CAA, Hachette, and Hachette UK; my Uncle Rob, Aunt Nila, and Aunt Mary, who gave me places to write when I needed them; and the Linnean Society, which is a real place, and contains the real *Flora Britannica*, which, on page 238, has a drawing of *Campanula trachelium* that is so much like my Mary Bennet that when I saw it I almost cried.

Thanks also to my niece Stella, who kept me writing with her regular queries of "Where is the book for me?" Here it is, Stells, the book for you.

Thanks and apologies to Mary Shelley and Jane Austen.

ABOUT THE AUTHOR

MELINDA TAUB is an Emmy- and Writers Guild Award–winning writer. The former head writer and executive producer of *Full Frontal with Samantha Bee*, she is also the author of *Still Star-Crossed*, a young adult novel that was adapted for television by Shondaland, and *The Scandalous Confessions of Lydia Bennet, Witch*. (She also wrote that thing about the Baroness in *The Sound of Music* that your aunt likes.) She lives in Brooklyn.